THE
MARTIAN
WAR

ACCLAIM FOR THE MARTIAN WAR

"I shall not reveal here the truth of our encounter with the Martians. I encourage you, dear reader, to purchase *The Martian War* and decide for yourself if you prefer the original tale offered by Mr. Wells, or this revelation of the facts. . . . You will find yourself greatly entertained."—SFreader.com

"Ingenious . . . a tight, brisk tale that fits nicely into the mold established by the pulp writers of a century ago. . . . A worthwhile supplement to the renewed fascination in one of science fiction's founding fathers."
—SciFiDimensions.com

"A terrific homage. . . . Fast-paced and action-packed."
—Harriet Klausner

"For a very different, utterly delightful reading experience, try [this] playful mix of fact and fancy."—*Daily Yomiuri* (Tokyo)

"Wells and Anderson fans should be delighted."—*Booklist*

"Smoothly mixes Victorian sober rationalism with the fast pace of the period's boys' adventure yarns."
—*Publishers Weekly*

"The author captures the spirit of the age in these linked tales that serve as seasonal witnesses to an age of invention and literary imagination."—*Library Journal*

THE MARTIAN WAR

A THRILLING EYEWITNESS ACCOUNT OF THE RECENT ALIEN INVASION

As Reported by Mr. H.G. Wells

KEVIN J. ANDERSON

TITAN BOOKS

The Martian War
Print edition ISBN: 9781781161722
E-book edition ISBN: 9781781161739

Published by Titan Books
A division of Titan Publishing Group Ltd.
144 Southwark Street, London SE1 0UP

First Titan Books edition September 2012

1 3 5 7 9 10 8 6 4 2

Portions of the first two chapters have been previously published as "Scientific Romance" by Kevin J. Anderson in *The UFO Files*, edited by Ed Gorman & Martin H. Greenberg, DAW, 1998; and "Canals in the Sand" by Kevin J. Anderson in *War of the Worlds: Global Dispatches*, edited by Kevin J. Anderson, Bantam, 1996.

A CIP catalogue record for this title is available from the British Library.

Printed and bound in the USA.

TABLE
OF
CONTENTS

PROLOGUE: CELESTIAL MECHANICS

PART I
SCIENTIFIC ROMANCE

PART II
THE FIRST MEN—AND A WOMAN—IN THE MOON

PART III
MARS AND ITS CANALS

EPILOGUE: THE SHAPE OF THINGS TO COME

To the imagination, genius, and sheer enthusiasm of
MR. HARLAN ELLISON,
who has raised the bar for all of us.

PROLOGUE

CELESTIAL MECHANICS

CHAPTER ONE

MR. WELLS AND PROFESSOR HUXLEY OBSERVE THE LEONIDS

1884

In chill November, the nights were as dark as the stars were bright.

Young Wells followed his professor up rarely used wooden stairs to the labyrinthine rooftop of the university hall. When he politely opened the access door for the older man, the damp air threatened fog or, worse, obscuring clouds. Yet he saw that the sky overhead was mercifully clear: a canvas on which to paint glorious streaks of light.

"The meteors will begin falling soon, Wells." The old biology professor looked just as eager as his student.

The minarets and gables of London's Normal School of Science provided a maze of nooks, gutters, and eaves interspersed with sooty chimneypots and loose tiles. Daring students could climb out on ledges and hold secret meetings, even arrange assignations with willing girls from the poorer sections of South Kensington who could be sweet-talked with pleasant and cultured words.

Wells doubted that any of his classmates had ever climbed out for such a lofty purpose as his own.

T.H. Huxley's creaking bones and aching limbs forced him to move with painstaking care along the precarious shingles, yet the famous man had a grace and surety about him. Wells knew better than to offer the professor any assistance. Although Thomas Henry Huxley was now an old man with yellowish skin and gray hair, the bright little brown eyes in his square face still held a gaze as sharp as a hunting falcon's. In his youth, he had spent years as a surgeon and naturalist aboard a sailing ship, the *Rattlesnake*, collecting and documenting biological specimens from around the world, much as his revered colleague Charles Darwin had done. Huxley had been through storms and hostile landscapes, surviving harsh climates and unfriendly natives; he could certainly negotiate a rooftop, even one slick with moss and mist.

With a weary sigh, the professor eased himself down beside a grimy brick chimney, adjusting his black wool coat. Leaning back, he propped his head against a chimney and scratched his bushy white sideburns.

"Is this your first meteor shower, Mr. Wells? The Leonids are a good place to start." Huxley's booming voice was startlingly loud on the rooftop.

"I've seen shooting stars before, sir, but never actually . . . studied them. Even in my youth, I spent more time with my nose stuck in a book than looking up at the sky."

The old man gave a wheezing laugh. "Exactly as I expected."

Huxley's private conversational tone wasn't much softer than the forceful oratory for which he had become famous. Whether he was lecturing students or shouting in vehement debate with pig-headed bishops, his confident delivery, wit, and obvious intelligence won him many friends, and created as many enemies.

A flash in Wells's peripheral vision took him completely by surprise. "There, sir!" He gestured so rapidly that he nearly lost his precarious balance on the slanted roof. A streak of white light shot overhead then evaporated, so transient it seemed barely an after-image on his eyes.

"Ah, our first meteor of the night, and you spotted it, Wells. Of course, your eyes are younger than mine."

"But your eyes have seen more things, sir." Limber enough at eighteen, Wells arranged his legs into an awkward squat, propping his worn shoes against a gutter for balance.

"Don't flatter me, Wells. I won't tolerate it."

"Sorry, sir."

Wells would have accepted any number of rebukes in exchange for the insights he received during the professor's biology lectures. Here at the university, his mind had been opened to a whole universe that dwarfed the dreary lower-middle-class existence to which his mother and brothers had resigned themselves.

Wells's dour mother had resisted the idea of an "unnecessary education," afraid her boy Herbert might put on airs above his social station. But the young man wanted to be a teacher, not a tradesman like the rest of his family.

When only seventeen, Wells had taken matters into his own hands by talking his way into a modest position as an assistant student teacher at the Midhurst School. Anxious to be free of his draper's apprenticeship, he had written a beseeching letter to the schoolmaster, Horace Byatt, begging for any post. The letter was embarrassingly manipulative, but at the time Wells had been young and desperate.

Byatt had found him an enthusiastic and dedicated pupil. In order to advance himself, Wells crammed immense amounts of knowledge into his hungry brain; he spent a great deal of time in school libraries or rifling through volumes in the Uppark manor library, while his mother worked. Each time Wells, or any one of his students, earned a high mark on special exams provided by the government, the Midhurst School received a financial reward. And young H.G. Wells was very profitable to schoolmaster Byatt. In fact, he did so well that he was admitted to the prestigious Normal School of Science, much to Byatt's disappointment (and loss of income).

There, Wells had met T.H. Huxley.

Although his mother sent him only a few shillings a week to pay for his schooling, Wells would rather have starved than return to his former terrible apprenticeship to a draper. He was destined to become a learned man. Huxley always said, "Ideas make mankind superior to other creatures . . . and superior men have superior ideas."

With a lean face and hollowed eyes, Wells was scrawny—even cadaverous, according to his roommate and friend, A.V. Jennings. Sometimes, taking pity on him, Jennings would fill him with beefsteak and beer so they could return replenished to the workbench in Huxley's laboratory. As the son of a doctor,

Jennings received a small weekly stipend, but even he could little afford such generosity.

Wells shivered. But though his garments, a thin coat and an old shirt, were insufficient to combat the chill, he had no desire to go back inside when he could be out here with the professor. He wiggled his foot, fidgeted his hands, always moving, trying to get warm, as he continued watching.

Around them, a miasma of night-time noises rose from the streets of London. Horse-carts and hansom cabs clopped by; prostitutes flounced into dim alleys or waited under the gas street lamps. Across the park, in the boarding house at Westbourne Grove where he and Jennings shared a room, the residents would be engaged in their nightly carousing, brawls, singing and drinking. Here, high above it all, Wells enjoyed the relative peace.

A second meteor appeared overhead like a line drawn with a pen of fire, eerie in its total silence. "Another!"

Bright in the western ecliptic, the ruddy point of Mars hung like a baleful eye. Mentally tracing the meteor's fiery line back to its origin, Wells saw that it radiated from a point in the sky not far from Mars itself, as if the red planet were launching them like sparks from a grinding wheel.

"Do you ever imagine, Professor, that these meteors might be signals of a kind? Even ships that have crossed the gulf of space?" Wells often spoke his odd speculations aloud, sometimes to the entertainment of others, sometimes to their annoyance.

Huxley's eyes held a bold challenge, as did his tone. "Ships? And from whence would they come?"

"Why not . . . Mars, for instance?" He indicated the orange-red pinpoint. "If Laplace's nebular hypothesis of planetary formation is correct, and Mars cooled long before Earth, then intelligent life could have evolved there much sooner than any such spark occurred here. Therefore, the Martian race would be more ancient, and presumably more advanced. Their minds would be immeasurably superior to our own—certainly capable of launching ships into the realm of space."

A third shooting star passed overhead, as if to emphasize Wells's point.

Huxley took up the mental challenge, as Wells had known he would. "Ah, Martians . . . interesting. And what do you suppose such beings would look like? Would their bodies be formed like our own?"

Wells resisted making a quick reply. Huxley did not tolerate glib answers. "Natural selection would ultimately shape a superior being into a creature with a huge head and eyes. Its body would be composed almost entirely of brain. It would have delicate hands for manipulating tools—but its mentality would be its greatest tool."

Huxley leaned forward from the chimney. "But why would Martians want to come to our green Earth? What would be their motive?"

Again Wells paused to think. "Conquest. Mars is a dry planet, sir—cold and drained of resources. Our world is younger, fresher. Perhaps even now the Martians are regarding this Earth with envious eyes."

"Ah, a war of the worlds?" Huxley actually chuckled at this. "And you believe that such superior minds would engage in an exercise as . . . primitive as military conquest? You must not consider them so evolved after all."

Wells kept his thoughts to himself, for he suddenly wondered if perhaps T.H. Huxley might be a bit . . . naive. He might be a font of knowledge about varied species and their adaptations to the environment, but if the professor could see no reason why Martians would want to invade the Earth, then Huxley did not understand the ambitions of those in control. A hierarchy existed between powerful and powerless. As with bees in a hive or wolves in a pack, social castes were part of the natural order.

Growing up in a poor family, Wells had witnessed the gross divisions of the upper and lower classes, how each fought against the others for dominance. As a miserable apprentice, he had labored as a virtual slave. After escaping that fate through calculated incompetence, Wells had lived with his mother, who was the head domestic servant in a large manor, Uppark. His lackluster father had once been a gardener, then half-heartedly ran a china shop, but for years had found no better employment than occasional cricket playing . . . .

Wells answered his professor carefully. "It is survival of the fittest, sir. If the Martians are a dying race, they would see Earth as ripe for conquest, full of resources they need, and humans as inferior as cattle."

Huxley shifted back to his former position, where he watched for further Leonids. "Well, then, we must hope your mythical Martians do not invade us after all. How would we ever resist them?"

The two sat in silence, looking into the clear sky. Wells shivered, partially from the cold, partially from his own thoughts.

They watched the stars fall as the malevolent eye of Mars blinked at them.

* * *

Fighting the feverish pounding in his head, Wells tried to concentrate in the noisy biology laboratory. He wondered if he had caught a chill from the previous night's meteor vigil. His constitution had always been weak, aggravated by poor nutrition; he suffered from coughs and was never surprised to find a spark of scarlet in his phlegm.

Eventually, though, he became absorbed in setting up microscopes, coverslips, eye-droppers of specimens, and experimental apparatus. His preoccupied mind flowed along with the sound of clacking beakers, the chatter of fellow students, the smell of chemical experiments and alcohol burners.

One of Huxley's Irish assistants—a copper-haired demonstrator who delivered occasional lectures when the professor felt too ill to speak—prepared the day's laboratory activity. The Irishman wore a wool jacket and a maroon tie, far too fine for real analytical work, since he would not deign to step down from his podium and wade in amongst the experimenters. As if he were a prize-winning French chef, the demonstrator presented a pot in which he had prepared an infusion of local weeds and pond water. The resulting murky concoction was infested with numerous fascinating microbes.

Jennings set up their shared microscope on a narrow table against the windows, while Wells went forward with his glass slide to receive a beer-colored droplet of the infusion, as if it were some scientific communion. He slid a coverslip on top and returned to his workbench partner.

Under watery light that shone through gray clouds, Wells focused and refocused the microscope. On his sketchpad, he recorded the odd creatures: protozoans of all types, alien shapes with whipping flagella, hair-like cilia vibrating in a blur, blobby amoebas, strains of algae. As Wells scrutinized the exotic creatures swarming and multiplying in the tiny universe, he felt like a titan looming above them.

Jennings tugged at his elbow. Blinking up from the eyepiece, Wells realized that the other students had stopped their conversations and stood at attention, as if a royal presence had entered the room. Professor T.H. Huxley—who rarely saw students outside the cavernous lecture hall—had come to visit his laboratory.

The intimidating, acerbic old man strode around the workbenches where his students diligently studied the infinitesimal creatures on their microscope slides. Huxley nodded and made quiet sounds, but offered little conversation as he moved from station to station.

When the great man came to where Wells stood proudly beside his apparatus, Huxley bent over to study the slide and adjusted the focus ever so slightly as if it were his due to man the instrument. "Ah, lovely euglena you have here under the light." He made another noncommittal sound, then moved on. Jennings ducked to peer down at the slide, rushing to complete his sketches.

Wells stared after his mentor, disappointed. Huxley had made no mention of their shared experience with the meteor shower, their lively conversation. The old man had come for no purpose other than to scrutinize his insignificant students . . . in the same way that Wells and Jennings studied the microbes.

His cheeks flushed, Wells perspired, and a feverish chill swept over him. His head pounded with ideas, but he had trouble focusing his thoughts. What if other powerful beings were scrutinizing *Earth* in the same manner, curious about the buzzing and swarming colony of London?

The hair on the back of his neck prickled, as if he could sense those probing eyes watching from afar. His vision became blurred, distorted. Wells found it difficult to keep his balance.

Jennings regarded him oddly. "You don't look at all well, Herbert." With practiced ease he reached over and touched Wells's forehead. "You're burning up! You stayed out all night in the damp cold just to gawk at shooting stars, and now look what's happened. You should go home and rest before this grows more serious."

* * *

The fever caught hold of him with nightmarish strength. Wells fell into a trap of delirium fed by his own imagination.

He saw meteors falling and falling, huge cylinders accompanied by green fire that blazed across the sky. Explosions. Flames.

Accompanied by his hot thoughts of delirium, he watched visions of invading ships that crashed to Earth, pummeling the British Empire like quail shot, and there wasn't a thing Queen Victoria could do about it. Fire, blood, slavery. In powerful war machines, the belligerent aliens trounced Russia, America, France, and Prussia. A red tidal wave crashed across civilization.

Conquerors. Slave masters. Even the most insignificant of these creatures had a military intellect superior to the combined genius of Napoleon, Agamemnon, and Alexander the Great. The clanking destructive devices surpassed even the imagination of Leonardo da Vinci.

And they had come to conquer the Earth.

Wells saw men, women, and children corralled, kept as food, their blood drained as they screamed. Infernal machines strode across the English landscape, equipped with weapons that dwarfed all human mechanisms of destruction, powerful heat rays that burned everything in sight. Flashes of light. Incinerating fire.

Hot like Wells's fever.

And overhead the meteors continued falling, falling . . . .

* * *

When the fever finally broke, Wells awoke in his narrow, lumpy bed to find Jennings laying a cool rag on his forehead. A patch of bright sunlight spilled through the window, warming his skin.

Wells croaked, and his normally high voice was uncooperative. "Are you practicing to become a doctor like your father, Jennings?"

The other man's eyes were red-rimmed, as if he hadn't gotten much sleep. "You've had quite a time of it, Herbert. Been feverish for days, haven't swallowed a thing but a bit of broth and some beer."

"Worse, you've missed three of my lectures," said a stentorian voice, as if the affront was too much to bear. "Excellent ones, too, I might add."

Wells managed to prop himself up on shaky arms to see Huxley in the small, stuffy room. "Since you are one of only three students who have proved worthy of a first-class passing grade, Mr. Wells, I wanted to see why you had been so rude as to abandon my class. Do you believe you've learned everything already?"

"I'm sure Mr. Jennings took good notes for me, sir."

His roommate smiled. "I even considered storing dissection specimens in your chest of drawers, Herbert. Best be careful when you go rummaging for a clean pair of socks."

It embarrassed Wells that the professor was seeing the squalid conditions in which his student lived. He supposed many students lived similarly, but he wanted to appear better than those others, for Huxley was a great man. Boarders came in drunk at all hours, and brutish noises carried through the walls. The air was cold—no one had brought up coal for some time—and smelled rank from unemptied chamberpots in the hall. It gave him little comfort to think that Huxley had endured worse conditions aboard the *Rattlesnake* in the South Seas.

The professor maintained a mock stern expression. "I should have been quite disappointed had you died, Wells. Though you are only eighteen, I see great potential in you. Please don't crawl into a moist grave until you have accomplished something worthwhile." The older man paced the room as if searching for significant words. "Ah, quite humbling, isn't it? A superior creature such as yourself, highly evolved and possessed of a grand intellect—laid low by something as crude and insignificant as a germ."

Wells gave a wan smile in response. "I'm sorry, sir. Henceforth, I shall try to prove my evolutionary superiority."

Huxley paused at the room's warped door, ready to leave. "You may wish to know, Wells, that this will be my last semester teaching at the university."

In his alarm, Wells managed to struggle his way into a half-sitting position. "But, sir, there's so much more we can learn from you!"

"Ah, I have wasted far too much time and energy in debates over Darwinism. I've explored the world, furthered the cause of science, and taught countless students, many of whom will use their knowledge for nothing more interesting than to add to lively chat at the pub. I have earned myself a quiet retirement."

"You have made an impact on many of us, sir," Wells said, swallowing back the lump that was rising in his throat. "Indeed, you are the greatest man I should ever hope to meet."

"Then you must continue to meet other men in the hope of proving yourself wrong." The professor's dark eyes twinkled. He tugged open the door, adjusted his hat, and frowned back at his sick student. "With your imagination, Wells, I expect you to make something of yourself. Don't disappoint me."

After Huxley left, Wells collapsed back on his bed. Jennings stared at him in awe. Neither man could believe what he had just heard. "That was quite a benediction, Herbert."

Wells closed his blue eyes, dizzy with residual weakness from the fever, but his mind was already spinning with a thousand thoughts, ideas, ambitions, and challenges for himself. "I'll rest for a bit, Jennings. I have to regain my health before I can begin my life's work."

CHAPTER TWO

PERCIVAL LOWELL AND DR. MOREAU
SEND A MESSAGE TO MARS

1893

In the sweltering Sahara, Percival Lowell stood at the open flap of his tent. Though the constant dust and unrelenting heat were bothersome, he reveled in his vast construction site, glad to be far from Boston and civilized industry.

The excavations extended beyond the vanishing point of the flat horizon. Thousands of sweating laborers—mostly illiterate Tuaregs and sullen French prisoners exiled here to Algeria—moved like choreographed machinery as they dug monumental trenches according to Lowell's commands, scribing deep lines in the sand. It was like a tattoo on the Earth's skin, a huge design that went nowhere and served no purpose, as far as most people could see. But Lowell had never made his decisions based upon the opinions of "sensible people."

As a boy on his rooftop in Boston, and later under the clear skies of Japan, Lowell had used his best telescopes to see similar marks on ruddy Mars. Long canals extending thousands of miles across the red desert. Straight lines, networks, intersections, all obviously of artificial origin. His observations and his imagination had convinced him that such markings must be indicative of life, an intelligent civilization. What *were* the canals? Why had they been constructed across the vast waterless continents? Were the Martians perhaps building great works—irrigation systems and pumping stations—to enable their race to survive on a dying world?

Lowell wanted to send them a message that intelligent life had sprung from the womb of the Earth as well, that the Martians were not alone in the universe.

Other astronomers claimed not to see the canals at all. It reminded Lowell of the trial of Galileo, when high church officials and Pope Paul V had refused to admit seeing the moons of Jupiter through the astronomer's "optick glass," denying the evidence of their own eyes. Lowell couldn't decide if his contemporaries were similarly bullheaded, or just plain blind. But he would show them, provided the work could be completed according to the rigid schedule he had imposed.

When he took a deep breath, the fiery heat and dust and petroleum stench curled the hairs in his moustache. He fished inside the pocket of his cream jacket and withdrew his special pair of pince-nez with lenses made of red-stained glass. Through the oxide tint, he could look out at the blistering Sahara, imagining instead the scarlet sands of Mars. *Mars*. Dr. Moreau, his new colleague in this undertaking, had given him the spectacles. They were a very effective tool, especially out here.

In such a great desert, how could one not intuitively understand? Water covered sixty percent of the Earth's surface, while Mars was a vast planetary wasteland. The Martians must have found it necessary to construct the magnificent canals as their parched world withered with age. By now, those once-glorious minds must be desperate, ready to grasp at any hope . . . .

Lowell strolled from the encampment to the long ditch his army of workers had cut through the shifting sands. From atop a crate, barrel-chested Moreau bellowed at the laborers. "Dig! Dig, you bastards! It's only sand."

If Lowell's calculations were correct, they had little time. The Martian emissary would be on its way, but lost, forging toward the wilderness of Earth. In the whole civilization of humanity, Lowell believed only he maintained an open mind. Only he was a legitimate and acceptable emissary for dignitaries from another planet in the solar system. Unless he sent his signal, the Martian would not know where to go. The alien emissary would become lost in a bureaucratic tangle of skeptics and Luddites.

If the approaching Martian craft saw Lowell's signal, then it could alter its course, go to a welcoming ear, someone who could become a champion for two planets. Lowell had exorbitant plans, but he did not believe he had delusions of grandeur. He wanted to do this for the betterment of humanity, not for his own glory, but because it was the right thing to do.

Lowell would bring the Martian emissary to the halls of Earthly government. He would accept his kudos, nod to his rich father and see if the old man might be proud. Then he would change the course of history.

But only if he could transmit his message in time.

Lowell prayed his workers would do their jobs swiftly enough, or his signal to the Martians would be in vain.

* * *

Months earlier, freshly returned from his sojourn in mysterious Japan, Lowell had spent a frustrating night at the Harvard Observatory. The skies were not far enough from the smoke of men, thus the seeing had been murky. But it was the best telescope currently available to him.

Lowell paid for his private observing time here with large donations from his family fortune, but he had already decided that he must fund a new observatory in a location chosen for its seeing, weather, and altitude—not for the convenience of Harvard astronomers. Most important, his new observatory must be completed in time to study the upcoming 1894 opposition of Mars.

A young Harvard assistant, Andrew Ellicott Douglass, stood inside the echoing dome, waiting for Lowell to relinquish the eyepiece. The wooden-plank walls exuded a resinous scent. From where he sat, pork pie hat turned backward on his head and sketchpad in his lap, Lowell could sense the young man's impatience. But he did not remove his eye from the wavering ruddy disk, where fine lines appeared and disappeared.

"Mister Lowell, sir, I understand your eagerness to use the refractor, but I have the proper qualifications—"

Lowell looked down from his seat on the padded ladder. "Qualifications, Mr. Douglass? I have exceptionally keen eyesight—and an exceptionally large fortune. Therefore I am also fully qualified." Tact was a commodity that served little purpose as far as Lowell was concerned, but now he made a half-hearted attempt. "You are welcome to devote any other night to the study of the heavens, but this is *Mars* and it is near opposition. Please indulge an unworthy amateur."

Within moments Lowell had become totally engrossed in the view again. With his hands guided by the image in the eyepiece, Lowell deftly sketched Mars, copying the lines he saw. He had never been an armchair astronomer and would go blind before he allowed himself to be considered one. He had already recorded over a hundred of the canals he saw on Mars.

After midnight, his eyes burning, he flipped to a fresh page in his sketchpad where earlier in the day he had already scribed a circle as the outline for another drawing of the red planet. At some time in the past hour, Douglass had left. Lowell hoped the young man was at least doing work at one of the other telescopes, since this evening's seeing was so extraordinary. He oriented his pencil on the map pad, then looked through the eyepiece again.

A brilliant green flash leaped from the surface of Mars, a jet of vivid emerald fire as of a great explosion, or some kind of cannon shot. A huge mass of luminous gas trailed a green mist behind it.

Once previously, Lowell had seen the glint of sunlight on the Martian ice caps, which had fooled him into seeing a dazzling message, but it had not been like this. Not so green, so violent, so prominent.

He noted the exact time on the pad in his lap, and his excitement grew as he formulated an explanation. The phenomenon was obviously a stupendous *launch*, a ship exploding away from the gravity of Mars into space!

Where else would they go, but to Earth? The Martians were coming!

* * *

Naturally, no one believed him . . . but Lowell didn't care.

Laying plans for a great project to signal the Martians, he calculated the largest possible excavation, then set off immediately to Europe on his way to French Algeria, and thence down into the deepest Sahara . . . .

In order to generate support and receive the blessing of a man he revered, Lowell traveled by way of Milan, Italy. Though he was not easily intimidated, he found himself stuttering in awe when he met the great Giovanni Schiaparelli, original cartographer of the canals of Mars and director of the Milan Observatory since 1862. Using only an eight-inch telescope, he had discovered the asteroid Hesperia and created original maps of the Martian *canali* in 1877, only a year after Lowell graduated with honors from Harvard.

"When I made my drawings," the old astronomer said, struggling with his English, "I was meant for those lines to represent only channels or cracks in surface. I, myself, never thought of *canali* as more than blemishes. I am told that the word *canali* suggest a different thing to non-Italian ears, maybe man-made canals—"

"Not made by men," Lowell interrupted, "but by intelligent beings. Geometrical precision on a planetary scale? What else can it be but the mark of an intelligent race?"

The old astronomer poured from a bottle of Chianti on a side table. He took a sip and blinked his rheumy eyes. His rooms were filled with books, oil lamps, and melted lumps of candles in terra cotta dishes. A pair of spectacles lay on an open tome, while an enormous magnifying glass rested within easy reach. Lowell felt a rare flash of sympathy—losing one's eyesight must be the worst hell a dedicated astronomer could imagine.

"I wish you could see what I have discerned, Signore Schiaparelli. Think of a dying world inhabited by a once-marvelous civilization. The very existence of a planetwide system of canals implies a world order that knows no national boundaries, a society that long ago forgot its political disputes and racial animosity, uniting the populace in a quest for water. The dark spots are pumping stations, obviously. Or oases."

Schiaparelli took a quick swallow of his Chianti, only to begin a brief coughing fit. Outside on the open balcony, pigeons fluttered in the sunlight. "But if Mars is so arid, Signore Lowell, surely all water must evaporate from the open *canali* . . . if the temperature is above freezing, of course—and it *must* be in order for the water to stay in its liquid state."

Lowell paced the room. "What if the lines we see are aqueducts, with lush vegetation thriving in irrigated soil, much as the Egyptians grow their crops in the Nile flood plains? I estimate the darkened aqueduct fringes to be about thirty miles wide. Vegetation would not only emphasize the lines of the canals, but would also shield the open water from rapid evaporation. Simple, you see?"

The old astronomer seemed more amused than captivated by the concepts. Lowell came closer to his host, barely controlling his enthusiasm. "My proposed plan in the Sahara follows a similar principle, Signore, but on a much smaller scale, since I am only one man and, alas, our own Earthly civilization has no stomach for such dreams. But someone must send a signal to our star-crossed brothers."

"And how will you accomplish this?"

"I have already dispatched surveyors and work teams to southern Algeria. I will excavate three canals, each one ten miles long, across an otherwise featureless basin, to form a perfect equilateral triangle. A geometrical symbol impossible to explain by random natural processes. Therefore, it will be a clear message that intelligent life inhabits this world. I will emphasize my puny canals with lines of fire, filling the trenches with petroleum products and igniting them under the cloudless desert skies. It will be a brief but dramatic message, blazing into the night. But I am confident the Martians will see it."

His eyes sparkled, his voice rose in volume. Based on his own celestial calculations, Lowell had estimated how much travel time the Martians would require to reach Earth. He lowered his voice. "I believe the Martians have already launched an ambassador to us."

Schiaparelli appeared surprised at such a bold assertion, but Lowell spoke with absolute confidence. "We must show them where to land. The Martian representative will receive an open-hearted welcome from us. Signore Schiaparelli, *I* intend to lead that party. I will be the first man to shake hands with a Martian."

* * *

He first met Dr. Moreau in an Algerian coffee shop, of all places.

The beefy man sat alone, drinking a glass of sweet mint

tea and taking apart an orange as if preparing to perform an autopsy on it. When he finished with the juicy sections, he turned to a plate of almonds and proceeded to crack the shells with his bare fingers, methodically eating one nut at a time.

Entering the café to escape the North African heat, Lowell waved his hat in front of his face to cool the sweat. He took another chair at the bar, cautiously nodding to the large Englishman. Outside, from the minarets of the mosques, mullahs let out warbling calls, like territorial songbirds competing with each other.

Lowell had just learned of delays at the Sahara construction site: Tuareg digger crews that had wandered off, French prison workers who had escaped, even supervisors who had taken money earmarked for wages and run off to Cairo. Here in Algiers, one Foreign Legion commander had accepted a retainer fee with the promise of finding Lowell other workers, but had never returned at the appointed meeting time.

Lowell was disgusted, impatient, and growing desperate. "If a work ethic exists on this continent, I'm damned if I can find it," he said aloud so the other man could hear him. "No wonder they're all so frightfully poor."

The bearish man did not seem interested in conversation, but Lowell continued to vent his frustration. "When a man agrees to do a job, and accepts money for it, I should be able to count on him. Lazy bastards. They do bad work, they leave the site, they simply vanish—and there is not enough time to do it all over again!" He set his hat on the counter.

The other man's eyes were a piercing blue, set in pale skin that had been subjected to the rigors of much sun but had never achieved more than the blotchy coloring of repeated burns. His hair was reddish gold, as was his beard; the matted strands on his forearms were thick enough to be called a pelt. In a gruff voice he said, "They abandon you because they are not afraid of you."

"I beg your pardon, sir?"

"Just a matter of incentive . . . and terror." He paused, as if considering. "My name is Moreau. A medical doctor by trade, at least where I'm still allowed to practice."

He cracked another almond and continued to stare across the tiled counter. The Algerian waiter asked in Arabic if he wanted another tea. Moreau motioned to Lowell as well, and the waiter stuffed two glasses with fresh green mint leaves then poured boiling sugar water over the top. The smell made Lowell dizzy.

"You're Lowell, right? I heard about your massive project out in the desert." Moreau did not even glance at him. "No one can understand why you are doing it."

"No one attempts to understand. They prefer to scoff."

"Then explain yourself. I am a man of some education."

Lowell sipped his tea, made a face at the syrupy sweetness, then told the broad-shouldered doctor everything. He had nothing to gain by keeping a secret about something so vast and ambitious.

Moreau didn't commiserate, but his broken-ice eyes showed true understanding. "I know how it feels to be ridiculed for one's passion. I am a researcher into anatomy and physiology. I, too, have my ignorant detractors."

Lowell had heard horrific tales of aspiring surgeons who paid grave robbers to provide fresh corpses for dissection. "I see. You are a . . . resurrectionist? Or a vivisectionist?"

"Neither, or both. In my time, I conducted . . . extreme investigations into the fundamental differences between humans and animals, and the mutability of the physical form. I was a colleague of the outspoken Darwinist T.H. Huxley in London, but my work was too extraordinary even for his comprehension. He called it 'unethical,' when it was really no more than unorthodox." He cracked another almond. "Ethics! What do ethics have to do with pure discovery?"

Despite himself, Lowell was interested in this man. Moreau's personality seemed as overpowering as his own. "And why are you here, in this godforsaken place?"

"Because Huxley discovered my work before I was ready to present it to the Imperial Institute. Damn him! I barely escaped England without being arrested. I am a wanted man there, probably reviled in all the newspapers, called a monster."

"Oh. I think I read something about it. In the *Hong Kong Post*?"

Moreau swept the crushed almond shells onto his plate with surprising delicacy. He turned to Lowell so abruptly that it startled the other man. "If I help you accomplish this strange task, will you promise me one thing?"

"I haven't asked for your help, sir."

"Nevertheless, you need it. If your scheme turns out to be true, if creatures from the planet Mars do arrive here, then I must be the one to study them, physiologically." For a moment, Moreau looked vulnerable. "It will restore my reputation in the scientific community."

Lowell finished his tea, then rubbed his teeth with his monogrammed handkerchief, removing bits of bright green leaf. "Just like that? You don't think I'm mad?"

"I have been called that myself." Moreau extended his hand. "Remember, *I* will be the one to study the Martian. Agreed?"

Lowell reached out to grasp the hand of the criminal vivisectionist.

* * *

Tuareg work crews and criminal laborers toiled day and night to move the sand. Some complained; some were happy for the meager pay or a reduction in their penal sentences; some shook their sweat-dripping heads at the insanity of this wealthy American's incomprehensible obsession, and the bearded doctor who drove them as fiercely as if they were animals.

The florid-faced surgeon allowed no slacking in the construction, and he was not above whipping the men if necessary. "Savages!" He often left Lowell behind in the camp, riding a horse up and down the miles of diggings.

Shovels tossed sand up over the ditches; half-naked boys ran back and forth with ladles and buckets from camels that strained to drag barrels of water along the dry canal that went from nowhere, to nowhere. Every third day, Lowell himself went to inspect the other two straight-line trenches that were moving with excruciating slowness to intersect with this one.

For the past month, when the teams grew too tired to continue, he had sent word to any oasis, tribal camp, or village, as far as Timbuctoo and Tripoli to hire more workers. Lowell had spread his inexhaustible funds as far as Alexandria, Tangier, and Cairo. He had bribed port officials and paid for the construction of a new railroad spur from Algiers out into the stark heart of the dunes, so that a private train could deliver supplies and workers directly to the diggings.

Blown sand hissed in the breeze. A drummer pounded a cadence to give the workers a steady rhythm, like galley slaves. Moreau had suggested the technique, and it seemed to be working. "They're being paid for this labor, Lowell, and they volunteered. Don't feel sympathy for them."

Smoke curled into the air, carrying an acrid, sulfurous stench as French convicts dumped wagonloads of hot bitumen into the trench. The sticky black flow would seal the sands with a thick, flammable mass that would also hold fuel. Even so, the walls still shifted, and the tarry bitumen ran soft and smelly in the heat of the day.

If one of the great dust storms of the Sahara swept across the dunes, God could erase all of Lowell's handiwork with one mighty breath. But he needed his luck to hold until he sent his signal. By now, the Martian vessel had to be close.

Moreau strutted up and down, a dusty bandanna wrapped across his face. The immense line in the sand stretched into a shimmer of mirage. Just a ditch, many miles long, extending to meet two others in what his surveyors guaranteed would be a perfect equilateral triangle . . . .

Looking at the plans in the tent with Moreau on their first night, he thought their symbol looked laughably small when viewed in perspective against the backdrop of the whole African continent. Lowell despised the thought that his work might prove to be *insignificant*. "Even if we achieve our goals, Moreau, we have accomplished little more than a gnat, compared to what the Martians have done."

"Nonsense!" Moreau always talked too loudly, as if he had

never learned a normal conversational tone. "Their task would have been much simpler, given that Martian gravity is only a third of Earth's." He thumped his fingers on the top of the small worktable. Moreau's numerous notebooks lay around the tent. "Based on current theories of evolution, such Martians could be twenty-one times as efficient and have eighty-one times the effective strength of an Earthman." He held the kerosene lamp closer to the map. "For such a species, the project of planetary canals seems neither difficult nor unlikely."

Lowell had done the excavation mathematics himself, letting the engineers double-check his work. Three trenches, each ten miles long, five yards wide, filled with liquid to a depth of an inch or so, equaled thousands and thousands of gallons of petroleum distillate, naphtha, kerosene. Convoys traveled endlessly across the Sahara.

Although it was a huge investment, what better way could Lowell spend his money, than to make a mark upon the Earth itself—and upon history?

But they had to hurry. Hurry.

* * *

Finally.

Finally. Lowell had never been a man of extraordinary patience, but the last week of waiting for the trenches to join at precise corners had seemed the most interminable time of his life.

Now, under the starlight and residual heat that wafted off the sands, Lowell stood with torch in hand like a tribal shaman, ready to send a symbol of welcome to aliens from another world. Moreau would be standing at a second distant corner of the triangle, along with his work crew supervisor.

The stench of petroleum distillates stung his eyes and nostrils. The convict workers had all been shipped back to Algiers or distant Saharan outposts. The chemical smell had driven off the camels and most of the workers. A few European foremen had stayed to watch the spectacle, and curious Tuaregs gathered by their tents to observe. This would be an event their tribal storytellers would repeat for generations.

Lowell turned to the telegraph operator beside him. Miles of overland cable had been run to the vertices of the great triangle. "Signal Dr. Moreau and Mr. Lewisham at the intersections. Tell them to light their channels."

The telegraph operator pecked away at his key, sending a brief message. When the clicks fell into silence, Lowell stepped to the brink of his canal in the sand. He stared into the bitumen-lined trench at the foul-smelling black mass that was now pooled with kerosene and gasoline.

Lowell tossed his torch into the fuel, then watched the fire rush down the channel like a hungry demon. The inferno devoured the petroleum, its flames hot enough to ignite the sticky bitumen liner so that the triangular symbol would burn for a long time.

Across the desert night, rifle shots rang out, signaling to torch-bearers stationed along the miles of each canal, who also tossed their burning brands into the ditch.

Lowell's family had amassed its fortune in textiles, in landholdings, in finance. His maternal grandfather was Abbott Lawrence, minister to Britain. His father, Augustus, was descended from early Massachusetts colonists. But Percival

Lowell himself would make the greatest mark—on *two* worlds instead of one.

An unbroken wall of flame roared into the night. He prayed the Martians were watching. He had so much to say to them.

* * *

Even long after the inferno had died down, Lowell found it difficult to sleep. He lay on his cot, smelling the dying smoke and harsh fumes, listening to the whisper of sand sloughing into the trench from the burned walls. Far off in the Tuareg camp a pair of camels belched at each other.

Lying awake on his cot, he spoke aloud to the apex of his tent. "I am an experienced ambassador to foreign cultures. I have diplomatic credentials. How could Martians be stranger than what I have already seen?"

If only they would arrive . . . .

* * *

Days later, the cylinder screamed through the air with the wailing of a thousand lost souls, trailing a flaming banner from atmospheric friction and a bright green mist from outgassing extraterrestrial substances.

Lowell scrambled out of his shaded tent to see the commotion. A burnt smudge smoldered like a scar across the ceramic-blue sky. Booms of sound came in waves as the gigantic projectile crossed overhead.

Moreau was already outside. "It's the emissaries from Mars, Lowell!" He raised his hands in the air. "The Martians!"

The cylinder crashed into the desert, spewing a plume of sand and dust. Lowell felt the tremor of impact in his knees. He and Moreau both laughed aloud and pounded each other on the back.

After the burning of the enormous triangle, the place had rapidly turned into a ghost town, but Lowell and Moreau had remained here to wait. Now, as the dust settled in the distance, Lowell cried, "We are vindicated!"

Moreau clapped him on the shoulder. "It is a very good feeling, Lowell."

The last Tuareg helpers retreated in panic, thrashing their camels to an awkward gallop across the dunes to a safe distance. *Fools*. They did not realize the magnitude of what was happening here.

"The world as we know it is about to change, Moreau. Come, we must welcome our visitors from space."

Together, they set off toward the pit.

PART I

SCIENTIFIC ROMANCE

CHAPTER THREE

A MESSAGE FROM AN OLD ACQUAINTANCE

1894

Another day of writing finished already, and the morning was still fresh. H.G. Wells set his handwritten pages aside and fairly leaped from his desk, satisfied with what he had done and ready for the rest of the day with Jane. Despite its lack of great literary merit, he was confident the article would bring in a few more shillings from the *Pall Mall Gazette*.

Such pieces were easy to do, and the readers certainly enjoyed them, though few of his writings contained any profound insights. Earning money as a writer was certainly better than being a teacher, a shopkeeper, or—he shuddered—a draper, handling bolts of cloth in a dreary warehouse. No, writing suited him best and, at twenty-eight years old, Wells had little chance for a more active profession since his latest collapse and the continued decline of his health.

Five years earlier, one of Wells's hateful students had intentionally hurt him while they were playing football in the schoolyard. The bully had viciously kicked his teacher in the kidneys, though he later claimed it was an accident. Wells spat blood for months and never really recovered.

In the seven years since Wells had graduated from the Normal Academy in South Kensington, he had accepted various teaching positions. But one night when returning from the train station he'd begun coughing blood, a relapse of his old kidney injury. The hemorrhage had continued, leading to a severe breakdown, which now required a long convalescence. When he first gave up teaching, he had stared at the specter of poverty—until he realized that he could write his little articles, and sell them.

Now he was attempting to be a full-time writer, producing short stories and essays and a constant stream of ruminations that the magazines liked. Luckily, the 1870 Education Act had opened schooling to many formerly illiterate British children, and now the population had a new crop of readers hungry for fiction and articles. Wells was happy to fill the need. As long as he was with Jane, nothing could be so bad after all.

He glanced at the pages he had finished, picked up the pen again and instinctively scratched out a few words, scribbling in corrections. Before he realized it, another ten minutes had passed. He forced himself to stop. *Priorities, Wells!* old T.H. Huxley would have told him, ten years ago. The lovely Miss Jane would be waiting for him, probably already dressed to go out.

He grinned like an eager schoolboy as he pulled open the door to his makeshift study. Spending time with her was far more enjoyable than writing inane articles.

Jane had tied back all the curtains and opened the windows to let in fresh breezes, since their rented rooms in Euston were far enough away from the dirty factory smoke in London and upwind from the smelly waters of the Thames. Now, in spring, the flowers the landlady had planted around the small house were in bloom. Starlings sat in the trees, and blackbirds flew over the nearby hedgerows and fields.

Jane was indeed there, ostensibly waiting for him but preoccupied with her own studies. She sat at the window with a guidebook of the birds of England on her lap, a pair of opera glasses obscuring her dark, wide-set eyes, as she stared out at the trees and the nearby meadow. Her loveliness always took his breath away.

"My dear Miss Robbins," he said, a smile appearing below his thin moustache. He sketched a bow. "I am sorry to have kept you waiting."

"Indeed, Mr. Wells," she answered, setting her book and her opera glasses aside and standing up to offer him a curtsey. "I believe we had an appointment?" She wore a long white skirt and black boots. A lacy shawl covered her shoulders, though Wells doubted the air would be cool enough to require it. Her high-cheekboned face was finely featured, and the irises of her brown eyes were lenses to a clever mind that showed the sharpness of her wit and intelligence. "Besides, this close to home I am not likely to see anything more interesting than a robin or a pigeon. On our walk, perhaps I should take my *Guidebook of Wildflowers?*"

"I shall not be looking at anything but you, my dear."

"You are a liar, H.G."

"I am a writer, Jane. There is a difference."

She was quite the opposite from Wells's newly estranged wife, Isabel. Years ago, as soon as he'd been able to support himself after graduating from the Normal School, he had ill-advisedly married his cousin on the recommendation of her mother and his own parents. It had been a terrible error in judgment. Isabel Wells had a calm personality, a beatific acceptance of things, and an utter lack of curiosity. She was unworldly, shy, and—worst of all—uninteresting. Within weeks of their marriage, they had both known that they'd made a mistake.

"Shall we go for our walk?" Jane asked him now, taking her opera glasses and the guidebooks for birds and flowers. "I've been waiting all morning."

"I can think of nothing better to do with the rest of the day."

She sniffed. "Really? So much for your supposedly refined imagination." Jane came forward to give him a quick kiss, then a longer one before reluctantly pulling away with a long sigh.

"Let me think on it."

For a time, Wells had loved Isabel well enough, but she possessed no spark, nothing to engage his furiously working mind. One of Wells's students, however—Amy Catherine Robbins, whom he called "Jane"—held the fire he needed. Meeting Jane was like sipping fine wine after he'd had only vinegar all his life.

Now, while Jane adjusted the pale yellow hat that perched on her neatly coiffed auburn hair, he admired her. "Of all the discoveries made by men of science, I believe that you, Jane, will always be my greatest discovery."

She took him by the arm, guiding him to the door. "The day awaits us, H.G., and if you continue with this flattery, we will never be about our business."

"We certainly could be about *some* business," he joked, but followed her anyway.

Since it would still be some time until his divorce from Isabel was final, he and Jane lived together quietly in their new Euston home, calling little attention to themselves. The starry-eyed couple had already been ousted from one set of rooms when a suspicious landlady insisted that they produce their marriage certificate.

As she took the lead down the path, Jane said, "Shall we go boating today? Or bicycling? Or just take a romantic walk down the lane?"

He donned a straw boater hat to protect his pale skin from the sun. "Since I finished another *Pall Mall* article, let us celebrate by renting bicycles."

"Can we afford it?"

"Not at all, but with our debts, what difference will a few farthings make?"

In addition to their own expenses, circumstances required him to support his old mother, who still toiled as a servant at Uppark. His father, long separated from her, had never been able to hold a job or make a success of anything in his life. Sadly, Wells's brother Frank seemed to be following in their ne'er-do-well father's footsteps. Frank tinkered with clocks, fancying himself a skilled mechanic, but he had no business sense and little ambition to do any work that did not set itself in front of him. It was left to Wells to pay for Isabel's needs. It never seemed to end, and he kept "writing away for dear life."

Times were hard . . . but they had always been hard, and he was accustomed to having no more than a few coins in his pockets. Though Wells had not achieved the goals he had hoped for in his life, he was happier than he had ever been before. He was with Jane. What could be finer? He would find a way to survive, somehow.

After they reached the bicycle shop and Wells paid for their rental, he helped Jane situate herself, adjusting her skirts. "Someday a great man will invent a bicycle with two seats, so that you and I can be even closer."

She pedaled ahead, weaving in circles as she waited for him to join her. "It sounds impractical."

"Impracticalities have never stopped the common man from doing anything he found amusing." Wells rode beside her, and they turned down a lane overshadowed by elms. Puffy white clouds scudded across the blue skies, and the day was warm.

"Someday we should rent one of Mr. Benz's new four-wheeled motorcars to drive around the parks," Jane suggested. "Noisy new machines, all that clatter and smoke!"

"If you desire such a vehicle, my dear, then we'll do more than rent one—we shall *own* one. I read in the newspaper that Henry Ford in America has begun to market his own automobile."

"You always look to the future, H.G."

"On the day that everyone owns a four-wheeled motorcar, Jane, you and I shall have to ride horses—just to be different."

They talked together, barely paying attention to where they were riding. The mention of Karl Benz's four-wheeled car led to a discussion of German industrial dominance and growing aggressiveness, now that Prussia and Germany had been fused into the Second Reich. Kaiser Wilhelm II had just signed a commercial treaty with the Russians that would make them into a much more powerful nation, and many Britons were worried.

Next, Jane wanted to discuss the unusual art nouveau movement sweeping across Europe, after which Wells insisted on talking about Nansen's departure from Norway on an ambitious expedition to reach the North Pole. When the conversation turned to politics, they discussed the Independent Labour Party, which Wells hoped would assist the downtrodden working class created by the Industrial Revolution.

The lively exchange of ideas reminded Wells of just how different this was from his painfully silent afternoons with Isabel, who never even read the newspapers and couldn't tell the difference between a starling and an ostrich, a thistle or a rose. At first Wells had talked with Isabel a great deal, but she had always remained quiet, listening with a flat, unengaged smile, her expression as devoid of interest as a porcelain doll's might have been . . . .

After two hours of slow riding, he and Jane made their way back to the bicycle shop, before they would incur an additional rental fee.

* * *

When they returned home for a late tea, the landlady was waiting with a letter in her hand. "Mr. Wells, this note was delivered for you this afternoon. It looks to be important, but the messenger would tell me nothing of its contents." She seemed to expect him to open the message in front of her and read it aloud.

Wells stiffly thanked her, knowing the woman already had

her suspicions about him and Jane. "I'm exhausted from my bike ride. Jane, let's rest for awhile and then look at this at our leisure." They closed the door, leaving the frustrated landlady behind.

Wells quickly looked at the note, fearing it might be from Isabel's solicitor, or someone demanding payment of a long overdue bill.

"What is it, H.G.?"

"A mystery." The amorphous glob of sealing wax reminded him of the single-celled amoebae he had studied under a microscope in biology class long ago. When he saw that it came from the Imperial Institute, he withdrew the letter and was astonished to learn the identity of its sender.

"Professor Huxley! He was my teacher long ago, but I thought he'd retired. He certainly hasn't been in public view for years. But why would he write me?"

Jane did not hold back the obvious explanation. "If you were his student, H.G., he must be proud of you. Perhaps he's read your articles."

"I can't imagine that he would." Wells went to the light by the window and read the note.

To Mr. H.G. Wells:

Please forgive this intrusion, if such you find it, but I have a matter of utmost importance that I wish to present to you.

After encountering some of your recent writings, I recalled with no small degree of pride how you excelled in the course I taught. Ten years ago I considered you to be a young man of ambition, vision, and intelligence, and your articles and essays have convinced me that my judgment remains sound.

With this in mind, I offer you a proposition. As you must be aware, the Imperial Institute was formed last year to promote higher education. What you do not know is that the Institute also has a vital and secret purpose. I invite you here to visit me for a week to learn what that purpose is.

I offer you my personal guarantee that it will be one of the most important things you ever do. I require the advice and input of the author of "Man of the Year Million."

"Your Professor Huxley is very mysterious," Jane said. "But he did read your article."

"And I am naturally intrigued . . . exactly as Professor Huxley expected, no doubt." He leaned close and gave her a kiss. "But how can I bear to be away from you for so long? You are my sounding board, the genesis and regulator of my ideas."

She gently pushed him away, then removed the pins from her hat and let her beautiful hair fall free. "I will miss you too, H.G. But we both know that you simply must go. Your imagination and intellect are up to the task, even without me."

CHAPTER FOUR

IMPOSSIBLE DISCOVERIES AT THE IMPERIAL INSTITUTE

When he arrived at the Imperial Institute, Wells stood at the ornate wrought-iron gates with a small suitcase in hand and imagined himself a young student again, eager to learn but knowing so little. He lifted his gaze to the imposing brick structure that housed so many great educators under one immense roof, feeling that he couldn't possibly belong in such an auspicious place. But he was no intruder here. He, Herbert George Wells, an invited guest of the great T.H. Huxley, was seizing an opportunity.

Holding his chin up, he stepped through the gate and into the well-manicured grounds.

Though he was eager to embark on something new, he

wished the old professor had given him some hint as to why he'd been called here. What could Wells possibly offer this impressive institute?

He climbed the stone steps of the main building and stopped at the imposing front doors. Again, Wells felt terribly out of place in the echoing halls that smelled of oiled wood and polished stone.

Students hurried by, talking with one another and ignoring the shabbily dressed stranger. The upper-class young men carried new books under their arms and wore fashionable clothes that were far superior to the threadbare clothing Wells had been able to afford as a student ten years previous.

Wells drew a deep breath and reminded himself that he was here because of Huxley's invitation, which he kept folded in his jacket pocket like a shield. Gathering his nerve, he marched directly to the school office and announced himself.

The male secretary behind the desk looked up, checked the appointment book, and nodded. "Yes, Mr. Wells, you are expected." He rang a bell, and a young volunteer arrived, obviously a student working for the office. "Please take a message to Professor Huxley. Let him know that his visitor has arrived."

Another young man came through a side door and relieved Wells of his small suitcase, which contained only a single change of clothes, as well as paper and lead pencils for taking notes or writing letters to Jane. "I will take this to your room, sir. Everything will be in order when you arrive."

Before Wells could splutter questions or even a thank you, the student hurried away. The secretary returned in a bustle, carrying a tray with a pot of tea and an arrangement of biscuits. Wells ate everything in sight before realizing that he was showing his nervousness. He sat back and tried to relax as he sipped his second cup of tea.

Wells was bursting with curiosity by the time an imposing old man entered the room. He leapt to his feet as T.H. Huxley settled his eyes upon him. The professor loomed just as tall as Wells had remembered him from the lecture hall, his white sideburns as bushy, his eyes just as bright. "Mr. Wells, I'm so glad you accepted my invitation."

"I could not do otherwise, sir. But . . . I thought you had chosen to remain out of the public eye. I heard a rumor that your health was poor."

"Ah yes, young man, I *supposedly* retired, but do not believe every story you hear. Occasionally there are other reasons for what a person does."

"Do you . . . do you have a teaching post for me, sir? Is that why you've called—"

"Not at all, Mr. Wells." Not noticing his crestfallen expression, Huxley continued. "It is something much more important than that. Come with me. Observe and consider, and when you finally choose to speak, I hope you can be a bit more . . . articulate?"

"I will try my best, sir."

The old man's stride was careful but still surprisingly brisk for a person of his age, as if he was impatient to be at his destination. With barely a sideways glance, he led Wells past the hubbub of lecture halls and demonstration labs, beyond student rooms and inner courtyards lined with benches and chess tables.

Huxley took him into a completely separate wing that ended in a locked door. With a flourish, the professor removed a key and twisted it in the lock, swinging the door wide on well-oiled hinges. "You are about to enter the future, Mr. Wells. Here, away from the prying eyes of spies and the merely curious, we perform vital work for the queen."

After Huxley conscientiously locked the door behind them, they walked past cavernous rooms with glass skylights and long tables covered with beakers and retorts of chemicals, long tubing, alcohol burners, and hand-cranked pumps. These laboratories were far more extravagant than the simple teaching studios the Institute allowed the students to use.

"These rooms look large enough for full-scale production . . . of something," Wells commented.

"Indeed."

Passing door after door, Wells smelled odd mixtures of chemicals and smoke, heard assistants chattering, saw chalkboards covered with equations. Intent men stood before designs and theorems, arguing over various consequences and derivations.

Huxley gestured proudly. "Mr. Wells, in this institute we have quietly gathered the greatest minds in the British Empire to pursue a high calling. We have chemists, engineers, mathematicians, biologists, architects. Not even Socrates ever encountered such a cadre of clever brains."

Wells stood overwhelmed, but he remembered Huxley's admonition to be articulate when he spoke. "But . . . why am I here, sir? I took only a single course from you, years ago. Surely, I could not have made such a lasting impression."

"Ah, I've enjoyed your interesting articles in the *Pall Mall Gazette*, Mr. Wells. Many are simple diversions, but others contain glimmers of true insight. I wanted your objective view about a certain important matter."

Wells cleared his throat. "What matter is that, sir?"

Huxley placed a strong hand on his thin, bony shoulder. "Very soon, we will hold a momentous conference here, a secret symposium." He met Wells with his intense dark gaze. "The fate of the world is at stake."

* * *

With a boyish delight, Huxley continued to show him the technological marvels quietly being developed behind the Institute's closed doors. Wells felt as if he had followed Lewis Carroll's Alice down the rabbit hole.

As the professor made his way down the halls, however, Wells noted that the old man's movements had a slow fragility. His joints obviously gave him great pain, and his breathing had a labored quality. Wells remembered Huxley's charisma and stentorian voice as he lectured about the wonders of biology or scoffed at the persistent challenges to Darwin's theory of evolution.

Wells peered through broad hall windows into research rooms filled with experiments in progress. Voltaic battery piles flashed electrical arcs; purple, brown, and green smokes rose from various beakers. They paused to admire a long, bubbling train of distillation tubes and fractionating cylinders. "This all reminds me of *Gulliver's Travels*—the third section, where the scientists of Laputa levitate their flying island by using a lodestone of prodigious size."

Huxley frowned. "This is deadly serious work, Mr. Wells, not a satirical scheme to extract sunlight from cucumbers. Our laboratory facilities are the finest in existence. Our equipment is superior even to the best Prussian instruments. We will have to surpass the Germans, Wells, if we are to defeat them in the coming war."

"War? War with the German Empire?"

Huxley cocked his bushy eyebrows. "Ah, surely you can read the newspapers and make obvious extrapolations?"

The recent unification of thirty-nine German states, including Austria and Prussia, had created the Second Reich, adding more strength to the historically aggressive Empire. This had raised concerns across Europe, especially considering the Reich's direction under the firm statesmanship of Chancellor Otto von Bismarck. Then, four years ago, not long after the beginning of his reign, the new Kaiser Wilhelm II had ousted Bismarck, and many in Britain had heaved a sigh of relief.

Now, the British Empire was apparently making contingency plans, looking to the future and preparing for the worst eventuality. Wells was embarrassed that he had not previously grasped the seriousness of the situation.

Huxley explained, "When setting up this secret portion of the Imperial Institute, Queen Victoria told me to let no possibility go unexplored, no idea unconsidered, no possibility ignored. Without restrictions, our chemistry labs are developing new explosives and exotic materials." He pointed to the heavy vault doors of yet another facility. "Behold our hermetically sealed germ laboratory where microbiologists study virulent diseases such as the bubonic plague and cholera."

Wells peered at the earnest doctors inside the sealed lab. "If these geniuses are as talented as you say, Professor, they are sure to find a cure."

Huxley raised his eyebrows. "Ah, but they are not seeking

a *cure*, Mr. Wells—they are attempting to derive military applications. Think what weapons such bacilli could become, if the germs were trained to recognize the difference between an enemy uniform and a loyal British soldier!"

Wells chuckled at what he thought was a joke; Huxley did not. He moved on before the younger man could articulate his questions and skepticisms.

With a grand gesture, Huxley opened the door to the next lab, covering his nose against the potent stench of acrid fumes. Wells rubbed his moustache and blinked stinging tears from his eyes. A single window near the ceiling struggled vainly to exhaust the noxious smokes.

Waving to clear the air in front of his face, Huxley strode into the lab. "Allow me to introduce Dr. Hawley Griffin, one of our most brilliant, if unorthodox, organic chemists."

A dark-haired man worked diligently alone amidst a forest of test tubes and bubbling retorts. He looked up, clearly annoyed at the distraction. His stiff hair stood up like a spiky boar's-bristle brush. His reddened, chemically irritated eyes wavered from Huxley to Wells, then back again, as if looking for something interesting enough to seize his attention. "I'm on trial number fifty-six. As you can see, I have nearly achieved success."

Huxley explained. "Dr. Griffin is devising an invisibility formula that can make anything completely transparent. Ah, imagine the opportunities for espionage, spies with perfect camouflage."

Griffin interrupted him. "More than just spies. An invisible man could be a thief, an assassin, or a detective. A hero."

Considering the bristle-haired chemist's eccentricities and his disjointed thoughts, Wells wondered about the possible damage his brain might have suffered from breathing chemical mists all day long.

Huxley said in a mild voice, "We have finally acquired a sufficient supply of laboratory animals for Dr. Griffin so that he stops testing his formulas on himself." Off in the corner, a cage full of white rats squeaked, as if complaining to the guinea pigs in an adjacent container about the conditions of their confinement.

"Numbers seven and twenty-one had particularly offensive flavors." The chemist juggled various containers of powders and liquids, all of which were unlabeled and chaotically arranged. Wells didn't know how Griffin could keep his precise mixtures straight and reproducible.

The scientist looked up again, as if surprised to find his visitors still there. "I have already conceived enough variations to attempt fifty different formulae. One of those concoctions will certainly prove effective!" Griffin drew a long sigh. "I hope the appropriate one tastes good enough to swallow."

Huxley took Wells by the elbow. "We must not disturb Dr. Griffin's researches further."

They closed the lab door behind them, and Wells breathed deeply of the corridor's fresh air. "Invisibility? Is he serious with his idea?"

"Oh yes, Wells. And he may actually have a chance at success, though I admit he is one of our more . . . unorthodox researchers. Next, allow me to show you a more traditional laborer, though his designs and discoveries are no less remarkable than Dr. Griffin's."

From directly ahead came the sounds of pounding and hissing, conversation and bellowed orders. The wide double doors were already open to an immense manufacturing bay where grease-smudged workers tended chemical furnaces, production benches, and intensely hot crucibles. In the center of the room, others hammered away at a large spherical framework supported by heavy braces.

"Unlike our friend Griffin, Dr. Cavor uses a team of assistants. He prefers to supervise the large-scale operation while others follow through on his ideas. That way, he accomplishes everything he can imagine as swiftly as his concepts occur to him."

Cavor was a short, broad-shouldered man with thick eyebrows, a stout neck, and hairy forearms. He issued gruff orders, directing the installation of curved milky-white plates onto the armillary framework. The layers of translucent tile were attached like dragon scales to the spherical vessel.

Cavor noticed the visitors and turned, clapping his meaty hands and shouting to his team. "You! Keep up the work while I meet with Professor Huxley." The squat man jumped down from his raised podium. Like worker bees, the assistants continued without interruption. Cavor stumped toward them on short legs, his puffy eyes alight. His extraordinarily square chin forced his lower lip to protrude slightly, as if he were about to pout. "An inspection tour, Professor? I assure you, I shall have substantial news to announce for the symposium."

"Delighted to hear that, Selwyn. I am simply introducing a protégé of mine, a student I taught back at the Normal School. He'll be joining us for the meeting."

Wells reached out, and Cavor's grease-stained grip was strong and calloused; he wasn't afraid to do hands-on work himself.

Glass-blowers pushed molding trays into orange furnaces that melted hard substances into a thick paste that was poured into shapes. He could not immediately identify the milky substance or its pearlish translucency; he had never seen a metal, glass, or porcelain with a similar construction. "Next you're going to tell me that Dr. Cavor is creating invisible iron."

"Oh, not invisible," Cavor said, "but extremely lightweight. I intend to manufacture an incredibly effective armor with sufficient density to stop projectiles, yet virtually without mass."

Huxley nodded toward squat Cavor. "Lighter than any substance known, Wells. Perhaps it can be made opaque to gravity itself."

Cavor's brows beetled with deep concentration. "The material remains in an unstable equilibrium state. Its crystalline structure needs to be shocked with an appropriate energy pulse to drive it beyond the structural boundary to that next level."

Huxley continued, "With the doctor's amazing 'cavorite,' the British Empire can manufacture feasible and effective ironclads for land or sea."

The workers in the manufacturing bay shouted to each other and barely averted disaster as a pulley chain slipped and a section of shaped cavorite swayed unsteadily. Cavor spun in alarm, calling brusquely to his visitors. "I apologize for being impatient, gentlemen, but the symposium approaches and we are on a deadline. My crews have been working around the clock to finish this demonstration sphere. I must get back to work." He hurried off.

Shaking his head as the professor led him out of the work room, Wells didn't know whether to be filled with wonder or skepticism. "All of your people seem to have been reading too much of Monsieur Verne's fiction."

Again Huxley remained serious. "I would not be surprised if the French themselves have an institution similar to this one, and no doubt their Jules Verne is an active part of it. However, Queen Victoria is more concerned with the Second Reich than with the French. That is why we must plan."

CHAPTER FIVE

FOOTSTEPS IN THE CORRIDOR

That night, Wells retired to his small but comfortable guest room in the secret wing of the Institute. He was no longer a penniless student living with A.V. Jennings in austere rented rooms; now he was a distinguished visitor of T.H. Huxley, accorded the hospitality of the Crown.

Exhausted both physically and mentally from all he had seen, Wells sat at a small desk under the flickering gaslight glow. He sharpened one of his lead pencils, then got out a clean sheet of paper. His imagination was fired with images, ideas, speculations; he wanted to share them all with Jane, who loved to debate with him and imagine possibilities. What would she think of the grand schemes of the Imperial Institute? Though he'd been gone only a day, Wells had promised Jane a letter every night. He had so much to tell her that he didn't know if he could get it all down on paper by dawn.

Though it was laughable to think she might be a German spy, he restrained himself from describing details of the Institute's research. Still, he was good at speaking in broad generalities, a technique he had practiced in his *Pall Mall* articles, in order to seem like more of an expert than he actually was.

After he had jotted down only a few paragraphs, though, his thoughts turned toward Jane herself. Her face appeared before his imagination, and he smiled like a love-struck fool. Though she would have been much more interested to hear about the innovative scientific work, his letter quickly devolved into repeated and persistent declarations of how much he missed her. He told her that his guest room was large enough for two, and it seemed vast and empty without her.

He finished by filling the margins with amusing doodles of himself with a big frown on his face and hands clasping a clownishly large heart. Among his correspondents, Wells was famous for the imaginative cartoons that adorned his missives. He sealed the letter so it could be posted the following day.

Seeing that it was well past midnight, he turned down the gaslight and began to undress for bed. Before he could turn in, though, Wells heard noises from the other side of his door. A whisper, then a strange mixture of chuckles and moans, growing louder, quieter, then louder again.

Puzzled, he opened the door a crack and cocked his ear to listen. The eerie noises echoed up and down the shadowy corridors. He thought he heard the sound of bare feet slapping on the wooden floor.

Then, resoundingly clear, came cackling laughter that was either the giggling of a child or the raving of a lunatic. But as he stared up and down the hall, Wells saw nothing but the flickering gaslight from covered jets on the walls. None of the other doors were open; all the other guest scientists were asleep. He could discern no movement.

When he heard the rapid footsteps again, he whirled to his left, half expecting to see a ghost burdened with clanking chains like Jacob Marley from Dickens's *A Christmas Carol*. Again, the corridor was empty.

The next noise was quite distinctly a startled indrawn breath. The footsteps stopped.

"Hullo?" Wells said in a quiet voice, not wanting to shout.

Accompanied by a faint chuckle, he heard running steps, bare feet receding toward the far end of the hall. Wells rubbed his eyes, but could see nothing.

Intrigued and determined to investigate this mystery, he stalked off in the direction of the footsteps. His stockinged feet were silent as he crept down the hall past closed doors. Wells followed the sounds into the wider corridors that led to darkened laboratories. Inside the enclosed research rooms he saw only low flames from gas jets on the walls. All of the labs appeared to be securely closed. Nothing moved inside the industrial bays.

He lost track of the footsteps and could hear no breathing except his own. His heartbeat pounded in his ears, but other than the hiss of gas jets, the night silence remained complete.

Perhaps he had dreamed up this hobgoblin, but he doubted it. Wells had a very vivid imagination, though it had always been at his beck and call. His wild fancies did not trick him with auditory hallucinations in the middle of the night. He was sure he had been wide awake.

He reached the end of the research wing, finding nothing. Putting his hands on his hips, he let out a long, frustrated sigh. After waiting a few more moments, he walked back toward his room, shaking his head.

When he rounded a corner that led back to his guest room, he was astonished to come upon a man standing entirely naked in the middle of the corridor. He recognized the eccentric chemist, Dr. Hawley Griffin. Yellowish-orange light from the gas lamps shone on his pallid skin.

As Wells stood speechless with surprise, the stark-naked man sprinted up to him like a foolish prankster. Before Wells could react, the grinning chemist playfully slapped him on the top of the head—then dashed off.

"You can't see me! I'm invisible!" Griffin sprinted away, chuckling as if he had played a very clever practical joke.

"Here now, Dr. Griffin! Wait!"

Griffin kept running, his bare feet slapping on the waxed wooden floor. He called in a singsong voice, "I'm invisible, *invisible*! Ha ha!"

Wells brushed his hair back into place, indignant that the unclothed man would do such a silly thing. He trotted after the nude scientist, following him down the hall, but Griffin picked up speed.

Rounding a corner, Wells saw the naked man skid to a halt. Barrel-chested Dr. Cavor stood in the middle of the hall, beefy arms crossed over his chest. Cavor's lower lip protruded from his square jaw in an expression of great disapproval. "Hawley Griffin, what on Earth are you doing?"

The naked man snickered as if concocting a devious plan.

He bobbed back and forth, then tried to dart around the other scientist, but Cavor reached out and snatched Griffin's arms.

The chemist squawked. "Stop! You can't catch me. You can't even see me."

"You're having delusions again, Hawley."

"No, I'm invisible! How did you catch me? You can't know where I am."

"Yes, we can, Hawley."

Breathless and panting, Wells arrived. "Dr. Cavor, what is he doing?"

The materials scientist just shook his head. Griffin turned around, his bristly hair glistening with sweat. He tried to break away again, but Cavor held the man's wrist with all his strength. Wells helped to keep Griffin steady.

"It's rather like *The Emperor's New Clothes*, you know," Cavor muttered.

The naked man finally stopped struggling. His shoulders slumped as he looked around in dismal disappointment. "You . . . you can really see me? Both of you?"

"Yes," Wells and Cavor said in unison.

With a deep sigh, Griffin surrendered. "Then it must have worn off."

"I'm sure it did. Come now, Mr. Wells and I will escort you back to your room. You've had enough excitement for tonight, and you need some sleep. Our symposium starts in two days, you know."

"Yes, yes, and I must perfect my formula by that time!"

"Does he have a . . . smoking jacket or something?" Wells asked.

"Yes, but it's invisible, too!" Griffin insisted as the two escorted him back to his room.

CHAPTER SIX

AN UNINVITED GUEST AT THE SYMPOSIUM

On the day of the symposium, Wells arrived in the lecture hall early enough to get a spot in the front row. He wasn't entirely sure what Huxley expected of him, but he did not intend to disappoint the professor. It was an unparalleled opportunity.

He settled himself in a varnished wooden chair and took out his papers and a lead pencil. He didn't want to miss a word that was said. In the center of the oratory stage, a dark wooden lectern stood like a pulpit. Remembering Huxley's showmanship when lecturing his biology students, Wells hoped the old professor still had his rhetorical abilities.

One by one, scientists filed in. Some still wore stained laboratory coats; many had tousled hair and bloodshot eyes, as if they had continued working through the night and all morning, trying to squeeze out one more result. Several men wore formal jackets, as if they expected an audience with the queen.

Wells was surprised to note impressive representatives filing in on the other side of the room. He recognized Prime Minister Gladstone himself, who had served in his post four times since 1868 in an alternating dance with his conservative rivals, the Marquis of Salisbury and Benjamin Disraeli. Numerous admirals and generals of the Imperial armed forces sat beside the prime minister in stiff, formal uniforms.

Wells surveyed them with amazement. The presence of such people drove home the importance of what would be discussed here. Self-consciously, he straightened his brown hair and moustache, then brushed imagined lint from his sleeves. His mother would swoon if she knew where her "Bertie" was now—and probably try to shoo him out of the auditorium so that "his betters" could do their important work.

T.H. Huxley entered from a side door, full of confidence. He wore a fine new suit and a perfectly knotted cravat. As he passed Wells, he paused. "Sit quietly and listen. Take notes of what is discussed and, most importantly—*think* about it. I may ask you questions afterward. I will make up my own mind, of course, but I would appreciate your analysis."

The whispering from the audience grew louder, then fell off as the old professor took long-legged steps across the lecture stage. Huxley bowed to his audience, then made a special show of recognizing Prime Minister Gladstone, the various lords, Members of Parliament, and military officers. When he was finished with the formalities, he grasped the lectern as if he were about to teach a class full of fresh students.

"The greatest minds of the British Empire serve this institute. Some arrived openly, some in the middle of the night. Each one knows the importance of what is discussed and developed here behind closed doors."

The professor summarized the familiar threats to the Empire, including the growing danger of the German Second Reich and her unexpected alliances with Russia, and the always-unruly French. Huxley swept his gaze across every listener. "How, then, is the British Empire to prepare? By leading the march of progress, rather than allowing ourselves to be trampled by it!" He turned to the dignitaries. "Gentlemen, distinguished M.P.s, your Lordships, Mr. Prime Minister, I present to you the secret work of the Imperial Institute."

While the symposium continued, Wells feverishly took notes and wondered how he could possibly help reshape the world.

The next two speakers, Professor Redwood and Mr. Bensington, were quite ordinary-looking fellows. Redwood cleared his throat, and Bensington did the same, only with more gusto, as if competing with his partner. Professor Redwood began, "We have created a food substance called *Herakleophorbia*—"

"I thought of the name," Bensington said. "Sounds quite impressive, doesn't it?"

"Though it's the devil to spell!" Redwood retorted, then returned his attention to the talk. "When used as a food source, Herakleophorbia greatly promotes growth and increases the size of any living creature."

Bensington leaned closer to the lectern. "Ideally, we will be able to create giant warriors who can overthrow any enemy army."

Redwood held up a hand. "For now, though, our amazing foodstuff has been tested only on laboratory animals."

"But with extraordinary success!"

Both men gestured to their assistants, who disappeared behind the stage and then returned, tugging two heavy wooden carts. In each cart rested a large cage that contained a snarling, ferocious-looking brown rat as large as a sheep, with a rope-thick pink tail, flashing eyes, and long sharp teeth. Their shrill squeaking could be heard all the way to the back of the lecture hall. The mammoth rodents clawed at the cages, gnawing on the criss-crossed bars with jaws powerful enough to sever an oak sapling in a single bite.

While some of the lords and generals stared wide-eyed, Prime Minister Gladstone applauded. "Bravo! With such a substance we could feed the hungry, grow crops and meat animals large enough to fill every need. The trade unions and syndicalists and downtrodden poor will no longer have anything to complain about."

"Well, Mr. Prime Minister, that is certainly one application," said Mr. Bensington. "Very astute of you to grasp that promoting social harmony is in itself a method of defending Britain."

Redwood scowled at his partner. Wells couldn't understand how the two men could work together without coming to blows. "Unfortunately, sirs, there are still certain . . . inconsistencies in the formula. For instance, Herakleophorbia seems to promote a great deal of aggression in the subjects."

Bensington would not be brushed aside so easily. "Yes, aggression—which is an advantage if we mean to create soldiers!"

"On the other hand, no one wants our pigs to become so vicious we cannot butcher them for their gigantic bacon!" Redwood added.

A few chuckles rippled across the audience.

With piercing squeaks, the enormous rats hurled themselves against the bars of the cages. One of the bars looked perilously loose, and Bensington signaled for the assistants to wrestle the swaying cages away. He sketched a quick bow to the prime minister and his cronies. "Nevertheless, you can certainly see the potential of Herakleophorbia." He tugged Professor Redwood from the stage, beating a hasty retreat as the rats' clamor grew louder.

For the next presentation, Dr. Hawley Griffin walked onto the stage. The eccentric chemist looked much tidier today: he was well groomed and wore a clean lab coat, but his expression shifted with extraordinary swiftness. Running hands through his bristly dark hair, Griffin presented his ideas about the military benefits of his experimental invisibility formula.

"Unseen soldiers could win every war, gentlemen. How could an enemy succeed in killing them, except by accident? Invisible spies could ferret out any secret, steal any document. Transparent assassins could slip in anywhere, kill any target. The possibilities are endless!" Griffin's face was flushed. "He who possesses my invisibility formula could rule the world!"

Huxley stood abruptly to cut off the other man's rant. "Ah, thank you very much, Dr. Griffin. None of us needs to be reminded that the aim of Britannia is to protect herself and carry on the burden of the Empire, not to conquer the world—as, perhaps, Kaiser Wilhelm wants to do."

Without much subtlety, Huxley escorted the chemist away from the lectern, turning to smile reassuringly at Gladstone. "Dr. Griffin's formulas have already succeeded in significantly increasing the transparency factor. Before long, he will have an effective demonstration. For now, ponder the applications and possibilities, should his work come to completion soon."

Next, Dr. Selwyn Cavor talked about his extremely lightweight alloy. "My demonstration sphere is fully armored and impenetrable to even the heaviest artillery shell, yet it weighs less than a hundredth of a similar vessel covered in iron plating."

"A weightless ironclad? Amazing." The admirals and generals were abuzz with excitement.

"Well . . . not entirely weightless yet, Mr. Prime Minister. However, I believe I'm on the cusp of making a material that is opaque to gravity itself, immune to the tug of the Earth."

For hours, one by one, prominent researchers gave brief demonstrations of their schemes. Wells continued writing his furious notes, and all the listeners continued to be amazed.

A medical expert and bacteriologist named Philby spoke about isolating the deadly cholera bacillus. He had already separated, purified, and concentrated the germ, which he kept in a locked container in his laboratory. Hearing Philby's scheme, one of the uniformed generals blew through his long moustache, then grumbled with anger. "This is preposterous! A truly horrendous means of waging war, and very ungentlemanly."

"But is it not something we must consider?" Philby insisted. "One small vial contains more ammunition than a hundred thousand bullets. We must not blindfold ourselves to reality. Certainly the Germans have already considered such a thing." The general was obviously sobered as he pondered the implications.

Late in the afternoon, the auditorium door opened with a loud crash. Everyone in the audience turned as a disheveled but arrogant-looking man strode in as if he were a king. In the corridors behind him, incensed security men hustled forward, blowing whistles and shouting for the man to stop. But the barrel-chested intruder strode down the central aisle.

At the side of the stage, Huxley wore a terrible expression on his face. "Moreau! How dare you enter here?"

Moreau squared his shoulders, and his voice boomed out. "I dare, Thomas, because I must save you all from becoming fools." His eyes were bright and defiant. "The Imperial Institute has a much too narrow view of the true threat that is upon us."

Huxley struggled to regain his composure. "Guards, remove this man. He is not welcome here, nor in any facility of higher education in the British Empire. In fact, Scotland Yard has several outstanding warrants for his arrest."

"Thomas Henry Huxley, you pride yourself on being a scientist, but you are pathetic when you allow emotions to rule you." Moreau crossed his arms over his chest. "I know you dislike me. You and I have a bitter history, and you have accused me of committing heinous crimes." He pointed an accusing finger at the professor. "But will you—before all these other researchers and the prime minister himself—*refuse* to hear what I have to say, though it may have a bearing upon the survival of every man, woman, and child on Earth? Where is your much-vaunted scientific objectivity?"

Huxley glowered. Wells had never seen the professor so angry. Moreau directed his words to Prime Minister Gladstone, but his voice still held an overconfident sneer. "I swear to you that the coming war will not only encompass all of the British Empire, but the entire world—nay, two worlds. You sit here clucking like old hens, worried about an insignificant shadow when the whole sky is falling on you."

"What is this man saying?" Gladstone said, flustered. Guards had come into the auditorium, ready to drag Moreau away, but the unwelcome scientist did not budge. Wells wondered how Moreau had learned of this gathering of great scientists, when the entire research wing was supposedly a closely guarded secret.

Huxley fumed. "Very well, Moreau. What is it? Be succinct and make your words pertinent. Do not waste our time here."

The audience members stirred and grumbled. "Silence! So that I may speak!" Moreau bellowed. The hubbub dwindled, and he waited for complete silence. "You will consider my information vital, though some may have been squeamish about my past methods. If you would drive me out now, you would blind yourselves to the most terrible danger the Earth itself has ever known!"

Huxley tapped the lectern impatiently. "Enough grandstanding, Moreau. What threat is greater than the Germans, or the Russians, or the French?"

Moreau said a single word in a deep, forbidding tone. "*Martians.*"

The lecture hall resounded with gasps, then chuckles.

"Enough! I assure you this is not a joke." Moreau turned to the anxious-looking guards still standing in the doorway. "You there! Haul in my specimen. Go on!"

When the men hesitated, Moreau looked as if he intended to chase them into the corridor himself. "Come, come! Men entrusted with protecting this facility should be capable of lugging a single crate!"

While Wells watched with intense curiosity, the guards returned through the doors. Grunting and straining, they dragged a heavy rectangular crate nearly as large as the cages that had held the enormous rats. The crate was covered with a tarpaulin that hid its contents from view.

Moreau strode up to the crate and clutched the fabric with both hands. He looked back at Huxley. "Now you shall see. You all will see." With a flourish, he yanked away the sheet to reveal an abominable, misshapen creature contained inside a glass-walled aquarium. "*This* is the true face of our enemy, gentlemen."

The lecture hall resounded with gasps and exclamations. The unearthly creature was obviously dead, preserved in murky formaldehyde. The bulbous, brown-skinned thing was composed mostly of a gigantic brain sac. Huge milky-white eyes looked like overcooked eggs. Snake-like tentacle appendages dangled from a soft and hideous body.

"It looks like that deformed Merrick chap," cried Philby, the medical researcher. But Wells, who had seen pictures of the "elephant man," knew that this supposed Martian was much more disgusting in appearance.

Wells scribbled notes furiously, attempting to record or even sketch what he witnessed. He swallowed hard as he scratched with his lead pencil, sure he had blundered onto the doorstep of history in the making.

He looked at the blustering bearded man. His immediate reaction was one of distaste. Moreau seemed to be a person of some genius, but little tact. Wells preferred Huxley's approach to the mysteries of science, yet Moreau's convictions stood taller and more impregnable than all of Wells's book learning. The abrasive man did not seem to care that he was liked among his colleagues, so long as he was proved *right*. Moreau stood buffeted by the wash of the audience's distaste, but showed no sign of backing down. His shocking announcement had at least shaken them, forced them to listen.

Smug now that he had their full attention, Moreau raised his voice. "This Martian died in the crash of a first cylinder in the Sahara, apparently a scout ship from the red planet. I have dissected and analyzed it thoroughly and recorded the full details here in my personal journal."

He removed a bound volume from his suit and held it up in a large hand. "This specimen is only the first—the first of an entire invasion force from Mars!"

CHAPTER SEVEN

THE MARTIAN CYLINDER OPENS

FROM THE JOURNAL OF DR. MOREAU

Grand discoveries require careful documentation. I am a participant in events that will change the course of human history, and therefore I have determined to set down all that I have observed and pondered. History must remember what occurred in the Sahara, on the Atlantic steamer, and at Percival Lowell's observatory in Arizona Territory.

If the impending Martian invasion is not thwarted, then this journal may be all that remains of our civilization. I will tell what happened, and how the human race failed in its time of greatest crisis. I am fully aware of my obligation to the truth.

* * *

After the silvery cylinder had torn a smoky line through the sky and crashed near our still-burning canals, Lowell and I rushed forward, awestruck and eager. We were impetuous men, and neither of us wasted time with undue caution. Hesitation results only in lost opportunities: that is a motto by which I choose to live my life. Now was not the time for us to be cowards.

A plume of dust curled into the air from the distant impact crater. "I hope the Martian ship did not explode when it struck the ground!" Lowell shouted.

"Impossible!" I replied over the rumble of the fire from the raw impact wound. "They would be too advanced to make such a foolish mistake."

Both Lowell and I were accustomed to leading, not following, and so we climbed the lip of the fresh crater in tandem. Together, we gazed down at the steaming ruin.

Deep below, I could make out a silver cylinder with snub ends like a bullet. It was mirror-bright, dazzling our eyes, though the hull was stained from entering the atmosphere like a giant meteor. But this was no meteor: the cylinder was clearly formed by the hands of an intelligent race.

I confess that I had a more scientific curiosity than a diplomatic one. If the alien civilization had sent a spacecraft across interplanetary distances, then Martian technology was obviously far superior to anything our greatest industrial nations had developed. I was eager to learn what these creatures could teach me.

The heat from the pit rose in a tremendous wave, preventing us from approaching closer. We could only stand to observe for a few seconds. Lowell dropped back, coughing, but I remained hunched over, shielding my watering eyes, until I, too, had no choice but to stagger back. With savage disappointment, Lowell clenched his hands at his sides. "I have waited years for this moment. I can tolerate a few more hours—but not much longer."

Impatient and frustrated, we retired to our shaded tents. We both felt as if our life's work was coming to its climax. Lowell fetched toiletries, shaved with a basin of tepid water, then changed into a fine new suit and straightened his collar. All the while he kept his gaze intent on the still-glowing pit visible through the propped-open tent flap.

And the hours dragged on.

After eating a quickly prepared meal, we shared a celebratory brandy and a cigar. Lowell told me of his longstanding passion for Mars and his intention to use part of the family fortune to build an observatory dedicated to the study of the red planet. His young assistant, A.E. Douglass, had already been sent to scout appropriate locations in the American Southwest, Mexico, and even South America. Then he talked about his journeys as an ambassador to Japan and the insights he had gained from the Eastern mind and its philosophies.

Oh, our frivolous conversation seems so absurd now as I record it, and I cannot in good conscience set down all our inane thoughts on paper. Let us say that Percival Lowell and I were equally naïve and optimistic, and I shall leave the matter at that.

Soon, we would have a chance to meet a real Martian face to face.

* * *

When evening cooled the desert, we set off again. I commanded the remaining Tuaregs to follow with crowbars and pickaxes from the trench excavations, as I thought the Martians might need assistance in opening their armored spacecraft. The superstitious natives accompanied us, though reluctantly.

Although their culture retained its belief in mysteries and demons, the Tuaregs had seen locomotives and white men coming in large ships. To them, a spaceship cylinder or a creature from Mars was no more fantastic.

Lowell was mulling over an appropriate speech to welcome the alien visitors, and I wondered if he had considered that the Martians were not likely to speak English. Still, Lowell had a knack for languages. On impulse, he reached into the pocket of his cream-colored jacket and withdrew the oxide-red spectacles I had given him, placing them over his eyes. Now he saw the world as a Martian would, the better to understand them.

When we finally stood on the crater rim, I could see a dull glow, but most of the cylinder had cooled. The immense object, larger than two railroad cars, made a ticking and crackling sound as its temperature continued to adjust to our environment.

Lowell noticed the hatch first, and excitement intensified his Bostonian accent. "Look there, Moreau! A circle protruding from the side of the cylinder." Indeed, a rounded cap was moving like an immense screw, rising from the cylinder's hull.

"Someone inside is trying to open it," I said.

Before Lowell could say anything, I scrambled down the

loose slope. The thin crust of vitrified sand broke beneath my feet, but I dug in my heels and skidded to a halt at the base of the crashed Martian projectile. Breathless, I gazed up at the curved cylinder, awestruck by its sheer size.

Lowell called from above, "Moreau! Are you all right?"

Without waiting, I reached forward, amazed that I could feel no heat radiating from the hull. Tentatively, I brought my hand closer and then, with brash resolve, touched it. The metal was still warm, but not unendurable. "It's completely safe, Lowell." He needed no further encouragement to join me.

Above, I heard a scraping sound, and the screw-hatch rotated visibly by a quarter of a turn, then gradually a quarter more. "Perhaps they are too weak to open it the rest of the way," I said when Lowell stood panting beside me.

He bellowed to the desert workers gathered around the rim. "Come here and bring your crowbars! We must get this cylinder open." He glared up them, his wavy pale hair ghostly under the starlight. "There will be no pay for anyone who hesitates."

Three of the dark-clad workers disappeared from the edge, and Lowell and I never saw them again. Four other men—either braver or more desperate for money—came down brandishing their crowbars like weapons, though we meant for them to be used only as tools.

The screw-hatch turned slightly again, then stopped. The skittish Tuaregs backed off, but Lowell clapped his hands. "Go on, you brutes! See what you can do to help."

The robed nomads clanged their bars against the hull, searching for some notch that would catch their bars.

Eventually, as Lowell and I supervised, the men managed to get their bars into the hatch seam. Working together, grunting and cursing in their incomprehensible language, the natives dragged the hatch cover around. It finally began to turn freely.

Eager to see the first light from the open crack, I wanted to push forward. My own face should be the first human the aliens saw—or, at the very least, Percival Lowell's. But the heavy screw made its last turn and fell off into the cooked sand. The Tuaregs scrambled back as hissing air gushed out like the steam from a tea kettle. Alien air, I thought, from the skies of Mars.

I saw only darkness inside the open hatch high up on the cylinder's hull. When the venting atmosphere had faded to silence again, one of the Tuaregs pulled his face close to the opening.

Suddenly an enormous shape thrust itself forward from within the cylinder. It had slick leathery skin, huge eyes, and a Medusa's cluster of tentacles. It made no sound as its appendages grabbed the Tuareg by his robes. The man screamed and thrashed, tearing his garments.

Despite their fear, the Tuareg's companions protected their own. Howling, they drew curved swords from their dusty robes and lunged for the Martian beast. The tentacled thing loomed up, seemingly furious at us.

For the briefest instant, Lowell and I stood stunned and amazed. Such a creature was unlike anything I had imagined in all my biological studies. I reacted more quickly than Lowell when I saw the Tuaregs with murder in their eyes. "No swords! Do not harm it. It is a creature from another planet."

With a swift stroke of his blade, one desert man slashed the fabric of his comrade's robe, cutting him loose. The terrified victim tumbled to the sand and scrambled away. The other Tuaregs, glowering at me, seated their swords back in their belts and took up the crowbars as clubs. In a group, they rushed the open hatch and pummeled the Martian, which scuttled backward into its large ship.

The Tuaregs paused at the dark opening, none of them willing to venture inside. Lowell came close with the kerosene lamp he had brought. "Stand aside, but be ready to defend us."

When I saw Lowell hesitate at the hatch opening, I snatched the lamp from him. This was no time for doubts and reservations. Without a thought for my own safety, I thrust the lamp into the cylinder's interior.

The kerosene glow reflected from strange shapes and curves, objects no human had ever seen. Inside, the Martian squirmed away on its lumpy tentacles. It did not manage to avoid the light, but it did avoid us.

"It appears to be weak, perhaps injured," I said when Lowell came up beside me. "It has backed off, so we can enter safely."

Before Lowell could nod, I swung my leg over the lip of the hatch and climbed inside, pushing the lamp in front of me.

The Martian scuttled away without voicing any sound; I wondered whether it had vocal cords. Many animals on Earth were speechless, as I was aware from my vivisection experiments. Perhaps Martians were mute, or they communicated in another manner entirely.

I shouted back to Lowell, "Call some of the Tuaregs inside.

Look there, the Martian is backed against that bulkhead. I want them to keep it at bay, so we can explore the rest of the ship. Maybe there are other survivors." Lowell relayed the orders, and two Tuareg men reluctantly entered what must have seemed a demon's lair to them.

With the known survivor accounted for, we ventured deeper inside, breathing the remnants of flat, dusty Martian air. I turned slowly around, shining the lamp inside the spaceship's large open cavity. I saw a sight that I shall never forget.

The crashed spaceship was a charnel house. Inhuman bodies—fifteen, we later counted—were strewn about like rag dolls on the interior deck, no doubt jumbled from the violence of the cylinder's impact. It seemed a tragedy to me that so few of them had survived the long and perilous voyage across interplanetary space. They had come so far . . . .

The dead creatures were slightly smaller than adult humans, the majority of them with whitish-gray skin and smooth shells on their body parts. These specimens clearly belonged to an entirely different phylum from the tentacled Martian.

Unlike a clipper ship or an ocean steamer, the Martian vessel did not contain a large cargo hold or numerous crates of supplies. The white-shelled aliens had been kept in a separate section of the vessel, like cattle in a corral. The advanced Martian—the creature with the soft body and the enormous brain—had apparently operated the controls, such as they were. The Martian projectile had apparently been launched from a giant cannon on the red planet, fired ballistically toward Earth, with only a few attitude-adjustment rockets to guide its course. Either these creatures were fools, or optimists. Either way, they had achieved their desire, and the cylinder had arrived at Earth.

Lowell, being more mechanically minded than myself, inspected the "bridge" of the cylinder, a strange curved affair that would never have been designed by the shipbuilders of the Royal Navy. He studied the levers and knobs designed for a race equipped with tentacles instead of manipulating digits. He could not decipher the Martian written language scribed onto the buttons and switches, nor could he comprehend the basis of the alien guidance system.

Since my background was in biology, I had other priorities, however. I knelt to perform a cursory study of the cadavers. They seemed oddly desiccated and shriveled, as if their bodily juices had been sucked away. Only mummified husks remained.

"Moreau! I've found a second large Martian." In the reflected lamplight, I could see another of the brownish brain sacs—this one clearly dead, its tentacles clenched to itself like the legs of a poisoned beetle. It, too, had been desiccated, drained.

"The crash could not have killed them all. Not in this fashion." Lowell pursed his lips. "I wonder if this Martian and these others died of some sickness. Or maybe they were murdered during the voyage."

I was not, however, worried about those answers for the time being. My immediate delight was in knowing that I now had so many specimens to dissect.

CHAPTER EIGHT

A WELCOME VISITOR AND UNWELCOME NEWS

After Moreau had delivered his shocking news to the symposium audience, the Institute scientists, military officers, lords, and even Prime Minister Gladstone, surged to their feet and gathered close to see the nightmarish specimen.

Moreau clearly understood the tumult his revelations would cause, and Wells could see that the bearish man enjoyed the effect of his announcement. Moreau stood confident and arrogant in the middle of the uproar.

Professor Huxley's words cut across the excitement and confusion in the lecture hall. "In light of these new developments, I hereby adjourn this symposium until we can further assess the news Dr. Moreau has brought us."

Griffin shot to his feet, his face reddened with anger, his bristly hair standing up as if in indignation. He did not even glance at the alien's tank. "We cannot stop the symposium! We must compile all knowledge so we can fight the Germans! We must not allow ourselves to be distracted by . . . Martians. My formula is too important."

Huxley gave the eccentric chemist a conciliatory look. "Dr. Griffin, much as I dislike Dr. Moreau, we have an important new factor to consider. It may be that the entire focus of our symposium will change dramatically."

"No! It can't." But his voice was lost among the shouts of amazement or disgust as people peered into the aquarium. Huxley paid no further attention to Griffin.

Moreau walked across the stage like a conquering general. "I think you will agree, Thomas, that my intrusion is warranted."

"If your words are indeed true." Huxley turned down his lips in continued skepticism. "Numerous hoaxes have been perpetrated upon a gullible public. The circus man P.T. Barnum in America has made a living at it, and let us not forget the Cardiff Giant, which many scientists insisted was real."

Wells hurried up to them, notepaper in hand, his mind full of questions. But he did not interrupt the conversation—or was it a confrontation?—between the two men.

"This is no joke." Moreau sounded dangerous. "We have known each other for many years. At one time, you respected my biological investigations. I realize that you disagree with the morality of my experiments, but have you ever known me to be a liar?" Moreau thrust the bound volume forward. "Here, take my journal. It documents everything. It includes sketches I made of dissections and a full account of my dealings with the

Martians." His eyes were full of challenge. "Read it and see if you still consider this a hoax."

Huxley took the book. "I will make up my own mind."

Wells fought back a smile. This was precisely what Huxley taught all of his students: to study the facts for themselves and to make their own decisions.

Moreau continued, his voice louder than before. "Something must be done immediately. Toward the end of this year, Mars and Earth will be at their closest point at opposition. Already, the two worlds are approaching each other inexorably along their orbital paths. We must stop the Martians before they launch their invasion upon Earth."

Huxley stared him down. Wells looked from one man to the other, holding his breath.

"Even if what you say is true, Moreau, exactly how do you expect us to fight a distant planet? Shall we shoot fireworks and hope they reach escape velocity? How can we possibly defend against invaders from Mars?"

Moreau gestured toward the scientists clustered around the aquarium. "You claim this Institute has the greatest minds in Britain. Think of something."

* * *

Wells retired to his small room and feverishly documented everything he had witnessed, adding parenthetical comments of his own, which helped him put his thoughts in order. He hoped that Huxley meant for him to do such editorializing. It was unlikely he would ever be able to publish these accounts— certainly not as factual articles, due to Britain's national security.

A student assistant rapped sharply on the door of his room. "Mr. Wells, you have a visitor in the front office. We could not allow her to come to the secure wing, but she wishes to see you—most insistently, sir."

Wells's heart leaped. Jane had come! With a happy expression and a light step, he hurried after the volunteer to the administrative office. Jane's face lit up as soon as he passed through the door. Her expression, her eyes, her gently pointed chin all reminded him of a perfect sunset on a beautiful summer day.

"Jane! I did not expect you, but I certainly can't complain."

"I have been sitting here for the past hour, H.G., trying to think of an appropriate excuse as to why I have come. I tried to divert my mind by studying the flowers and birds and butterflies in my guidebooks. At night, I worked on memorizing all the constellations. But nothing seems as interesting if I don't have you to share it with. I'm sorry if I'm disturbing your visit here, but I've missed you so."

"You and I need never make excuses for wanting to be together, my dear." He kissed her, much to the embarrassment of the frowning secretary who sat at his desk. The poor man shuffled papers and made an inordinate amount of noise to remind the two that he was there and watching.

At that moment the door swung open and T.H. Huxley strode in. "Have you drafted those letters yet, Henderson? They must be posted immediately. I require the advice of other experts—" He looked up, distracted. "Ah, Mr. Wells! I should have *you* write my correspondence. Then my demands will be clear and concise, and my urgency made plain."

Wells chuckled in disbelief. "Professor, you are one of the

finest writers of our age. I wouldn't presume to have a literary ability equivalent to your own."

"I do not require *literature*, Wells, simply a request for information." He looked at Jane, and suddenly his personality brightened. "And who is this? She appears to be a fine specimen."

"Indeed she is, sir." Wells beamed. "One that should be included in every textbook of the female form and mind."

Jane extended her hand. "Apparently H.G. doesn't believe I have a name. I am Miss Amy Catherine Robbins. I'm very pleased to meet you, sir. H.G. speaks of you often."

Huxley said, "Wells is proving to be a shining star just as I had hoped. Especially after today, I need his insights more than ever."

"Then you need Jane's insights as well, Professor," Wells said impulsively. "She has an imagination as sharp as my own, and often sheds light on questions in a way I have never before considered."

"Excellent. We could certainly use a fresh perspective on these matters. Will you be staying with us, young lady?"

"Professor, we have no rooms available," said the dour secretary. "Especially not for a lady."

"I would love to stay, if I'm invited," Jane said, ignoring the secretary. "I can, of course, share a room with H.G. We are to be married soon anyway."

Henderson appeared extremely embarrassed, but Huxley was too distracted to show any reaction. "Can you vouch for her loyalty to the Crown, Wells? Are you certain she's not a Prussian spy? More importantly, are you convinced she will not be bored by our technical discussions and scientific talk?"

Wells squared his narrow shoulders to look as imposing as

he could manage. "Jane has one of the most insightful minds and interesting perspectives of any person I know. She was once a student of mine, by far the best. I have decided to keep her."

"It is settled then," Huxley said. "You two follow me back to the research wing. After Moreau's announcement today, not even a woman could disrupt my researchers further. Tell her about our Martians, Wells, and see what she thinks about the whole matter."

"Martians?" Jane arched her eyebrows as they followed the professor into the private wing.

Huxley took his leave of the pair while Wells showed Jane to their room. Once inside, they became much more interested in each other than in interplanetary invasions. With all the privacy they could wish for, the two occupied themselves with kissing, laughing. Reacquainting themselves with each other involved the tedious and time-consuming task of removing the appropriate layers of clothing. They did not begrudge the time, but went through all the necessary steps . . . .

Later, finally able to concentrate on other things, Wells got around to telling her everything, and she listened with rapt attention as they lay naked together, cozy in the narrow bed.

In the joy of seeing her again and talking about the Institute's wonderful projects, as well as the Martian specimen, Wells overextended himself. Jane was suddenly more concerned about his health than an invading fleet from Mars. She touched his moist forehead and frowned as she brushed his brown hair aside. "You must not tax yourself too much, H.G. If you have another breakdown, you can't help Professor Huxley at all."

"But there is too much to do, Jane!"

"I have no wish to become a widow before I have a chance

to be your wife. You must not have another relapse from your old kidney injury."

Tonight, though, he felt too excited to lie back and rest. Having Jane naked beside him did little to calm him either.

He grasped her hand, and their fingers intertwined. "All right, let us talk about the consequences of the astonishing things I've been shown. I'm sure you'll think of possible repercussions I haven't yet considered." He knew Jane could understand the implications of Moreau's warning and see the overall perspective, but she also saw smaller problems and human difficulties. "Will humans be able to change their priorities? If Moreau is correct, then the Martian invasion will be a war that encompasses the entire world. No, in fact more than our world, both Earth *and* Mars."

"People will do what they need to do. You can't solve all the problems yourself, H.G."

"No, but with all the talent in this Institute, we have a good chance. Professor Huxley has already contacted the world's governments. Surely we can work together on a problem of obvious mutual benefit? Humans are intelligent creatures, after all. How can the Prussians, the French, and the Americans, not *see* that we must cooperate to face this peril?"

"I have always loved your dreams, H.G." Jane leaned over to kiss his forehead. "But you must temper them with a healthy dose of practicality."

CHAPTER NINE

THE DISSECTION OF INTERPLANETARY SPECIMENS

FROM THE JOURNAL OF DR. MOREAU

That night we stationed uneasy Tuareg guards around the crashed cylinder, containing the live Martian without provoking it overmuch. It was the only plan we could think of to keep the creature safe until Lowell and I decided what to do with it.

Two of the uneasy nomads retrieved a typical specimen of the desiccated pale creatures from inside the cylinder and transported it back to camp. I myself assisted in carrying the first dead Martian, brown-skinned and trailing limp tentacles. On the way, I grunted and strained like a burly carter. It was a long and strange procession as we delivered the pair of alien cadavers to our tents.

After supervising the trench-digging in the Sahara, I had been weary beyond anything I had experienced even in my most obsessive days of medical experimentation. But I now felt the adrenaline of heady accomplishment and the joyous possibility of making a discovery that would shatter the very precepts of science. Thus, I felt no need for sleep. Not now. My movements were frenetic, my breathing fast, and I knew I had to organize my priorities. I could think of so many remarkable things to do. Though there was no immediate time limit, I wanted to learn everything *now*.

I set up two large plank tables under the tent fabric and hung three kerosene lamps from the supports overhead. Fascinated, Lowell stood beside me, getting in the way. We spread the two specimens in the brightest pool of light, where I could properly dissect them.

I couldn't wait to begin. I was about to become the first biologist to learn about extraterrestrial anatomy. My old colleague and rival, Thomas Huxley, would be so envious! Perhaps he would even regret his decision to oust me from London. But no, not Thomas. Huxley is as arrogant and set in his moral rectitude as I am in my willingness to pay the price to acquire new knowledge.

I devoted my surgical attentions to the lesser being first. By its fundamental external structure and, as I later saw, its arrangement of internal organs, the whitish creature seemed to derive from an utterly different Adam than the blobby, big-brained, tentacled Martians.

I bent closer to the corpse of the pale creature we had extracted from the crashed cylinder. With its pair of arms and legs, a head on a stalk-like neck, the whitish alien looked much more human than the tentacled Martian. Its overall appearance reminded me of a worker ant. Perhaps a Martian drone? The creature appeared flimsy, its limbs designed to survive gravity significantly lower than that on Earth—lower even than that on Mars, but I knew that couldn't possibly be.

Its body was covered with a tough membrane, not quite skin, nor entirely a shell. Its spade-shaped head had a large, thick cranium that, when cracked open, revealed a rather disappointing nodule of brain matter, that seemed to be only a substation in a larger network of intellect. Or perhaps it was merely a stupid beast, like a cow. Huge dome-like eyes covered a quarter of its flat face. Probing with my fingers, I found a small mouth tucked under its chin, surrounded by tiny cilia or feelers. Obviously not a predator or even a scavenger. This creature's mouth and digestive system seemed equipped to handle little more than jelly or gruel.

I decided to have a more detailed look inside the creature. With a surgical saw and pry blades, tweezers and probes, I cut open its skull and chestplate, whereupon a greenish-blue jelly oozed out. If this specimen had not been desiccated, would this ichor have run freely, like blood?

The pale creature had a surprisingly limited set of internal organs, which made me wonder just how high on the evolutionary ladder its ancestors had managed to climb. Its muscles slid like rods within exoskeletal tubes. I identified what I thought were the equivalents to heart and lungs, but the bulk of the specimen's interior was devoted to a large nervous system that came to a nexus inside the skull with a small fleshy nodule embedded at the base of its skull—a rudimentary brain? It was certainly not a very large organ, so I supposed I wouldn't be discussing higher mathematics with this creature, had it survived the crash. I concluded that this being was a lower form of life.

Lowell sat beside me, observing every moment of my work. With a sketch pad and a sharpened lead pencil, he deftly made detailed drawings of the creature's physiology. I would have done the same after completing my initial study, but I was glad to have an objective and enthusiastic artist drawing what we both could see. Detailed records were the very bugaboo of science! Lowell had made enough superb sketches of the canals of Mars that I trusted his eye for detail. I could label the drawings later with my speculations about the functions of the organs and musculature.

I wondered if Lowell intended to publish these reports. He is a man with a large ego. After spending so much money to fund this expedition, he may want to claim the credit for himself, though I'll insist on being included. This discovery alone will redeem me in the eyes of the scientific community.

Anxious to move on—there was so much to learn!—I let Lowell finish sketching the ant-like drone Martian while I moved to the larger specimen on the second dissection table.

The huge sac of brain was obviously more evolved, and thus superior to the lesser being. The superior Martian lay spread out in a shapeless hulk like a squashed spider. Oddly, the larger specimen was based on an entirely different evolutionary blueprint from a human being or the drone. How could they both have sprung from the same tree of life? Though this more highly evolved creature seemed less physically complex than its pale-skinned counterpart, it had a more impressive character, a majestic *brain*. The round dead eyes were glassy. What secrets had they seen?

First, I ran my hands over the smooth brownish skin. It was soft and pliable, a bit like the rubberized fabric of a mackintosh. I could sense no internal structural support, no bones or cartilage. Had it evolved beyond the need for a physically mobile form? The creature's "body" itself was little more than a sac to contain the vital Martian thinking organ. Everything else seemed superfluous to its functioning.

I stretched out one of its boneless tentacles. Each appendage seemed loose and elastic, but with a potential strength like braided steel cables. Such a thing could have gripped a victim's throat like a garrote—if it were a carnivore, of course.

As I continued my inspection, I wondered what sort of motivation lay behind this expedition to Earth. Peaceful contact with a fellow intelligent species? Did the Martian race intend to share their knowledge and culture with us?

Or were they planning something more sinister? Yes, even then I had my suspicions.

With my sharpest scalpel, I cut through the soft wet-leather skin and peeled back the head covering to expose the creamy contours of Martian brain tissue. Such an enormous organ! It would require a bucket to hold! As I stared, I mused about the thoughts that might have passed through such an enormous and intricate cerebrum. Another planet, another intellect.

In my numerous vivisections, I had studied the open brains of apes and pumas, as well as lesser specimens of dogs and cats. This Martian brain surpassed any I had ever seen before, even in human cadavers. The rills and valleys, the ridges and swirls provided a map of alien mental geography. It would have taken me a year just to note every subtle twist and curve, every branching line, every blood vessel.

I was immensely careful. While I had many of the drones stacked like cordwood inside the crashed cylinder, this superior Martian was my only opportunity to study the greater race—unless the other Martian died, of course. Opportunities abounded.

Lowell and I worked deep into the night.

* * *

Far out in the Sahara, the nights were incredibly dark. The stars shone so brightly they made my eyes ache.

The nervous Tuareg guards remained out at the crater, armed with metal rods but with strict instructions not to kill the remaining Martian. They sat by a small fire made from dried camel dung. The pungent character of the smoke was surpassed only by the stench of their own long-unwashed bodies.

After the Moon set an hour before dawn, the darkness grew deep and mysterious. The red planet hung near the horizon like an evil eye, accusing me for what I had done to the bodies of the dead Martians we took from the cylinder. While I rested on my cot, my mind was feverish with all I had learned. Although I had scrubbed my hands clean and disinfected them with alcohol, I still felt the aliens' gelatinous secretions.

Then a frightened cry shattered the calm night. The

words were indecipherable gibberish, but the tone was of alarm and excitement.

Off my cot in an instant, I pulled on boots and raced across the sands. My eyes were already adapted to the dark, and the starlight provided enough illumination. Lowell ran beside me. Neither of us asked questions, because we knew that we had no answers.

A faint orange glow still simmered from the crater. The three Tuareg guards shouted, waving their scimitars threateningly. One ran forward to clang his crowbar against the metal hull.

"What is all the fuss?" Lowell demanded.

Before the nomads could give a comprehensible answer, a ratcheting mechanical sound came from the half-buried cylinder. Standing on the rim, I watched as a segmented construction erected itself from an opening atop the spacecraft. It was an arm strung together with girders and connected with pulleys, made with salvaged components from inside the cylinder.

The towering appendage rose up like a questing probe. From its end depended a boxy device that appeared to be a camera fixed with a strange rotating lens. The segmented arm swiveled and bent, as if feeling its way, rising taller until it towered over all of us.

"Our captive Martian has been hard at work," I said. "Who knows what it assembled while we performed our dissections?"

"Perhaps the creature is trying to communicate," Lowell said.

I tried to imagine myself in the circumstances of our

unusual visitor: it was the only survivor of a crashed ship, and as soon as it had emerged onto our world, the Tuaregs set upon it with weapons. "We should try to understand it. Such a superior being cannot possibly mean us any harm."

The desert men brandished their crowbars and curved swords, as if the camera box-thing was the eye of a demon. The spinning lens brightened, and a throbbing sound pulsed from inside the cylinder. The segmented arm turned . . . as if searching for a target.

Lowell was more suspicious than I. "Moreau, that thing may be a weapon."

As I looked at the contraption, I too thought it seemed threatening. Even as we retreated from the crater rim, Lowell instructed the Tuaregs to knock down the segmented yardarm. In particular, he told them to break the flashing, spinning lens that I surmised might serve as a remote eye for the Martian. Needing no further encouragement, the men surged forward.

The tentacled Martian hauled itself out of the upper opening twenty feet from the ground. I was amazed at the creature's agility as it climbed the segmented girders and wires like a circus capuchin. Sparks sprayed from the rotating lens, and I felt a wave of growing heat.

Then the Tuaregs climbed up and battered the base of the metal arm with their crowbars, severing connections. The Martian flailed its tentacles as if in rage as it scrambled higher up the extended mechanical boom, which began to bend under its weight.

Unaccustomed to holding itself in the increased gravity of Earth, the heavy creature toppled. It looked like a gorged tick that had dropped off a dog's ear.

The Tuaregs scrambled away in horror. But once the desperate Martian hit the sand, it lumbered off at an awkward galloping gait. The creature scurried with surprising speed across the soft sands and over the crater lip.

"Don't let it escape!" I cried.

Smelling blood, the Tuaregs raced after the monster, brandishing their weapons and howling. Because of its soft musculature, the thing began to slow as it moved across the desert. The nomads surrounded it, keeping it at bay, jabbing with pointed blades. One man struck with the crowbar, clubbing the Martian, which reeled back, pathetically flailing its tentacles.

Lowell and I charged in among the men, knocking their blades aside. "Don't injure it, you fools! Have you no idea how valuable this specimen is? Its mind is immeasurably superior to ours."

The cornered Martian sidled back and forth, churning up the sands like an octopus cast onto shore. I searched for some way to communicate with this intelligent being, but could think of no frame of reference we shared.

Lowell and I devised a scheme by which the Tuaregs would shout and brandish their weapons and thereby herd the Martian back to camp. We would secure the creature within one of the tents and deprive it of anything that could be fashioned into a weapon for those powerful, tentacled arms.

We made our racket in front of the giant lumbering brain. The poor Martian must have been frightened and intimidated by the Tuareg brutes. Nevertheless, now was not the time for compassion. Compassion, I believe, has been the downfall of many scientists who are not willing to do what needs to be done.

Before long, the Martian seemed to understand where we wished it to go and that we had no immediate intention of killing it. As if with fearful resignation, it scuttled across the sands.

Once, in the London zoo, I had seen a heavy walrus attempt to move. The walrus might have been a sleek aquatic swimmer, but on dry land it was out of its element, padded with blubber and enormously ungainly. The Martian reminded me of that walrus, lurching across the sands toward our encampment.

Lowell had clearly come to a decision. He did not ask my advice or consult with me in any way . . . but then he rarely did. He was Percival Lowell, and he had paid for all of our work. Though I was our expedition's only real scientist, Lowell held the purse strings.

Watching the Martian approach our tents, he brushed his moustache. "We must take him to civilization."

CHAPTER TEN

THE UNSEEN SABOTEUR

Long after the rest of the Imperial Institute had gone to bed, Wells and Jane remained awake in their room playing cards while talking politics, culture, and the likelihood of winning against a Martian invasion. She demurely won twice, and he bested her once before leaning back against the bed and adjusting the pillow.

"Maybe we should simply move in here," Wells suggested languidly. "No more prying landladies, no more questions about our marital status."

"And no more afternoon bicycle rides," Jane pointed out, "or strolls along the lane, or boating on the canals. Our relationship would have more interesting science, but less romance."

"Less romance? Not necessarily." He kissed her again, after which she deftly beat him at cards for a third time.

Gracefully accepting his defeat, Wells yawned. "You tire me out, Jane, in more ways than one. We should go to bed. Tomorrow will be even more exciting. I'd like a close look at that preserved Martian specimen."

Before they could undress, Jane heard furtive creepings out in the hall. She gave Wells a perplexed look, and he sighed. "It's probably just Griffin wandering around naked again." He opened the door a crack, and Jane mischievously pushed in beside him.

He caught the unmistakable sounds of quick footsteps and heavy breathing, but he saw no one. Then, farther down the hall in the research wing, the door to Dr. Philby's biological laboratory opened of its own accord, swinging wide with a faint creak. Wells was sure that his eyes had tricked him. He heard muttered curses coming from inside the room, an indrawn breath of surprise, then the tinkle of breaking glass.

"What is it, H.G.?" Jane whispered. He put his finger to her soft lips.

The wooden door creaked again, accompanied by slapping footsteps that dwindled in the opposite direction. Jane's eyes widened as she looked both ways down the corridor, and saw no one.

Wells set his teeth. "Come with me—but quietly."

The two of them moved under the uncertain gaslight toward Philby's lab. Because of the deadly germs kept within the locked cabinets, the biological scientist always locked his research rooms. But when Wells tried the knob, it turned easily, and the door swung open.

Wells looked at Jane. "This is not as it should be." Bending to inspect the keyhole, he noted scratches on the brass plate. Someone had picked the lock.

Inside, the laboratory was dimly lit. Moonlight shone through upper windows, glinting off tables crowded with neatly arranged vials and beakers. Rats rattled against the wires of their cages, anxious to escape before Philby experimented on them. Everything else remained still.

"Here!" Jane hurried to a locked sample cabinet; someone had broken out a small pane of glass and removed six of the marked test tubes stored inside.

Wells's stomach clenched as he looked at the labels on the remaining glass vials. Philby's handwriting was dense but clear. "Some of the specimens of cholera bacillus and bubonic plague are missing! Someone has taken them."

"Who would want to steal a deadly disease?"

"Someone who no doubt wishes to use it, Jane. An anarchist, or syndicalist perhaps. Radical trade unionists, Marxists. Our society has produced any number of passionate and desperate men who feel the need to make their point through terror instead of rational discourse."

Jane's face hardened with determination. "I'll go sound the alarm."

"No, if we raise a hullabaloo, we may not learn what this man is up to. Besides, if he is cornered, he could simply shatter one of the test tubes and unleash the plague upon all of us."

Together, they hurried down the hall in the direction the stealthy footsteps had gone. Several lights burned inside Dr. Cavor's assembly bay. The large sphere, completely covered with lightweight armor material and ready for its symposium demonstration, glistened in the dim light of low gas jets.

The hatch of the armored sphere was open. Equipment around the room lay in disarray, as if it had been ransacked. He knew Cavor kept an eagle eye on his workers and insisted on an organized shop, everything put in its place. "This isn't right."

Among the paraphernalia on the equipment benches, Wells watched several tools move by themselves. A box was gently shoved aside by unseen hands. A floorboard squeaked on the raised assembly deck.

Realizing that they were out of their depth, he pulled Jane from the open door. "We've got to go before he sees us. We should tell Professor Huxley."

* * *

Wells rapped quietly but insistently, seeing the light that shone from beneath the old man's door. "Professor Huxley, sir! Are you still awake?"

Huxley peered out at them, cinching his striped lounging robe tighter around his sleep shirt and loose trousers. "Ah, Wells—have you had a thought of some importance? A revelation that cannot wait for the light of day?" He had been reading a thick book; Wells recognized it as Dr. Moreau's journal.

"Something much more urgent, sir." He and Jane quickly told him what they had seen. Huxley's bushy eyebrows drew together, and his forehead furrowed.

The professor tucked the book under his arm, pulled on slippers, and joined them. "I've always been concerned about enemy spies infiltrating the Institute, but after what I saw in the aquarium today, I can't believe anyone is concerned with national boundaries."

They hurried down gaslit corridors toward Cavor's lab. The door was open wider than before, the gaslights still burning, but the large engineering bay seemed silent and empty. Wells looked around the room, but saw no sign of anyone. "Whoever did it seems to be gone now."

Huxley swept his gaze over the clutter. "If we study which items have been disturbed, and which ones are missing, we can determine what this intruder was up to." He wrinkled his nose. "Something has spilled as well."

Jane moved purposefully to the open hatch of the cavorite vessel. Though the cavorite structural material was transparent, the interior of the spherical vessel had been paneled with sheets of thin metal, jointed like a roll-top desk in numerous adjacent sections; they appeared to be window blinds that passengers could raise to observe the outside. At present, though, they were all closed. "Professor, come look at this. The sphere is loaded with supplies."

Huxley put his shaggy gray head next to hers. "But it was supposed to be just a demonstration model. Look there— food . . . water . . . documents."

Jane climbed inside for a closer inspection. "Boxes of apples and carrots, loaves of bread." She picked up one of the brown bottles of beer. "It looks as if someone was preparing for a long voyage."

Huxley shook his head. "Cavor has not yet discovered how to make the vessel work. That was why we couldn't show it to the Prime Minister—ah, hullo!" When he saw a set of loose charts marked with thin black lines, he climbed in next to Jane and picked up the curling papers. "These are detailed nautical maps of the English coastline. I daresay we've uncovered something sinister."

Jane pointed to handwriting along the margins of the charts. "Those words aren't in English."

"It's German," Huxley said. "This is all some plot of the Kaiser's. I was concerned the Germans might be preparing to launch into a massive war. That was why I originally called the symposium."

Wells paced around the outside of the sphere, inspecting how it rested in the armillary cradle like a giant featureless globe. He completed his circuit of the lab, but found no sign of the intruder. He clenched his fists. He was not a large man, nor was he strong, but he intended to fight this rogue, if he should encounter him.

Huxley poked his head out of the hatch. "Alas, it may be Griffin. He is indeed mad, I think . . . but not in the way he makes it seem to the rest of us. I have noticed certain patterns of his behavior that lead me to suspect he has ties to Prussia. He may have been working as a spy all along, confident no one would suspect him so long as he acted the part of an eccentric. Griffin is not quite so amusingly eccentric as he lets on."

Jane said, "If you suspected this man, why did you let him continue to work here?"

Huxley sighed, rolling up the incriminating charts. "Griffin's genius was great, and we needed to take the risk. Given time, he may have developed a viable invisibility formula. Now though, I am afraid he is simply . . . mad."

Wells felt his skin tingle, as if with a ghostly movement of air. Then very close behind him he heard a sharp exhalation of breath. Before he could whirl to confront the mysterious presence, though, someone struck him on the head. Wells stumbled from the blow, his ears ringing; colored blotches swam in front of his eyes.

"H.G.!" Jane shouted.

Wild laughter rang out like crows flying in the air. "Mad? You fools don't bother to understand." It was the voice of Hawley Griffin, resonating from thin air. "The old order cannot be changed—it must be destroyed and stripped away, so that a new world can be built." He snorted with disgust. "I have spent more time thinking of politics and sacrifices than all your stuffy lords and Institute teachers have ever done."

Wells swung at him blindly, but his fist swept through the air, and he lost his balance again, feeling dizzy and a fresh rush of pain.

"You can't see me! You can't hide from me! You can't defend yourselves against me. I can go anywhere I wish." Griffin laughed again. "I can do anything I want."

Instead of continuing to strike out at the invisible man, Wells staggered toward the sphere, where Griffin had piled all of his stolen notes and supplies. He blocked access to the hatch. "I won't let you get inside this vessel. And I won't allow you near Jane either."

At a cluttered laboratory table, beakers and flasks suddenly flew in all directions, as if Griffin had petulantly swept his hand sideways. Equipment clattered to the laboratory floor. Griffin spoke again, angry now. "Your childish meddling cannot stop me."

Jars and boxes moved. Something scraped. Wells heard an object move on the cleared table, but couldn't see it.

"Not only am I invisible, Professor Huxley, but I have in my possession a nitroglycerin bomb." The chuckle resounded again, coming from nowhere. "It was the simplest thing in the world to create in my chemistry lab. No one thought to watch me."

From inside the sphere, Jane cried out as she found a new stack of documents by the supply boxes. "He's taken all the original papers from the symposium! All the notes and documents. He meant to run off with the secret research."

"Yes," Huxley said, "and no doubt he meant to steal away with the cavorite ship as well—if he could make it work."

When Griffin laughed again, the spectral voice came from a different part of the laboratory. "And I will blow up everything in my wake, killing the greatest scientists of Britain, erasing their knowledge. When Kaiser Wilhelm has your remarkable military developments, the Second Reich will conquer not only the British Empire, but the entire world! And I will be the real power, an invisible man spying on everyone, whispering into the Kaiser's ear." He let out a giggle. "Then, if he doesn't do exactly as I say, who could stop me from slipping into his chambers and slitting his throat?"

Wells refused to move from the sphere's hatch. His head throbbed from the blow, and his vision jumped about as if he were on the deck of a heaving ship in a storm. He clamped his teeth and breathed sharply through his nose, forcing himself to cling to consciousness.

"Now you three have ruined my careful plans. I warn you, I am holding the nitroglycerin bomb, which I have masked with my invisibility formula—but I assure you, I *do* have it. I will set it off, unless you leave the sphere immediately. I do not intend to be stopped."

Huxley's expression was one of stony indignation. "An invisible man with an invisible bomb. Very convenient, Griffin. I am not a man who simply accepts things on faith." The professor squeezed Wells's shoulder reassuringly, keeping him in front of the sphere's hatch. "I despise those who simply accept without proof, like Bishop Wilberforce."

Griffin's voice now came from near the door. "This is not an intellectual debate. Can you take the risk, Professor?"

Wells stared, hoping his eyes could distinguish some blurred outline, some murky shadow cast by the invisible man. Judging by Griffin's voice, Wells could guess where the man was hiding—for now. But the unseen intruder could easily stalk around the room, move to a different place. Wells didn't dare leave his protective position by the cavorite sphere. Griffin would watch every move he made.

Then, from behind the spot where Griffin apparently stood, a barrel-chested man strode through the open lab door—Dr. Selwyn Cavor! His dark eyes were bleary with sleep, but bright with anger. He moved quietly, balling his fists in annoyance. He evidently had heard everything they'd said.

Wells spoke quickly to distract the invisible man. "You'll never get away with this, Griffin. You can't kill all of us." He winced, realizing that if he had written such dialogue in a story, he would have immediately edited it out.

From the work table behind him, Cavor stealthily lifted a large flask filled with a sapphire-blue liquid and moved closer.

Griffin snorted. "This nitroglycerine bomb can easily—"

As soon as the unseen man revealed his location by speaking, Cavor raised the heavy laboratory bottle and brought it crashing down. The flask shattered against something unseen in the air, spilling blue liquid.

Cavor looked very satisfied with the impact. "You're a disgrace, Griffin."

The blue fluid took shape in the air, and now Wells could see the silhouette of the bristly-haired chemist, traced by the fluid. The stunned invisible man let out a groan of pain, swayed, and slowly crumpled.

Then some of the blue liquid dripped down onto an object in Griffin's hands—a rectangular shape, a box of some kind. The nitroglycerin bomb!

Griffin slumped forward, and his fingers let loose their hold.

With a yelp of alarm, Wells knocked both Jane and Huxley deeper into the sphere. "Back!" As he himself stumbled backward into the armored globe, he grasped the handle of the hatch, pulling it after him.

He almost had the door closed when the invisible bomb struck the floor.

The explosion was the loudest thunderclap Wells had ever heard, a giant fist of wind and energy. It pounded the cavorite sphere, hammering against the hatch as the detonation tore the whole laboratory apart . . . .

PART II

THE FIRST MEN
~AND A WOMAN~
IN THE MOON

CHAPTER ELEVEN

ADRIFT IN SPACE

A s the nitroglycerin explosion rang through the laboratory, the shock wave slammed the hatch shut on the cavorite sphere, and Wells tumbled into Jane and Professor Huxley amongst the boxes, crates, and papers.

The interior of the vessel was entirely dark, thanks to the closed blinds that covered the transparent walls. There was not a glimmer of light, no lessening of the intense shadows. No outside sound, though fire and fury must be all around them. His stomach gave a queasy lurch, and he had the oddest sensation of gentle, floating movement. He wished they could find a miner's light amongst the supplies the madman Griffin had packed aboard.

"Jane? Are you all right?" Wells scrambled about, bumping elbows, nearly sticking his left thumb in Huxley's eye. "Sorry, Professor."

The older man's gruff voice came from within inches of his ear. "She's behind me, Wells. We both appear to be intact."

"You can inspect me later, H.G. Do you think it's safe to go outside yet?"

In the darkness, Huxley made a skeptical noise. "There may still be fire and smoke from the concussion. Nevertheless, I'm pleased to learn, albeit accidentally, that Cavor's armor is exceptionally effective. Otherwise we should all have been blasted to smithereens."

"Oh, Dr. Cavor!" Jane cried. "He was right in the middle of the explosion."

"So was Griffin," Huxley said, his voice grim. "I do hope *he* didn't escape."

"With all this tumbling, I can't seem to find the hatch." Wells's hand slapped the inner wall, striking one of the pull-down blinds that covered a window. "Here, at least I'll let in some light." He fumbled with the catch on the bottom of the metal blind and slid it up to expose the incomprehensible scene outside.

The view made no sense: a tumult of darkness and starlight, glowing fires and billowing orange-white smoke—all receding rapidly. The armored sphere had hurtled out of the shattered laboratory like a cannonball, blasted upward by the explosion of Griffin's bomb!

Joining Wells at the window, Huxley looked down upon the burning wreckage of the Institute. The explosion had started a fire, and the sphere's violent ascent had knocked a hole in the roof. Many of the windows all along the building had shattered. Lights were lit; people scurried around.

Though Wells felt no change in his concept of up or down, he became disoriented again. As the view changed to a bottomless pit of open night sky studded with misty clouds, he realized that the sphere was spinning, rolling about like a great ball as it continued to rise high into the air.

"Amazing!" Huxley exclaimed. "The outer shell of the sphere is now opaque to gravity! The explosion in the laboratory must have unexpectedly provided the necessary impulse to the inert cavorite, changing its material structure."

"But how do we get down again?" Jane asked.

"Apart from falling," Wells added.

"Young lady, I do not even understand how we got *up*. If this were an artillery projectile, we would reach the peak of a parabolic trajectory and descend to the ground. But this vessel is not propelled by acceleration like a bullet. We simply appear to be . . . independent of the Earth's gravity, and presumably flying away from its surface at a tangent."

Trapped inside the cluttered sphere, they continued skyward at such a terrific rate that the main building of the Institute and the sprawling grounds were far, far below by the next time they tumbled round to get a view of the ground again. The metropolitan landscape of London extended below, thoroughfares and parks lit by tiny fireflies of street lamps. Wells made out the sultry curve of the Thames River, the unmistakable Tower of London, Buckingham Palace, Hyde Park. As the sphere continued its rotation, Wells once again saw only a bottomless pit of night sky studded with misty clouds. "This is making me dizzy."

Soon, they tore through a clump of cloud that left sparkles of moisture on the cavorite segments. The once-milky material had become perfectly clear now, since the shock-catalyzed phase change.

Working other rolling blinds, Wells and Jane exposed more of the cavorite windows and noted that the direction of their rolling movement changed each time they exposed one. By carefully selecting portholes on opposite sides of the sphere, they managed to stabilize their tumbling, and the seesaw of gravity evened them into a gentle, constant upward movement. With detached fascination, Huxley made notes as he pondered the views.

When the armored sphere finally rose above all impediments of Earth's atmosphere, they saw the full glory of the stars. The brilliant Moon shone more glorious and distinct than Wells had ever seen it from the ground. After more than an hour, their ascent had not noticeably slowed. Eventually they saw the curvature of the Earth itself, and a thin frosting of atmosphere.

"Ah, it seems we are leaving our Earth behind," Huxley announced.

Ever practical, Jane began looking through the supplies that Griffin had stored aboard the vessel. The sphere contained crates of food, bottled water, wine, and beer, as well as hard biscuits and fruit, such as might be packed as provisions aboard a seafaring craft.

Cavor, with his engineering mind set, had not gone out of his way to provide comfort and amenities. Small cushions tucked against the wall of the floating sphere might have been intended as comfortable seats—but only by a scientist who would never be required to sit in them. An empty covered tureen, now floating toward the sphere's ceiling, might have been meant as a portable privy.

But at least Wells was with Jane, and little else mattered.

Huxley conducted a brief, efficient inventory of the jumbled stockpile. "Since we don't know how long our journey might be, it's a good thing that rogue saw fit to leave us with provisions. I suggest we take inventory and portion out a logical distribution."

Wells asked, "Do you think the cavorite will . . . wear off, Professor?"

"Although I have read all the reports Cavor bothered to write—he was not very conscientious about writing up his research, I'm afraid—I do not claim to understand the physical mechanisms by which this unusual alloy functions."

As they rummaged through the boxes, setting aside the perishables, Jane found six stoppered and sealed test tubes casually stored among a set of engineering drawings. "Look, H.G.! The vials of cholera bacillus that Griffin stole from the medical research laboratory."

Wells paled. Huxley gently took the test tubes from Jane's slender hand. "I cannot believe my supposed colleague would have stooped to such a horrible method of warfare." With cotton wadding and strips of cloth, he carefully padded and wrapped the vials of deadly cholera germs. "We must make certain these are not damaged in any accident."

"Maybe we should just . . . open the hatch and throw them out," Jane suggested.

Huxley said, "My dear lady, we are out in space, beyond the atmosphere of Earth."

Jane caught her breath in alarm. "Of course! If we were to

open the hatch, all our air would escape. We would suffocate."

Wells put his arm around her. "I'd rather continue breathing for at least a while longer."

* * *

Though they hurtled far from their planetary home, the three explorers were safe enough within the armored vessel. Despite the obvious peril and uncertainty of their situation, the novelty soon wore thin. After several hours, they actually began to grow bored.

"I suppose this is not unlike your time on the H.M.S. *Rattlesnake*, Professor?" Wells asked. He and Jane huddled to share warmth and comfort.

Huxley talked to while away the time. "No, Mr. Wells, this is unlike any trip I have ever experienced. When I was but twenty-one, I secured a post on the *Rattlesnake* as their assistant surgeon. Though I had few qualifications for the job, it sounded exciting, and I wanted to be away from England. I spent the next four years sailing in the southern seas. The *Rattlesnake* was a scientific ship on a mission of exploration but, ah, it was a cockroach-ridden frigate. At least there were many fascinating things to see."

The old professor smiled wistfully. "I collected marine specimens over the side of the ship by using a wire-mesh meat safe as a dredge. I acquired fishes, aquatic plants, and small cephalopods. I wrote detailed summaries of my discoveries, which I posted home to England from each port. My papers were accepted by the prestigious journals of the Royal Institution and the Royal Society. They never guessed how young I was."

"I read many of those papers, Professor," Wells said. He had showed some of them to Jane as well, who was always fascinated with new specimens and the breadth of diversity of life on Earth. "When I was your student, I considered you quite a role model."

Huxley smiled with pleasure. "Ah, and look where it has gotten you, Wells. The three of us hurled far from Earth—farther, I daresay, than any human has ever gone before."

Jane sighed. "Out here in the space between planets, there aren't very many specimens for us to study. Then again, I didn't bring along my guidebooks or my opera glasses."

"Motionless tedium is the cruelest torture for the educated mind," Wells said. "Lesser animals, and even men without curiosity, can stare at the grass for hours. My own father was perfectly content to lounge outside his china shop, simply watching the road, greeting passers-by, but rarely stirring himself to perform any sort of work. Though the towns on the outskirts of London did well with the growth of industry, my father never managed to make a success of his shop. I don't believe he cared. He would rather have been playing cricket."

Jane snuggled closer to him in sympathy. "He sounds quite different from you, H.G."

"Oh, he was a good-hearted man, everyone's friend—but singularly without ambition. My mother was never happy with him. Even as a child I could sense the strain between them. Still, he took me to watch him play cricket sometimes. He was very good at it, you know, and—by a fortunate accident—one of those cricket matches made me into the man I am now."

"A cricket match?" Huxley asked. "I fail to see the connection."

"While my father played, one of his friends from the local pub liked to wrestle with me. I was only seven, and I found it deliriously entertaining. The man would toss me into the air, catch me, then toss me again. One time he missed—and down I fell onto a wooden tent stake, which promptly shattered my leg bone."

Jane stroked his hair. "It must have been terrible, H.G."

"On the contrary, my dear, it was a miracle. I had to spend the next several weeks bedridden, waiting for the bone to knit. And that is when I discovered *books*. My father felt extremely guilty—I'm sure my mother had something to do with that. He borrowed books of all kinds from the Bromley Institute Library: science, astronomy, and a wonderful natural history complete with illustrations. I simply couldn't get enough. That experience opened my mind, gave me new worlds to explore, new ideas to digest."

Jane slumped against the curved, cool wall of cavorite with a frustrated sigh. "If only we had books here to occupy us."

By the bright moonlight streaming through the exposed portholes, Huxley reached into his striped lounging robe and produced the thick volume he'd been reading when Wells and Jane fetched him from his room. "Ah. We do have Dr. Moreau's journal."

CHAPTER TWELVE

THE CRYSTAL EGG

FROM THE JOURNAL OF DR. MOREAU

For days, we kept the stunned Martian confined within a sweleringly hot supply tent. I imagined that conditions on Mars were colder than here in Algeria, probably colder than most inhabited places on Earth. The creature must have been abjectly miserable, but we had no better alternative.

Lowell sent riders to follow the spur rail line to the nearest Tuareg settlements for additional assistance. At last, two of the nomads returned hauling a dismantled iron cage on two complaining camels. The sturdy iron bars, which the men said had once been used to hold a lion, would provide the perfect confinement for our Martian. Lowell paid each of the strutting men a gold piece, and they seemed well satisfied with their efforts.

We had a long trek from the crash site to the train tracks at the far end of the geometrical ditches. From there, we would use our own narrow-gauge cars to meet up with the main rail line north to Algiers and the coast, where we could acquire transportation by Mediterranean steamer.

Staring at the horizon of tan dunes, Lowell wore his red-lensed glasses. They had become quite an affectation for him. He had a gleam in his bright, hawkish eyes. "Because of our Martian visitor, Moreau, you and I will not be swept into the dustbin of history like so many others."

Though I harbored no wish for endowments and museums to be named after me, I very much wanted to recapture the scientific respectability that Thomas Huxley had stripped from me. If the sun rose again on my career, perhaps my important prior work would not be so easily dismissed . . . .

Tuareg laborers worked to remove all fourteen of the remaining drone cadavers, which would be crated, preserved, and eventually shipped or sold to scientific institutions around the world. I insisted on maintaining watch so the nomads could not steal Martian artifacts to sell as trinkets in a market town.

The day's heat turned the creature's spacecraft into an oven, but despite the oppressive temperature, the men still had to carry kerosene lamps inside, as the cylinder had no windows or portholes. By the light of my own lamp, I searched for items of further scientific interest, studying the vessel's smooth walls and flat deck. How had those giant intellects occupied themselves during the tedious months of travel? I doubted their inferior white drones would have offered much conversation. I had an amusing vision of the two enormous brains holding playing cards in their tentacles, challenging each other to a round of whist.

The Tuaregs lifted one desiccated drone body after another and carried them outside. I heard the nomads jabber in their language, then their words became hushed and furtive. Suspecting that the men were hiding something, I demanded, "What is it? Show me what you have found." Though I knew perfectly well they could comprehend commands in English, they pretended not to understand me. "Show me what it is! The cylinder and all artifacts within it are the property of Percival Lowell."

I finally grabbed one of the shrugging men by his loose robes, ready to beat him with a stick like an animal. As my colleagues will be quick to agree, I have little patience when someone stands in my way. The man saw this in my eyes, and his companions knew they would be searched and whipped. He reached into the folds of his robe and withdrew a perfectly polished crystal egg as large as my extended hand. I glared at him, and he surrendered it quickly.

"The law of your Mahomet requires that the hand of a thief be struck off with a sword. Isn't that correct?" The man whimpered, while I happily held the crystal egg. "Fortunately for you, I have no patience for religious nonsense. But I do not abide thieves. You will all be searched at the end of the day. If we find anything that does not belong to you, I shall see that your *heads* are lopped off, not just your hands."

I had no idea what sort of artifact the crystal egg might be, whether it was some bauble dug from the Martian deserts, or an unimaginably sophisticated piece of technology based on glass and silica. When I showed it to Lowell that night, he was just as amazed and mystified. "Perhaps the Martian knows."

We opened the flap of the sealed supply tent, wary of an attack from the creature. But the Martian huddled in shadow, listless and weak. Lowell held up the crystal egg. "Can you identify this? Explain its function?"

The Martian's tentacles twitched. Its saucer-like eyes were alien and expressionless, like a squid's. Lowell snorted. "How can anything with a brain so large be incapable of communication?"

"They may communicate in a completely different manner. The skin on its head could be a tympanic membrane like a drumhead, or maybe they exude scents in a chemical language indecipherable to our primitive noses. Maybe he even forms words with his mind."

Lowell bent closer to the captive alien. "We are your friends, fellow scientists. We sent the signal. We came to greet you." He sighed. "I wish you'd give us some sign that you want to exchange information." But the Martian was as inscrutable as a cigar store Indian, and we left it alone . . . .

The next day Lowell commanded his workers to break down the camp. Three men assembled the lion cage and a platform to set atop a camel's back like a palanquin. The ornery beasts would carry the caged Martian to the rail line.

The iron cage was placed before the supply tent, its gate open. When the flap was lifted, the Tuaregs shouted and beat upon the fabric with their rods. The thumping noise and the ruckus chased the sluggish alien creature out into the desert sun. When the Martian saw the cage, it went wild and tried to escape. But the stern natives forcibly encouraged it into the confinement. They slammed shut the gate, then together lifted the heavy cage onto the palanquin platform. Even lashed down, it rested uneasily on the back of the camel.

Lowell left a few of the men to guard the empty crashed cylinder, while the rest of us set off to the rail line. It was a long and uncomfortable pilgrimage across the desert. The camel groaned as it plodded through the sands, while the Martian huddled in the cage, its tentacles wrapped around the bars as if testing the iron's tensile strength. It might have been a powerful creature on Mars, but the thing was now overburdened by its own weight in Earth's gravity.

At last, we reached the dead end of the narrow-gauge spur line Lowell had laid down to service his trench excavations. I had no doubt that desert bandits would soon blow up the line or steal the iron rails for salvage. It no longer mattered to me.

Tuaregs on horseback raced to where Lowell's private locomotive and cargo cars waited. For more than a week, the train had relayed prison supervisors and French labor camp workers back to Algiers. Now, forewarned by the Tuareg riders, the bored engineer was able to stoke his furnaces and get up a head of steam by the time we crested the dunes. Our nomads lifted the heavy cage from the camel's back and loaded it into one of the dim cargo cars. After Lowell paid them in gold, the desert men departed, anxious to be far from the hideous creature.

Lowell and I rode with the train's engineer up front in the locomotive, confident that the Martian was secure in its cargo car. The dry wind felt pleasant on our faces as the chugging train spat steam and cinders into the air. Though the engineer was rather ignorant, we were glad enough to have the conversation of another man who spoke English.

We traveled northward for hours until we finally reached the nearest sub-Saharan rail line that intersected our narrow-gauge spur. Then we prepared to wait. Schedules in the desert mean little. Hours or dates printed in a timetable are only useless numbers. A train would arrive whenever it came by.

We spent the night out in the darkness, but the following dawn we heard the distant rhythmic shunting and saw the plume of steam and smoke. Lowell and I stood on either side of the tracks to flag the train down. The locomotive slowed, then hissed and wheezed to a stop.

We learned that it was traveling from Algiers to Marrakech. We were quite pleased with that destination, for from Marrakech we could catch another train northward to the port city of Casablanca.

Lowell seemed to have an inexhaustible supply of cash. He paid the conductor for space aboard one of the nearly empty boxcars, and we spent an hour loading the caged Martian, the crated alien cadavers, and our equipment from the camp.

The other passengers on the train, most of them wrapped in Arab garments, stared out the windows at us while we worked. They didn't seem impatient, having no expectations for when they might arrive in Marrakech; they simply rode along, letting the day slip by without being marked off by the ticking of a pocket watch.

The train chugged off again, grinding slowly forward on

the rails, and Lowell worked his way from one passenger car to another, searching for a lounge where he could relax. Since I had no interest in conversing with anyone, not even Lowell, I climbed into the cargo car, where I could sit beside the caged Martian.

As the train moved along, the rolling wheels vibrated beneath the car. Golden ribbons of sunlight penetrated the uneven slats in the boxcar walls. The Martian's tentacles held on against the jostling of the train; it looked upon me with envious eyes, an indecipherable but seemingly malevolent stare. I watched it stir, trying to understand the language of its movements and reactions . . . .

From long years of practice, I had become adept at studying specimens that knew nothing but pain and fear. Sometimes their rudimentary brains comprehended their fates as I removed them from their cages and took them to the operating tables. Some struggled and slashed with claws or teeth. I've heard of animals caught in traps that become so desperate they gnaw off their own limbs.

Would this Martian do such a thing? Had it learned such terrible fear of me, the man who kept it in captivity?

For years working in university laboratories in London, I had pushed the limits of surgical techniques. My studies in vivisection and responses to pain expanded the limits of human knowledge. In exploring new methods of grafting from one species to another, I attempted to determine the plasticity of the animal form. In outward appearance, at least, I tried to fashion wild animals into creatures physically similar to human beings. With form, I hoped, would come function.

My dream had been to take a large animal with the potential for greater intelligence—a bear for instance, or a dog—and through deft manipulations with the scalpel, create a new species. I removed bestial teeth, enlarged the skull area to accommodate secondary brain tissue, reshaped paws into hands.

Because of the loud howls of my experimental subjects and the constant need for disposing of failed specimens, I was forced to do my work at night, in private. While I taught students at the Normal Academy during the day and performed seemingly innocuous experiments for the other schoolmasters to see, my real work went on in the quiet, late hours.

I came so close.

I remember bright lights shining down on the operating table, which glistened with red blood that leaked out of numerous incisions. I had flayed the skin from a baboon; while strapping its arms and legs to the table, I proceeded to cut it open so that I could add superior organs harvested from other animals. A formerly docile German shepherd dog lay whimpering on another operating table, still alive (I had removed several of its vital organs, and thus it could not survive long). I had also taken brain tissue and olfactory apparatus from a cat, and was attempting to splice them all into a singular hodgepodge being.

The baboon snarled and growled, the dog whined, and the cat let out hideous noises, but I was too intent on my work to understand how clearly the clamor could be heard far away down the halls. Before I knew it, Professor Thomas Huxley threw open the door to my surgery and stared aghast at what I was doing. "This is an abomination!" His bellow startled me, and my scalpel slipped, causing irreparable damage to the baboon's medulla oblongata, thereby ruining the specimen.

Huxley, Darwin's bulldog, a man supposedly unruffled by even the most challenging rhetoric, was struck speechless. Finally, he spluttered, "You are through at the Academy, Moreau! I will call the police, and I shall see that you go to prison for this . . . this *nightmare* of science."

"Thomas, you don't understand. Here, let me show you what I'm doing. The possibilities are—"

Huxley shocked me—and himself as well, I suppose—by vomiting on the floor. I found it rather disappointing, because this was a man who had performed a great deal of biological research and published numerous papers in respected journals.

"You are supposed to be a man of science and vision," I said. "Will you not even listen?"

From his expression of revulsion, I knew what Huxley's answer would be. Despite all of his challenges to religious-minded people whom he considered to be gullible fools, despite all of his admonishments to use logic instead of artificial morality and senseless sentimentality—T.H. Huxley was disgusted by what I had done.

He saw to it that I was immediately stripped of my position at the Academy. I was forced to flee the country and leave my work behind, simply in order to remain free of prison. In the ensuing scandal, I had no choice but to seek sponsors in foreign lands, visionary men who understood that potential breakthroughs can be purchased only through effort and pain. I was forced to work in isolated places: in Africa, on uninhabited islands in the Orient.

For all his eccentricities, my new friend Percival Lowell was a kindred spirit.

Peering through the bars in the lion's cage, I could see a terrible, unearthly intelligence in the Martian's eyes. Though the creature was weak and entirely at my mercy, it seemed to believe that it alone was in control.

I wondered for a moment if my own doomed experimental animals had felt the same way, just before I dissected them . . . .

* * *

When we finally reached the port of Casablanca, Lowell learned the names of officials susceptible to bribes, which forms he was required to fill out, and which fees must be paid. There was already a steamer in port bound for the United States, and he promptly booked us passage in separate cabins.

Knowing that seamen would be more curious than the nomadic and superstitious Tuaregs, we decided that the Martian's presence should be kept quiet. The cage was covered with a tarpaulin, and Lowell explained that he was transporting a large animal captured in Africa, bound for the Boston zoo.

We found a place in the dark, cool cargo decks where the Martian's cage would be left undisturbed. At first, the steamer captain showed little interest in what we were trying to smuggle, and then none at all after Lowell paid him an extra bribe to buy us more privacy.

I was glad to be bound for America. After so many years on the run, I looked forward to calm civilization. I wanted to go anyplace where I would find the freedom and facilities to perform all the experiments I had in mind. Though it was currently uncommunicative, the Martian would offer a wealth of opportunities—science, technology, philosophy—once I managed to break through the barrier of understanding.

Lowell and I found ourselves alone with the Martian in a small cargo room. We removed the covering tarpaulin and looked through the bars. "He will truly be a marvel when we get him to America," Lowell said. "My family can help me make the appropriate scientific announcements."

I was more concerned about the Martian's declining health than about its possibilities for fame in Boston society. "I will be pleased merely to get it to a safe place. Perhaps it is suffering from one of our Earth germs, to which it has no immunity. Right now, it looks very sick."

CHAPTER THIRTEEN

DR. CAVOR'S SPHERE PROVES ITS METTLE

According to Huxley's still-ticking pocket watch, it was past noon back in London, but out in space the passengers saw nothing but a starry night. Wells opened one of the interior blinds to expose the Sun's orb, but the illumination was so blinding he had to close the covering immediately. The incredible situation in which he found himself took his breath away.

Ever practical in the face of panic, Jane rolled up the opposite shade so she could gaze out at the pock-marked Moon. Its silvery-white surface seemed peaceful and soothing.

While the professor dozed, Wells and Jane stared at the lines and shadows, deep craters that might have been ancient volcanoes or asteroid impacts. Wells had never imagined such a sight in all his life, and he hoped he survived to write about it, someday.

He pressed closer, as excited as he was frightened. "It looks closer, Jane. See all the detail. It's as if we're seeing through a telescope."

"You promised to show me fascinating things and take me to interesting places." Jane touched his cheek. "So far, you have been true to your word."

The Moon had always fascinated Wells, but at the moment Jane intrigued him more. Seeing Huxley sound asleep, they slid away from the porthole. Under the shimmer of moonlight, he put his arm around her, and she rested her head on his shoulder. So far the excitement had kept them awake, but they swiftly fell into dreams in each other's arms . . . .

* * *

Huxley shook Wells vigorously awake. "I thought you'd both like to watch this—we're going to crash soon."

The urgency in the professor's voice made Wells snap to full alertness. Jane was already up and peering out the porthole. Filling the whole view, the Moon loomed in their path like an immense hammer ready to smash them. The craters now looked like yawning, hungry mouths fanged with cliffs and upthrust ridges.

"Our speed must be quite extraordinary," Huxley said, without a glimmer of panic. "I wish Cavor had installed some form of direct controls. I do not know how to guide our course or slow our descent."

Wells had a sudden idea and pulled himself to the nearest

exposed porthole. "If Cavor's material is opaque to gravity, how is it that we are being drawn so inexorably toward the Moon? Obviously, there must be some—"

The older man's eyebrows shot up. "Of course, the porthole! You've left one of the blinds up and a section of cavorite exposed. These blinds must block the action of the cavorite somehow, but with the uncovered section facing the Moon, lunar gravity has acted on all the items inside the sphere, pulling us along in that direction. Unfortunately, to our doom."

Jane understood. "The Moon is reeling us in like a trout."

Acting decisively, Wells rattled the blind shut. He mentally went through his own lessons on physics and astronomy, when Jane had studied at his side.

"That will stop the pull of gravity, but our momentum will keep us traveling in a straight line," he said, discouraged. "That is Newton's first law."

Huxley sighed. "What a pity. I should have liked to do a bit of exploring on the Moon."

Though the sphere was now dark, Wells scrambled to the other side of the sphere, bumping Jane's leg, knocking into Huxley's shoulder, but he had no time to waste. "All is not lost—we simply need to apply an equal and opposite force." He slid open a window blind, saw an empty field of stars, then slammed it shut. He opened another, then another, until finally one opened with a view of the blazing sun. He shielded his eyes from the burning vision. "The Sun is more distant, but much larger and has a stronger gravitational pull. It'll slow us, like applying the brakes on a bicycle."

"Brilliant, Wells!" Huxley said.

Jane braced herself, expecting a sudden lurch of deceleration.

"I'm glad we fell asleep looking at the Moon. If we had a porthole open facing the opposite direction, we might have been roasted alive before we could do anything."

The glare inside the enclosed sphere was harsh as the sun dragged them to a halt. Jane rolled up the Moon-side covering, glanced out quickly, and snatched the blinds back down again. "We seem to be safely high above the surface."

Wells slammed shut the Sun-side blind. "There. I would guess we're now just hovering."

Huxley seemed very pleased. "If we have discovered a crude means of maneuvering this craft out in space, then we are no longer in danger of immediate obliteration. With a judicious opening and closing of the blinds, we can ride the currents of gravity wherever we wish to go."

"That means we can make our way safely back to Earth," Wells said.

"Whenever we're ready," Jane added.

Huxley tapped his finger against his bushy sideburns. "Must we be so anxious to get back to our cozy homes? I would rather have a look around."

"Very well, then." Jane's expression was determined. "We shall do our explorations as a team."

Wells gave her a quick, enthusiastic hug. He had always known she was hungry to learn and discover, curious about the way the universe worked. "In *From the Earth to the Moon*, Jules Verne's heroes did nothing more than circle around the Moon and return home. We shall be the first to actually touch down—if we can manage it without killing ourselves."

Huxley went to the opposite porthole and slid up the blinds so that the lunar surface showed in its full glory. "Forward again, carefully." With a section of the cavorite exposed, the armored sphere began to move once more toward their destination.

The professor's joy and anticipation made him look much younger than he had appeared at the Imperial Institute. "History shall remember us as the first men on the Moon, Wells. Not a bad accomplishment, eh?"

"The first men *and a woman*," Jane insisted. "Or do you expect me to stay inside the cavorite sphere and cook you breakfast?" Wells chuckled.

"My apologies, Miss Robbins," Huxley said. "The female of the species always plays a vital role—frequently more important than the male's, for all our colorful plumage."

Flying by their best guess, the three passengers opened and closed the blinds to adjust their course, angling toward the pock-marked surface. They circled the alien landscape in fits and starts, approaching the shadowy boundary between daylight and the dark side of the Moon.

"Shall we select a place to land?" Huxley asked. "I am dubious, however, about our ability to exert such a level of control."

"All of the terrain looks equally bleak to me," Jane said.

They were settling toward the razor-edged line of dawn that crept across the surface as the Moon orbited the Earth. "Perhaps it would be best to make a landing on the edge of sunrise, which is likely to be the most temperate area. The day side may be baking hot and the night side intensely cold."

"An excellent deduction, Wells. Let us choose a level spot near a crater."

After so great a journey across such a vast distance, the last few moments swept up on them with the speed of a locomotive. They had slowed to a fraction of their former velocity, but still the craters and the rocky surface hurtled toward them. Wells yanked open the opposite window shades, letting the Sun's pull slow them like a parachute, and Jane slammed shut her view of the craters. They were flying blind.

Huxley said, "I hope we aren't crushed like an egg dropped onto a tile floor."

"We'll know in a moment," Jane said.

And they did. Cavor's remarkable armor cushioned them against the impact. The jolt rang through the sphere, throwing the three passengers together in a heap. The round space vessel rebounded into the sky again, tumbling, rolling, until finally gravity snagged the open sections of cavorite again like an anchor and pulled the sphere downward. After several more ricochets, each one smaller in amplitude than the previous one, the sphere came to rest with the exposed windows flat against the ground, where gravity could seize them.

Wells fumbled to find Jane in the darkness, and threw his arms around her. Huxley sounded as if he couldn't believe what he was saying. "We have actually reached the Moon."

Crawling on his knees, Wells opened all of the blinds at what he perceived to be the sphere's floor. "This should hold us to the lunar surface like a magnet. I wouldn't want the sphere to drift away while we are off exploring."

"What sort of clothes do you suppose one must wear when walking on the Moon?" Jane said.

"No one's ever done it before, so you will set the fashion," Wells said.

They had been so rushed when pursuing Griffin that he and

Jane were dressed only in the comfortable lounging clothes from their room. Huxley wore his striped robe, loose shirt, and trousers. "I would have preferred good, sturdy alpine boots, but under the circumstances I shall make do with slippers."

"First things first," Jane said. "Let us look out on this strange new world."

Wells opened one of the small blinds so they could see the silhouetted terrain. The sphere rocked slightly, but the larger bottom-facing windows held them to the ground. Together they watched sunrise on the Moon. A flood of light and warmth swept over them, bursting through a dam of darkness. The vivifying sunlight crossed the cold, black landscape. With it came mists that evaporated, rising gradually at first and then with greater fury in a constant exhalation.

"Ah, the air itself must have settled and frozen in the utter coldness of night," Huxley said. "Interesting."

When the line of sunlight passed over their cavorite vessel, the rumble of the pebbly lunar surface was strong enough that they could sense the vibration through the armored hull. Outside, the atmosphere thickened.

"Look, the sky is even turning a slight blue," Jane said. "It's as if the whole world is waking up with the morning."

Ice crystals sparkled like diamonds in the light. The rigid shadows became diffuse, then melted away. Never in his life had Wells seen such a magnificent dawn. "Do you suppose the air will be thick enough for us to breathe?"

"If it isn't, then our expedition of discovery will produce very little of value." Huxley's falcon-sharp eyes looked at both Wells and at Jane. "Our most important duty is to be explorers for science. We must see what we can, document our discoveries, learn what the Moon has to offer. One day other voyagers might come here to complete the detailed work, but we three are the first—and we must do it properly."

Gathering his nerve, Wells went to the hatch, which they had not opened since it had been blasted shut by Griffin's nitroglycerin bomb. "Well, as they say, we can't begin until we start. If we're all agreed . . . ?" He raised his eyebrows. Both Huxley and Jane nodded.

Showing no trepidation, Wells unsealed the hatch. With a hiss, their air rushed out, swirling and cold, fluttering the papers inside. Wells stood blinking out at the rugged ground before him. No one—not even Sir Richard Burton in Arabia, or Mungo Park in darkest Africa—had ever set forth into a land so strange. He drew a deep breath of the lunar atmosphere and braced himself, expecting to be struck down by poisonous gases from the strange world. "The air is fresh and sweet, though a bit chilly."

"It will warm as the day proceeds," Huxley said. "Go outside, Mr. Wells."

But he hesitated, turning back to his mentor. "Sir, the honor of being the first to touch this new world rightfully belongs to you. It is equivalent to Christopher Columbus discovering North America." Little more than a foot separated him from the dusty, crumbly ground.

"No need to make such a foofaraw, young man. It is but a small step."

Wells stood firm. "No, Professor. When history looks back upon this, it will be seen as a giant leap for mankind."

CHAPTER FOURTEEN

STRANGE CARGO

FROM THE JOURNAL OF DR. MOREAU

Our steamer left Casablanca, stopped at Tangier, and proceeded through the Strait of Gibraltar. While Lowell took in the Mediterranean breezes on the sunny deck, I spent my days tending our captive Martian and taking copious notes. I already had enough material to write at least one analytical book, possibly more.

The steamer passengers had no inkling that a creature from another planet was stored in one of the small cargo holds. By the time we headed west across the Atlantic, I had become accustomed to my small, dim room in the private parts of the ship adjacent to the cargo chamber where we held the Martian.

My cabin's former inhabitant had been rousted out to bunk with another sailor. Despite the captain's instructions, the disgruntled clod wanted back into his little room, insisting that he had left keepsakes there. But I found absolutely nothing, and I was sure the man wanted to accuse me of stealing. Besides, I had begun to let the sick Martian loose from its lion's cage so that it could move about the metal-walled chamber. I had no intention of letting this oaf see it.

The red-headed man had a squarish, stupid face that looked as if it had been pummeled into a barely human mold; his ears were swollen, his nose crooked, most assuredly damaged in street brawls. The crewman glared at me in front of the door to the cargo room, but I am accustomed to dealing with brutes and fools.

Taking the initiative, I pushed him away from the cabin with enough force to surprise him, then I promptly brandished a metal pipe (which I used when I needed to encourage the Martian back into its cage). "If I batter your nose into a pulp, perhaps the ship's doctor could set it properly this time, and you won't look like such an ugly gargoyle."

The man had obviously expected me to be a meek tourist to be bullied into submission. But when he saw that I was deadly serious and would not be intimidated, he slunk away, growling empty threats.

I slammed the cabin door and secured the lock, knowing that I must now be on my guard against this uneducated brute. If the Martian had come to Earth in search of intelligent life, I was glad it had first encountered men such as myself, rather than stupid apes like that one.

I did not tell Lowell about the threats. Although he wanted to be credited with great discoveries, he was willing to go only so far. At heart, Percival Lowell was a man of high society, raised in Boston to appreciate cigars, brandy, and gourmet foods. While I stayed in my dim room devoted to our work, Lowell secured a grand cabin for himself on the sun deck. He enjoyed all the amenities he'd missed in the primitive Sahara. He bathed, had his clothes laundered and pressed, and dined each evening at the captain's table.

Naturally, I was invited to join him. But how could I leave my Martian, whose health was clearly fading, its mysterious illness gaining a stronger hold? How could I dine on beefsteak and soufflé, while the most vital biological discovery in history lay plaintively weak below decks?

I offered the Martian everything I could imagine it might eat. I attempted to interest the creature with vegetables or fresh meat, sugar water, even unpalatable chemical compounds from my research kit, but the Martian refused every form of nourishment that I could imagine.

In my dissection of its desiccated comrade, I had found no obvious stomach, gut, or intestines, and I wondered if it might draw sustenance through photosynthesis in the manner of a plant. Making sure no one could see, I moved the creature to an outer cabin for a few hours, where a wide sunbeam shone through the salt-speckled porthole. But still the listless beast showed no response, and I returned him to the cargo chamber.

Recalling all of my experiments grafting the healthy organs of one species of animal onto the weaker set of another . . . I considered the possibilities. If only I could graft some human organs onto the Martian—a strong set of lungs, or even a heart, as I had done in my vivisections—then perhaps this superior being could live after all. But I did not have access to such biological resources. I could do only what I was able.

I was growing extremely concerned. How could I ever replace this live specimen if I, through my own negligence, allowed it to perish?

As a doctor, I was certain—judging by the increasing rubbery grayness of its skin and the rising and falling temperature of its body, which I acquired through the awkward use of a thermometer—that the Martian was suffering from some sort of Earthly *germ*.

Coming from a different planet, Martian life could be at risk from fevers and other morbidities to which humans had long since become accustomed. Our atmosphere was thicker, the gravity heavier, the moisture in the air higher than the red deserts of Mars. Such a creature had never been meant to survive here. This lone explorer would die here unless I could perform some drastic miracle.

In desperation, I gave it a radical series of injections, a course of strong drugs, stimulants, and vitamins. The Martian recovered some of its strength and vigor. In fact, its improvement was so dramatic and remarkable that I realized my own exhaustion and stress. When had I last eaten?

Thus, I finally decided to take Lowell up on his invitation. I went into the sunlight at last, leaving the Martian secured in its room. I wanted a bath and a change of clothes, a shave, and a good meal among civilized company. But what I most desired was to talk privately to Percival Lowell.

I need not recount in detail the mundane dinner conversation with the captain and all the vapid travelers, who had little intelligence and much money. After the meal, feeling clean and refreshed, my belly well satisfied and my chest warmed by a particularly mellow Bordeaux, I took Lowell down to see his prize specimen. When we returned, however, we came upon quite a shock.

The metal door to the isolated cargo chamber was ajar, forced open. I instantly had a sense of foreboding. "Damnation! Someone has broken in."

We rushed into the room, only to find it ransacked. My medical equipment lay strewn about, my doctor's bags, vials of serum and chemicals scattered. Worst of all, the Martian was gone. The lion's cage stood empty, the barred door hanging open.

"Blast! The brute is loose!" Lowell's expression showed annoyance rather than panic. "We must track it down. The thing can't have gone far on the ship."

I ran out of the cabin and into the lower passageways. "We will certainly hear a commotion if any other passengers see it."

But I didn't think the Martian would go near crowds of people. It would slink and hide belowdecks, maybe make its way to the engine room. I remembered the strange rotating camera construction it had built at its crashed cylinder and therefore we knew that it had a substantial mechanical aptitude.

Lowell and I hurried through the shadowy passageways. The tunnels were hot and dank, smelling of metal, bilge, and grease. The shielded gas lamps provided insufficient illumination. The Martian would have a thousand places to hide.

"The creature is frightened—doesn't know where to turn. When we find it, we'll have to corner it."

"Yes, Moreau, and a cornered animal is extremely dangerous."

We considered splitting up, but realized that if we came upon the alien specimen—if it was indeed energetic enough to have launched its impetuous escape attempt—one man would be unable to subdue it.

We opened doors, looking into unoccupied cabins and storerooms. The ship's engines throbbed, and we could feel a swaying motion from the restless seas around us. My senses were highly attuned. I knew the Martian was intelligent and its tentacle appendages sufficiently nimble that it could have picked the lock of its cage. But someone else had broken into the rooms.

A bloodcurdling scream echoed along the passageway, a shriek of pain and terror that suddenly broke off with a hollow, wooden-sounding snap.

"It came from just around that corner," Lowell said.

Wasting no thought on caution, we raced pell-mell to the cabin where our Martian had gone to ground. Anyone else would have frozen with terror upon seeing the monstrous Martian, its lamp-like eyes, its writhing tentacles. But when we saw what the creature was *doing*, even the two of us were shocked and revolted. Lowell turned away, but I could only stare, trying to understand.

The Martian had attacked the oafish redhead whose quarters I had taken over. I guessed that by the time the crewman broke open my sealed cabin door, the Martian must already have let itself out of the cage. If I'd been the one to return, no doubt the creature would have fallen upon me.

The crewman had paid a high price for his vengeful curiosity. Like a predatory spider chasing a fat beetle, the Martian had pursued the man, overtaken him, and brought him down with powerful tentacles. While the hapless man screamed and struggled, the Martian wrapped one of its snake-like appendages around his throat and snapped his neck. Blood still dribbled from the redhead's lips, and his dull-witted eyes were glazed in death.

Lowell had never seen a dead man before, certainly never a cruelly murdered victim with fresh bloodstains all around. But the most horrific aspect of the tableau was what the Martian was *doing*.

It's saucer-like eyes looked at us warily, like a wolf guarding its kill. Its multiple tentacles moved in a dizzying flow. It had seized hypodermic syringes from my medical kit, and I realized that the crewman had not ransacked my laboratory after all—it was the Martian itself.

Like an industrial harvesting machine, the Martian plunged hypodermic needles into the dead crewman, filling each syringe barrel with fresh blood, and then curled back around to inject the harvested life fluid into its own veins.

"It's . . . feeding." I allowed myself to feel intellectual interest once the initial unpleasantness had worn off. "Fresh blood, like a vampire."

Did human blood contain the proper proteins and nutrients the Martian required to stay alive? It seemed an impossible evolutionary adaptation. Knowing the physiology of the

Martian, I saw no natural apparatus on its physical form that was adapted to drawing or ingesting blood. I saw no signs that it was a blood drinker. Was it possible that the creature had traveled so high on the evolutionary ladder that it depended upon artificial apparatus to survive? Had it become utterly dependent upon tools, even in order to derive nourishment? It seemed unlikely to me, but the Martian civilization had clearly advanced far beyond anything on Earth.

I could see by the unnatural pallor in the crewman's corpse that he had already been mostly exsanguinated. I couldn't say I felt sorry for him. With a flash, I understood the reason for the desiccated condition of the other white corpses inside the crashed cylinder, the pale drones left as shriveled husks . . . even the other superior Martian, bled dry. *This creature had fed on them.* A terrible necessity to ensure that the mission succeeded?

"Good Lord, this is horrible!" Lowell reeled with growing horror and revulsion, then staggered to the wall, whereupon he retched up most of his fine dinner and the Bordeaux.

So, now I knew our specimen had murdered more than once. Had it been an honorable decision of survival among the two remaining superior Martians, or had this creature killed its companion just to drink its blood?

As these thoughts raced through my mind, Lowell recovered and turned with revulsion and anger. He raised his metal bludgeon and brought it down swiftly upon the Martian's brain sac. He struck again, sideways, scattering the hypodermic needles across the floor. Half-stunned, the Martian scuttled away from the crewman's body, but Lowell struck it a third blow.

I interposed myself between him and the Martian. "Don't hurt it. We have just made a substantial discovery about its very nature. Think, man! It must have been desperate, starving." I sneered at the dead redhead on the floor. "And this was probably the most valuable thing that cretin has ever done in his life. I doubt he'll be missed."

"It was murder, Moreau!"

"Is it murder when one species kills another? When a hunter shoots a gorilla in Africa, when a farmer butchers a cow? These Martians may be as superior to us as we are to our domesticated animals. It is an accident and understandable, but we must make certain it does not happen again."

Together, threatening with our clubs, we drove the sluggish Martian back down the corridor. I wondered if it moved slowly because it had gorged itself, or if Lowell's blows had injured it. Despite its feeding, I could see the marks of sickness still upon it.

We urged the Martian forward. It seemed to know where we were going and, as if chastened, it moved along willingly. I wondered if it was simply biding its time and building further schemes in its great brain.

When we had the creature safely secured in its iron cage, I added a second lock this time. Then I looked at Lowell. His hair was mussed, his eyes reddened and wild. Fortunately, I am adept at cleaning up after experiments that have gone wrong; the rest of the world has never needed to know the details of failed attempts.

"Lowell, you must go speak with the captain," I said, command firm in my voice. "Smooth this over."

He did not usually respond well to sharp orders, but

in this situation he was completely lost. "Yes. Yes, I must explain to the captain—"

I cut him off. "What you must *explain* is that this loutish crewman was bothering you in the afterdeck where you had gone to smoke a cigar. This man asked you for money, and when you refused, he tried to rob you. He attempted to land a crippling blow, but you were easily able to subdue him. After all, you lived in the Orient for many years and studied mysterious techniques used by the warriors of Japan. But he came at you again, and out of instinct you threw him."

"Yes," Lowell said, nodding, not entirely following the story I had fabricated. "I have studied what the Japanese call *judo* and *tae kwon do*."

"Yes, use those words. And to your horror, the bully was flung over the rail and landed in the steamer's wake."

Lowell blinked at me, astonished. "But how could I say that? It's absurd."

"Would you prefer to say that a rampaging monster from another planet killed him and then drank most of his blood? Believe me, I know how the superstitious and fearful commoners think. It will be a mob."

I could not help but remember how I had been driven from place to place, whether by ignorant people or by educated men such as Thomas Huxley. I knew precisely what would happen when the crew learned about their fallen mate. "Do it now, Lowell, or all is lost. No one will doubt you. And now I must go fetch the corpse before anyone else finds it."

Finally I got him to repeat the story to my satisfaction, and I sent him off, looking dazed—which was good, for it would make his words all the more believable. Then I raced back to where the dead crewman lay crumpled.

I had much work to do, and it would take me the rest of the night.

CHAPTER FIFTEEN

THE GARDENS ON THE MOON

Taking Jane's arm, Wells stepped forward onto the surface of the Moon. All around them, the lunar environment buzzed and popped, teeming with a million forms of exotic life. Toward the horizon where the sunlight had first appeared, Wells could already discern an expanding carpet of green, blue, and white, mixed with all the shades in between. Strange plant life emerged from the soil's night-cold dormancy.

"Normally, the Moon's gravity would be too weak to hold onto an atmosphere," Huxley said, "but here in this explosion of fertility, the outgassing of fresh oxygen is enough to provide pockets of breathable air for us." The professor was the only one who seemed to require an explanation; Wells and Jane were astounded just by looking around themselves, without a need for textbook explanations.

With a cry of surprise, Jane looked down at her feet as she stopped on the gray lunar soil to see spiky shoots thrusting through the pale dirt as if they were live creatures. Bulbous white lumps sprouted toadstool umbrellas, which kept growing in the nourishing sunlight; within moments, the mushrooms stood a foot high, then as tall as a person's waist.

"Look at the types! The colors and flowers—like nothing I've ever seen." She hugged him. "They're strange and beautiful!"

"Like the explosion of life in a desert after a rainstorm," Huxley said. "These organisms have only a brief window to live their lives and reproduce. We are witnessing a biological frenzy!"

Grayish-white sacs swelled up like balloons, pushing pebbles aside. When Wells bent over to touch the stretched-tight membrane of the growth, the fungal skin burst and showered him with spores. Jane laughed as the force nearly knocked him backward, and his sudden reaction sent him careening much farther than he had expected. Wells found himself sprawled on his back perilously close to a cluster of sword-shaped lavender leaves that waved in an unseen wind.

Embarrassed, he thrust himself to his feet—and continued to rise several feet into the air before slowly landing. "I feel light as a feather!"

Jane sprang after him, her step taking her high into the air, as if she were a pole-vaulter.

"It is the lunar gravity, of course," Huxley called from behind them. He drew a deep breath of the freshly manufactured lunar air. "Less than a fifth of Earth's."

With a mischievous glint in his eye, Wells bounded back

toward Jane. He soared over her head like a bird, then gently landed a hundred yards from their cavorite sphere.

Curious and excited, with no silly social expectations of supposedly proper behavior, Jane launched herself toward Wells. Here, they were as far from disapproving frowns and whispered gossip as any human could be. When he saw that she was about to overshoot his position, Wells jumped into the air to intercept her. They caught each other high above the ground and drifted slowly back to the surface.

"Professor, try it for yourself!" Wells's already reedy voice sounded even tinnier in the rarefied air.

Huxley attempted to appear dignified. "I have no need for such horseplay, Mr. Wells."

"Horseplay! I am merely conducting a valid scientific experiment. Where is your curiosity, sir?"

That was all the excuse the old man needed, and the distinguished T.H. Huxley jumped into the air. He laughed as he soared, his robe flapping, his white hair like a comet's mane around his head. "Ah, this is amazing!" When the professor drifted to a landing, Wells and Jane rushed toward him, but like a child playing a game of tag, Huxley bounded off in another direction. "I feel so young! I had forgotten what it was like."

Wells himself was delighted with his new abilities in the breathtakingly strange landscape. "For the first time in years, I am unhampered by my own injuries, the aches, the kidney pains."

The professor felt the same. "Back home my joints trouble me greatly. The weight of Earth pulls me down, but here I feel as if the strings have been cut. I could run to the edge of the world."

Wells bounded away, laughing. "It feels like I have on seven-league boots. Ah, the places I could traverse on Earth with so much stamina!"

"But at such a speed, Wells, would you have time to see anything?" Huxley called.

"Who knows how much time we have, Professor?" Wells answered. He set off on a chase after Jane, who laughed with him. "We cannot expect to see the whole Moon in a day."

"Best not to go too far," Jane said. "If we reach the dark side of the Moon before the atmosphere has thawed, we won't be able to breathe."

Around them, the landscape came amazingly alive, transforming into a bizarre forest of cacti and crawling lichens, swollen fungi and jeweled flowers that fluttered like frilly eyelashes. Professor Huxley landed in a thicket and stopped to inspect a cluster of exotic plants, shaking his head with a mixture of amazement and sadness. "Ah, the taxonomy! Would that I could spend a year with sketch pads simply documenting these life forms. Everything we see around us is a new species, never before studied. A single one of these cacti would make a name for us in the natural history community."

"I could be the author of the very first guidebook of lunar flora," Jane said, smiling.

Just then they heard a mournful blatting that echoed across the feverishly stirring landscape, but the rugged terrain made it impossible to pinpoint where the sound originated. Ahead of them, the ground rose in black cliffs toward the lip of an extraordinarily large crater, its circumference so great that the rim seemed a straight line. The mournful lowing sound came from one of the ledges that remained in shadow.

"Come, we must find what it is!" Wells sprinted off, prepared to offer aid to the distressed creature. The slope of the outer crater would have been impossibly steep for any Earthbound alpinist, but in the low gravity Wells hopped up to a broad ledge, balanced precariously, then sprang to another ridge. With the actual lip of the crater still some distance above him, he came upon a startlingly bizarre creature: a huge slug-like thing, fat and soft, its pearly skin blotched with discolorations.

It crawled forward like an immense caterpillar, its entire body rippling with the movement. It had two huge burnished eyes and a pair of slug-like antennae that quested above a round and dripping mouth. The creature let out a plaintive lowing like a cow lost from its barn. Seeing Wells, it blatted as if accustomed to handlers and glad for rescue.

Jane stopped short beside him. "Oh!" The mooncow let out another soft bellow. "So the Moon is home to more than just plant life."

"Indeed, one might infer an entire civilization."

Wells looked at the professor. "How do you extrapolate an entire civilization from one stray moon slug?"

"Observe the symbol stained on this creature's hide, like a rancher's brand. Obviously an artificial pattern." He indicated the circle and triangle emblazoned on the mooncow's bulk. "Also the remnants of a broken harness there on the far side. Some intelligent force has domesticated this animal, and I suspect there are many more—both herders and beasts." Huxley looked meaningfully toward the high rim of the crater, and the three set off.

The lost mooncow let out a despairing bellow as they left it behind, but Jane whistled for it, and the creature squirmed its fleshy bulk and began to ascend the slope like an inchworm.

Near the top of the crater, Huxley discovered a line of poles fashioned out of a yellowish metal, stakes forming a perimeter fence that was clearly falling down and not well maintained. "You see, Mr. Wells. This was also erected by intelligent hands."

Wells felt the heavy poles, examined the dilapidated wires strung between them, the collapsing fence. "It appears to be *gold*."

"Quite possible. The precious-metal contents of the Moon have never been tapped by industrialists. Lava flows, meteor strikes, and seismic events may have stirred the valuables to the surface. Who knows what mother lodes lie at the bottoms of these craters?"

Wells frowned. "When news of this comes to Earth, tycoons will doubtless attempt to launch exploitive journeys to the Moon. And they will bring poor workers forced to earn their livelihood and work off their passage back home." He shook his head. "I fear for the dramatic changes in social order this will bring."

Jane put her hand on his arm. "It doesn't sound like a dramatic change at all, H.G.—just more of the same old routine."

Huxley crested the rise and stood transfixed by the view of the immense bowl. Wells and Jane joined him, gazing with awe upon sweeping pasture lands covered with spiny plants, swollen mushrooms, and juicy foliage. Hundreds of mooncows grazed aimlessly, eating with dozens of mouths on their underbellies. As they traveled over the plants, they mowed, chewed, and digested the alien plants, leaving trails of slime.

Even more amazing, though, were the other creatures: spindly humanoids with whitish-gray skin and large ant-like heads. They moved like shepherds keeping watch. There were only a dozen of them, far too few for the slug-like beasts, but with frenetic movements they did their best to maintain the captive mooncows. They carried golden staffs that might have been weapons or cattle prods.

"We should attempt to communicate with them," Huxley said. "It will be the first encounter between Earthlings and, if we return to the Latin root, *Selenites*. Moon men."

Behind them, the lost mooncow lumbered to the top of the crater, saw the pastures and its fellow slug-creatures, and let out a joyous hoot. The slug-like beast careened at full speed, tumbling down the slope as fast as the convulsions of its slippery underbelly could take it.

The commotion drew the attention of the Selenite shepherds. They could not help but see the trio of human forms standing exposed on the top of the crater. The lunar shepherds reacted frantically, raising their cattle-prod spears, chittering in confusion, as if waiting for instructions.

Huxley raised his hands in greeting. "Both of you do the same," he muttered urgently to Jane and Wells. "We will be not only scientific observers, but Earth's first ambassadors to another civilization."

Jane pointed to a steep switchbacking path that led down to the crater floor. "Gentlemen, shall we go and meet them?"

The three set off, taking great strides toward the confused party of Selenites. Wells noticed numerous paths laid down on the lunar soil. Cave openings led into catacombs that passed through the crater wall and beneath the surface. Jane pointed out the ruins of house-like structures, collapsed towers and amphitheaters, obviously the signs of a once-great civilization now fading into nothingness.

As Wells noted the crumbling structures, the signs of once-vast pastures and industries, he was uncomfortably reminded of the old castle ruins he had seen in England. Once the golden age had passed, local peasants had used the bricks and stones of the great citadels to build minor cottages. For decades, the locals scavenged the ruins of great castles. The lunar civilization, once great, now seemed little more than the backbone and trappings for daily life among these uncivilized remnants.

The ant-like drones surrounded them, holding their golden spears and chattering in a buzzing, clicking language. Wells drew Jane close, but Huxley stepped forward boldly. "We come in peace, as representatives of humanity. From Earth!" He pointed toward the sky.

The Selenites paused, then formed a protective circle around the humans. One of the Selenite shepherds set off at a scuttling walk toward the nearest tunnel opening, while the others nudged the three visitors forward, leading them into the underground city.

"I hope they don't have a war dance and a cookpot waiting for us at the end of this passage," Wells said.

"I encountered headhunters in New Guinea," Huxley said. "They were most fierce and frightening, but in the end they proved to be no real threat—not at that time, at least. Let us hope we have similar luck here."

The tunnels snaked around, full of side passages and branchways worn glassy smooth, as if termites had bored through the crust, following some sort of grand geometric plan. After an interminable time—it could have been an hour or as much as a day—the Selenites brought them into a cavernous central chamber lit by phosphorescent fungus placed on the walls in artistic patterns. The blue-white bioluminescence gave an ethereal caste to the grotto. Everything shimmered with a pale silver glow.

At the center of the room another creature perched on a dais—grossly distorted but reminiscent of the Selenite species. Its body was atrophied and tiny beneath an outrageously enormous head, a quivering mind within a skull that seemed as large as a small asteroid. The head was so huge it was supported by a framework of rings and rods that held the brain upright. The creature's actual face was small, like a tiny speck on a globe, and it had a slit for a mouth tucked under a complex set of gleaming jewel-like eyes arranged in a pattern. Wells counted eight of the twinkling gem-eyes on its head.

The Selenite drones brought the three humans to a halt in the middle of the chamber, and they faced the scrutiny of the awesome brain of the Moon. Huxley stepped forward. "We come from the planet Earth, the blue sphere you see in your sky. We have no weapons—"

You are invaders. Words rang through their heads, a communication that appeared in Wells's thoughts with no voice attached. *You have come to destroy what remains of our civilization.*

"No," Jane chimed in. "It is only the three of us, and we came here by accident."

Wells felt a splitting headache pulse through his skull, as if nimble fingers were sorting through index cards in his mind. From the wince on Jane's face and the perplexed scowl on Huxley's, he knew they felt the tingling, high-pressure mental probe as well. Finally the communication resumed.

Now I have learned everything about you, and I see that you tell the truth. You are no threat to our civilization.

The Moon leader raised spindly hands, and the Selenite soldiers backed away from the captives, relaxing their hold on their pointed golden staffs.

I am the Grand Lunar, said the telepathic voice. *I am the ruler of a once-vast civilization. We Selenites were peaceful, productive creatures. We maintained a perfect social order— until everything was broken, most of our people lost, our entire way of life destroyed.*

Wells, thinking of the cholera bacillus in sealed vials within their cavorite sphere, asked, "What happened? Was it some awful plague?"

No, the Grand Lunar answered. *Selenites are immune to all diseases and infections. We eradicated them from our biology long ago.*

Huxley looked at the giant pulsing brain. "Then how could your utopia have been so completely destroyed?"

The Grand Lunar responded with a shudder of never-forgotten terror transmitted by thought waves. The three humans could feel the fear and revulsion within themselves.

This destruction was caused by the Martians.

CHAPTER SIXTEEN

THE MUTABLE NATURE OF THE MARTIAN FORM

FROM THE JOURNAL OF DR. MOREAU

The dead crewman lay on the shadowed lower deck of the steamer. Fortunately, no one had discovered him yet.

In the uncertain light, I gathered the syringes from where Lowell had scattered them. Only one of the glass barrels had broken; the rest lay intact—a fortunate occurrence, for I would need them to keep feeding the Martian. After pocketing the syringes, I put my hands under the dead crewman's arms. The bully stank of sour sweat, dirt, and urine. I was not surprised to find that he had fouled himself upon his death, as many animals will do.

Moving quickly, I dragged him along the dim corridors. It was well after dinner, and at night the ship grows quieter.

Every few moments I paused to listen, fearing that someone might come to investigate all the commotion. Still I heard no shouts, no pounding footsteps. Perhaps no one had heard the man scream after all.

I hid the corpse inside my small cabin until I could properly dispose of it, then hurried back to wipe up any remaining bloodstains from where he had died. No one would ever know what had really happened to the brute.

With my door firmly latched, I spread the pallid body onto a makeshift operating table and proceeded to drain the remaining blood from his circulatory system—I saw no sense in letting it go to waste, if this was indeed the nourishment our specimen required. When I finished, I had several beakers of fresh blood. The Martian regarded me hungrily as I worked. It made no sound, but its tentacles waved as if stirred by air currents.

I reassembled my medical kits, gathering up the vials scattered on the floor of my laboratory. I would have to begin the next step quickly, if I had any hope of success. After the crewman was dead, his delicate organs and tissues would begin to spoil.

Turning my back on the Martian, I surreptitiously slipped a potent sedative into an open beaker of blood. The Martian was as large as a bear, and I could only guess at the proper amount of anesthesia it would require. I came back to the cage, holding the beaker of scarlet fluid, and stared at my specimen, looking for some sign of communication in its eyes. If it was ravenously hungry, perhaps I could trick it.

The Martian reached out with its tentacles and touched the beaker. I let it draw the glass between the bars of its cage.

I then offered it two of the intact syringes, and the Martian rapidly began to inject the blood into itself. I watched with a morbid fascination as the beaker was drained.

I noted the signs of sickness on the Martian's flesh, discolorations, blotches. Maybe the fresh blood would keep it strong for a while, but I intended to effect a more permanent cure of the Earthly germ. As soon as it was time.

When the sedative rapidly began to take effect, the captive Martian seemed astonished that I, a lowly human, could have deceived it. As the alien struggled against imminent unconsciousness, I turned to the dead crewman on my operating table, stripped off his shirt, mopped sweat and grime from his pasty chest, then disinfected his skin. He must be clean before surgery.

I prepared my operating tools as best I could. Normally, I harvested organs from a still-living donor in order to ensure their freshness and integrity, but I had no choice right now. Much finesse is required when grafting organs from one species onto another. The pieces don't fit properly together, and junctures must be rigorously sealed. In addition, I had only a minimal working knowledge of the Martian anatomy, unlike other vivisection subjects upon which I had so often practiced. But I could draw some generalizations, and I did my best. The Martian's very survival was at stake.

I used a scalpel to cut into the redhead's flesh, after which I took up a heavy bone saw to crack open his sternum. Then I began my longest and most exhausting surgery ever.

I grafted the crewman's strong heart and fleshy lungs into the Martian's body. It was bloody work, but necessary. The two organisms were not meant to coexist, but I forced the issue. Neither the dead crewman nor the dying Martian had any choice.

With my surgical apparatus, and the expertise I had developed over years of working with dissimilar species, dragging them unwilling up the evolutionary ladder, I now applied connections and junctures. This was what the Martian needed to survive.

I took meticulous care that the tools were sterile, that the sutures were tiny and even, that the components from two different planets matched perfectly. I took no shortcuts with my vital work, in the hope that the grafts would heal properly and the organs continue to function, so that this hybrid creature could survive on Earth. It would be able to breathe our air and, with the crewman's blood, perhaps even find a bit of immunity to fight off our terrestrial germs.

In my travels around the world, I have discovered many unusual drugs and medicines from the jungles of Borneo and Thailand, from uncharted islands in the South Seas. I always keep a store of them in my medical kit. Some of these substances—poisonous lichens and fever-reducing fern leaves—proved to be quite beneficial in helping one body accept the organs from another. Otherwise, biological instinct leads to a rejection of what does not belong there.

Finished with the surgery, I sewed up the Martian's tough brown skin and applied sterile cloths. I wrapped more bandages around the incision sites and hoped the alien would heal quickly, for within ten days the steamer would reach New York harbor. I did not want the specimen weakened while we moved it down to Boston and Percival Lowell's family holdings . . . .

Much later, a shaken and half-drunk Lowell returned and looked stupidly at what I had done. But nothing else could shock him. He had told the captain his fabricated story, and the man believed him implicitly.

"That redhead was a rogue," the captain said, "always getting into brawls, never doing his share of work. I've had to club him several times myself, and I had more than half a mind to kick him off the ship once we reached port. You've saved me the trouble, Mr. Lowell. I doubt anyone will miss him, certainly not the man he was bunking with."

Stunned at how easily we got away with the crime, Lowell had downed three, perhaps four, snifters of brandy before coming back to find me finishing my efforts. He stared aghast at the redhead's mutilated body, but I soothed him. "The poor victim was already dead, Percival. But I used him to keep our Martian alive."

"Of course you did." Lowell's words were somewhat slurred. If I was lucky, he would go back to his cabin and drink even more brandy; by morning, he might have doubts about what had occurred here.

"I need your help in one last thing, Percival. The two of us must toss the body overboard."

At first Lowell quailed at this, but five minutes later he dully reached down to take the dead man's feet after I had wrapped him in a bloodstained sheet to keep his cut-up form together. We hustled along the silent corridors, climbing metal stairs. Each time, I took a careful look and waited until no one was there to see.

It was the darkest part of the night, when all other passengers were asleep and only a skeleton crew remained at their duties. We soon reached the open salty air and the starlit darkness, and wasted no time. The breeze was brisk, carrying the dampness of impending storms. The waves behind us were choppy.

"Come, Percival. No time to delay." We hoisted the dead crewman. "Up, up—heave."

In a flash, the redhead tumbled overboard, his loose arms and legs still flopping, pale skin showing through his torn clothes. The splash made almost no sound at all, and the steamer forged ahead, leaving him far behind within moments. Soon only the fishes would know what we had done.

Lowell and I stood together at the rail, quietly looking into the milky wake of the steamer. "It was what we had to do, Percival," I said. Without a word, he turned and went back to his stateroom.

I stayed on deck for a while longer and then went back to my patient.

CHAPTER SEVENTEEN

IN THE HALL OF THE GRAND LUNAR

In the underground chambers of the Moon, the Selenite servants prepared a banquet for the three humans. The pale drones brought forth platters of soft fungus meat and decanters of sap as sweet as honey.

At first, they hesitated to eat the proffered food, but they were far from their cavorite sphere and their supplies. Huxley inspected each item, sniffing it and frowning uncertainly. The aromas were certainly tantalizing and appetizing. Wells and Jane looked to the older man for his guidance. Finally, he surrendered to his hunger and took a bite, then several more. Seeing Huxley's implied approval, Wells and Jane fell to the banquet with great gusto.

After Wells had consumed much of the honey-like sap liquid, he began feeling giddy and fuzzy. Huxley and Jane decided to stop drinking, preferring not to become intoxicated at such an important moment under the awesome gaze of the Grand Lunar.

Next, they were served a buttery-tasting meat that purportedly came from the mooncows; the slug-like herd animals matured rapidly and were butchered for food each lunar cycle. It seemed that everything on the Moon moved at a frenetic pace, like desert flowers bursting into bloom after a rare downpour. Unfortunately, the once-admirable lunar civilization had not recovered so swiftly after the Martian attacks.

"We too have learned of the threat from Mars," Huxley said, between bites. "Precisely what happened when the Martians invaded the Moon? And when did it occur?"

The Grand Lunar studied them, its enormous throbbing brain supported by a heavy framework. Finally, a series of horrific images and memories poured into their minds, conveying the full spectacle of the disaster.

Once, lunar society had been a complex web with many different castes: drone workers, soldiers, thinkers, engineers, builders, shepherds, and farmers, all guided by the Grand Lunar's incredible intellect. Their hive-like society had been diligent and peaceful. They had no rivals, no enemies. For millennia the Grand Lunar and its predecessors had maintained the number of Selenites at the perfect level for proper functioning.

Then the Martian invaders had come.

Cylinder after cylinder had been launched from Mars to crash upon the Moon's day side, at the height of Selenite productivity. At first, even the Grand Lunar did not know what was happening. Large-eyed Selenite astronomers, who also spied upon Earth, had noticed the green flashes from Mars and so were able to determine the origin of these terrible spacecraft.

While the cylinders cooled in their new craters, the Martians assembled large mechanical walkers, giant tripod devices equipped with powerful weapons. Heat rays incinerated the Selenite observers who had gathered to welcome the visitors from the red planet.

The first Martian attack was immediate and terrible. Thousands of Selenites were slaughtered outright by the awful heat rays, and the Grand Lunar was forced to withdraw the soldier-drones until Selenite scientists could develop appropriate defenses. The Moon's engineers and thinkers turned their knowledge to building immense weapons.

Since lunar society functioned as a single vast and efficient machine, the Selenites could combine their skills with focused determination; thus, they swiftly developed and produced new defenses. As the Martians began their march of destruction across the lunar surface, the brave Selenites rallied. They used newly synthesized explosive devices to blow up the Martian cylinders, but more and more of the deadly projectiles rained down from space.

The Martian invaders attacked with their heat rays, forcing the Selenites to take even more violent measures. Desperate, the Grand Lunar authorized the most terrible bombs imaginable. The round craters of these incredible explosions now peppered the whole surface of the Moon.

The invaders from Mars had kept coming, and the heat ray decimated the Selenite population. The Grand Lunar bred and produced army swarms to defend the Moon, but the Martian conquest could not be stopped. Loyal drones and soldiers had massed here in this chamber in a last stand to defend their leader, the core and soul of Selenite society. They planned to fight to the death.

The Martians, however, had no intention of utterly destroying lunar civilization, nor of seizing the Moon as new territory. With their red world dying, the Martians needed more slaves, more food, and more resources. They wanted to take huge numbers of Selenite captives back to Mars, no doubt to be put to work on the Martian canals and industries. Their conquest finished, the hideous invaders loaded their return cylinders with hundreds of thousands of Selenites, cramming them in like packaged goods, and departed for the red planet.

Still tenuously connected to their leader, the captive Selenites had sent their last mental messages home. The voyage to distant Mars was long, and they had been crowded aboard the vast conquering ships. Cut off from the Grand Lunar, they did not know what to do. They were bullied and tortured by the dominant, tentacled monstrosities.

In the vision, Wells could taste their fear and helplessness. The drones could not fight back, and their puppet strings were cut once they'd been taken from the Moon. Aboard the transport ships they stood shoulder to shoulder, the bulk of the lunar population dragged off to another planet. Those who survived the journey became the seeds of an endlessly oppressed slave corps on Mars.

Without the bulk of the population, the once-magnificent lunar society had gone stagnant. The Martians left the Moon a devastated, barren place, its civilization broken. There were too few survivors of each Selenite caste for the Grand Lunar to rebuild the population. Thus, for many centuries, the beaten

Grand Lunar had barely held together the tattered remnants of a once great society . . . .

As the parade of images in his head ceased, Wells looked at the insect-like workers and servants. He remembered the dilapidated fences around the crater pastures and how few Selenite shepherds existed to watch all the mooncows. The remaining drones were barely enough to keep the Grand Lunar alive and functioning; they would never be sufficient to repair the war damage. Ever since the holocaust, the Grand Lunar's surviving astronomers had kept their telescopic eyes upon the Earth, watching small threads of civilization appear on the big blue neighboring planet.

Jane expressed her concern in a voice that rang out too loud in the chamber. "And the Martians have also been watching us! We know they've sent at least one scout, and they intend to launch an invasion force to Earth."

They will conquer you and destroy you, the Grand Lunar said.

Wells defiantly clutched Jane's hand. "No, they will not! Thankfully, we have had some forewarning. We can take our spacecraft directly to Mars—and prevent this."

Huxley looked at him in surprise. "Ah, you are most ambitious, Mr. Wells, to think that the three of us could stop the war plans of an entire planet."

"If not us, then who else is there?" Wells knew in his heart that he had to do something.

Perhaps there is help. The Grand Lunar lifted tiny hands to its shrunken face. With a deft movement of nimble fingers, it selected one of the faceted gemstone eyes, twisted it, and removed the jewel, leaving an empty socket in the insectile head. Holding it in the palm of a diminutive hand, the Grand Lunar extended the gem to Jane, who was closest.

Take this as a talisman. If any of my Selenites still survive on Mars, they will know this comes from their Grand Lunar.

Jane clutched the eye gem, looking at it. Then she smiled back up at the immense, quivering brain. "Thank you."

* * *

The remaining Selenite drones swarmed out, guided by the Grand Lunar to usher the human visitors back to the cavorite sphere. Other workers brought blankets, water, food, and other supplies, stocking the interior for a long voyage to distant Mars.

As the three humans climbed back into the armored vessel, the Selenites backed away, bowing their ant-like heads. Wells, Jane, and Huxley called out farewells, knowing that the mind of the Grand Lunar could see them through these lesser drones.

When they were secured inside the sphere again, Wells and Jane looked at each other, knowing their next step. Together, they closed the louvered blinds on the floor of the craft, sealing off the cavorite and severing all ties to the Moon's gravity.

As the armored globe rose from the cratered surface, the three of them opened and closed various blinds, searching the star-studded sky until they located the angry crimson eye of Mars. Committed to their course of action, they left that one porthole open so that the gravitational pull of the red planet could drag them across the emptiness of space.

They sat back to prepare their battle plans. Three mere humans would have to fend off an alien invasion.

CHAPTER EIGHTEEN

THE MARTIAN ARRIVES IN BOSTON

For many anxious days and nerve-wracking nights, I sat beside my recovering alien patient, tending it with all the diligence one might have attributed to Florence Nightingale. (An amusing comparison, since no one had ever uttered the names of Moreau and Nightingale in the same breath!)

Less than an hour after I finished my extreme surgeries, transplants, and organ grafting, the creature recovered from the anesthetic. I observed it closely from outside the iron-barred cage, watchful for any sign of hemorrhaging or convulsions. I saw neither. The creature simply looked at me with pain apparent in those ominous, saucer-like eyes.

During extreme courses of vivisection, I had learned to

gauge the levels of agony in my test subjects. I could sense within the Martian's great brain a burning will to live, perhaps even a fire of vengeance directed toward me. I did not mind. If such emotions gave this being the will to survive, then so be it.

To keep up its strength, I injected the remaining beaker of the crewman's blood. As the Martian healed, its body would require much more sustenance. That was going to cause a problem. Short of surreptitiously killing another crew member—and Lowell would never approve of that—I pursued the only other alternative to feed my Martian. Using tubes, rubber hoses, and hypodermic needles, I gave the creature regular transfusions of my own blood, hoping that when the Martian saw me draining my own life fluid so that it could feed, it might think more kindly toward me.

During long days sitting at the alien's side, I made further fruitless attempts to communicate with it. Occasionally I grew impatient and demanded that the creature respond; at other times I used a soft voice, hoping to coax some small gesture or sound. But the Martian appeared uninterested. Not listless, just . . . biding its time.

Only once did it exhibit a definite flare of attention, when Lowell let me borrow the crystal egg we had found inside the crashed cylinder. As I held the shimmering ellipsoid in front of the caged Martian, it attempted to snatch the ovoid with one of its tentacles, but I kept the treasure at a safe distance.

"Speak to me," I said. "Show me a sign that you want to communicate."

But when I took the crystal egg away, the Martian resumed

its sulking torpor. Discouraged, I returned the crystal egg to Lowell in his stateroom.

Finally, as the ship entered New York harbor, I cautiously removed the bandages from the caged Martian. The creature remained weak, but obviously had turned the corner to recovery, both healing from surgery and fighting off the Earthly infectious germ. Still silent, the alien watched me while I unwrapped the gauze and studied my tight little stitches, pleased to see that healthy scabs now covered the incisions. The wounds did not appear to be infected, and I was much relieved. The grafting had indeed taken!

As the Martian breathed, its skin inflated and deflated like a blacksmith's bellows, and I could tell that its adopted lungs were functioning well, processing the atmosphere of a planet to which it had not been born. The human heart was beating, supplementing the Martian circulatory system.

It would live and grow strong, and if the enormous brain was as intelligent as I hoped, the Martian would realize that *I* was responsible for its survival. But would this alien beast understand gratitude and obligation?

* * *

The moment that the steamer docked in New York, Lowell was once more in his element. He set to work arranging carters and equipment handlers to move our research apparatus as well as the recovering extraterrestrial specimen. He spent a full day on the docks negotiating with burly, thick-lipped men. I've never been good at such things, preferring that lesser men simply do as they are told and leave me to my more important work.

When all the transportation was arranged to ship our secret captive to Boston, I told Lowell that I was confident the Martian would survive the journey. I was, however, concerned about what Lowell planned to do once he reached his family home. We had discussed the matter numerous times during our travels, but Lowell still refused to think through the consequences. Our specimen and our announcement would shake the Lowell family dynamic to its core. No matter what these supercilious blue bloods thought, I did not want my Martian to become a circus specimen! Did Lowell mean to show off the creature to his stern father as proof that he had been correct in his eccentric aspirations?

This return to Boston was extremely important for Lowell. He had been born with a silver spoon in his mouth, the eldest son of a Brahmin family that had amassed an enormous fortune in the textile industry. His father was a humorless man with no vision beyond practical business concerns, and he was grooming Percival's younger (and more responsible) brother Lawrence as the true successor to the family fortunes.

"I have always been the maverick in my family, Moreau," he told me as we watched Boston approach out the side windows of the train. "I can think of nothing more maddening than to devote my energies to running a textile business. But because I am the oldest son, my father expects it of me."

Percival Lowell has the drive and passion often seen in the wayward sons of the rich, desperate to make a name in the history books. Though he obviously enjoys the finer benefits of his wealthy upbringing, Lowell resents the expectations of his family. He does not recognize the opportunities he has. His resentments make him weak, for he does not choose to turn them to his own advantage.

Some of my disparaging comments in this journal should not be misconstrued to imply that I dislike Percival Lowell. He is a most accomplished man, who graduated from Harvard with distinction in mathematics at the age of twenty-one, and he received the Bowdoin Prize for his essay on "The Rank of England as a European Power Between the Death of Elizabeth and the Death of Anne." He has traveled the world, studied the classics, experienced numerous foreign cultures, proved his facility in languages, even offered to fight in the Serbo-Turkish War.

Lowell sailed for Japan ten years ago, in 1883, where he was asked to serve as Foreign Secretary for a special diplomatic mission from Korea (though at the time he had never even seen Korea). Returning to Tokyo, he was later asked to help write Japan's new constitution. In attitude, personality, and behavior, Lowell is similar to me in many ways—and that cannot help but create certain frictions.

Knowing that his father had been annoyed by this long and expensive expedition in the Sahara, Lowell now wanted to stride through the gates of the city in a triumphal march. Lowell had already wired home about his imminent arrival, and a fine social reception was planned for him. He was gruff and confident, ferociously proud of what he had done, though I could sense a nervousness in his manner.

The question remained: should we explain our awesome

achievement to the family, or leave them blissfully content with their predictable lives that allowed no room for the mysteries or majesty of the universe?

* * *

As I had feared, the society party thrown by Lowell's family was as excruciatingly dull as watching the Sahara sands.

Though Lowell claimed to be a fish out of water in such situations, he adapted remarkably well. I had seen him at the captain's table aboard the steamer, chatting with upper-class people from different countries. I'm sure that his doting mother noted that he wasn't his old self, but he had not been home in years. I hoped his resolve would not falter now.

Lowell was careful to give few details about me, for we didn't know how far word of my scandal had spread. Those who spoke with me did so only out of polite obligation, for Lowell was the hero of the party. Everyone flocked around him, wanting to hear his stories of Japan and the Oriental mystics, and the wild Tuaregs of the Sahara.

Lowell mentioned nothing about the Martian. That tale we would tell later, when we were ready. These people were not the right sort to appreciate the magnitude of our discovery. They would either be titillated or horrified . . . but worst of all, they would not be truly *interested*. The revelation of our Martian's existence must wait for the proper appreciative audience.

I amused myself by treating the tedious party as a scientific experiment, studying herd behavior and mating patterns. It was clear that the scions of Boston families were offering their daughters for marriage consideration to the eccentric but well-bred Percival. I found it amusing—like horse breeders comparing their best brood mares. Lowell seemed oblivious to the nuances, though by now he was thirty-eight years old and no longer perceived to be young enough to continue his rebellious lifestyle. He had to think of his future. I was certain his mother was pressuring him to marry into an acceptable family.

Finally, late at night when the guests had departed and Lowell's mother had retired to bed, he came to me to share a last brandy for the evening. The two of us held our snifters, barely sipping, playing the part of drinkers. After having observed the shallowness of the average Bostonian, I whispered to Lowell, "We can't possibly do our work in an environment such as this. They will always be watching, prying. Your parents will beg you to attend parties, picnics, luncheons. You will be forced to accept speaking engagements. Our Martian will fare badly, I fear."

His face had a pinched look. "I know that all too well, Moreau. We must be away from Boston."

"But where can we go? Is there a safe place?"

"Yes, completely safe and far from here. My parents won't like it . . . but they have not liked many of my decisions." Smiling, he slyly reached into his jacket pocket and removed the red-lensed spectacles I had given him. "We will go to Arizona Territory, Moreau, where I am building my own observatory, far from the closed-minded fools of Harvard."

"Arizona Territory? Out west in the American wilderness?"

Lowell settled the red-lensed spectacles on his nose. "The Arizona desert is the closest thing to Mars one could find here on Earth. There, with the Martian, we can perform our work in total privacy."

PART III

MARS AND ITS CANALS

CHAPTER NINETEEN

AT THE MARTIAN ICE CAPS

During the long voyage to Mars, H.G. Wells, Thomas Huxley, and Jane Robbins occupied themselves by reading Dr. Moreau's journal. Wells absorbed the information with cold fear and a hardening resolve. "These Martians are ruthless enemies, Professor."

"All creatures have a mandate for survival, Mr. Wells, and the Martians' dying environment drove them to take such desperate measures." Huxley scratched his sideburns. "Unfortunately, since our race is to be the target of their depredations, I find it difficult to rouse sympathy for them."

When at last the dusty orange sphere filled their view, Jane drew her finger across the transparent cavorite. "Look at the canals, H.G."

Wells could make out the cat's cradle of artificial lifelines that linked the population centers of a waning old civilization. "No telescope on Earth has the aperture to discern these details, but now that we are here, it all seems so plain."

Huxley frowned. "No doubt the Martian astronomers have more sophisticated equipment to watch our lush green planet. They must covet all the things Earth has to offer."

"They are not welcome to it." Jane crossed her arms over her chest. "Not if we three have anything to say about the matter."

They prepared themselves for landing. After they entered orbit at an extreme angle, which carried them in a near polar trajectory, they spun the sphere around, balanced on the fulcrum of gravity, and plunged toward the polar ice cap at the southern extreme of the Martian globe.

Huxley looked strangely amused. "I always imagined someone would conquer the south pole on *Earth* first."

They tried to use the same techniques of opening and closing blinds over the cavorite segments in order to balance the pull of gravity. Because of their greater distance from the Earth and Sun and Moon, however, the opposing tug was not sufficient to assist them. Though they uncovered every cavorite pane on the opposite side of the sphere, hoping to stall their descent, the surface of Mars rushed toward them with extreme rapidity.

"Hang on!" Wells shouted at the last moment and grabbed for Jane.

Out of control, the armored globe struck the bleak fields of rubble near the outer edge of the ice cliffs. A blizzard of crates, bottles, and papers swirled around them. Huxley grabbed the padded case that contained the vials of cholera bacillus and shielded them with his body.

The sphere struck the ground and rolled, plowed through the loose ground, tumbled into the air again, and finally came to rest, with a slow grinding motion. While debris fluttered all around, the three of them blinked at each other, panting.

Rusty powder obscured the uppermost cavorite windows, blocking most of the dim sunlight. The sphere's hatch was at shoulder height, thankfully not buried or inaccessible.

"I seem to be intact," Huxley said, cinching his striped robe tight.

"We're on Mars, H.G." Despite their perilous situation, Jane's eyes were bright with wonder as she peered through the rust-smeared porthole.

Wells smoothed his shirt and trousers, then helped to straighten Jane's hair. "But there's so incredibly much we don't know about the Martians."

"Like anything else, we must learn, Mr. Wells—and then apply what we have learned," Huxley said. "If there are different political factions, perhaps we can turn one group of Martians against another and prevent the invasion."

Jane stood next to Wells at the hatch, forceful and optimistic. "Then we have everything to discover, a veritable treasure-trove of science. We'd best get on with it if we mean to save our planet."

Huxley joined them. "We know from Dr. Moreau that Martians can breathe our air. Therefore, it is reasonable to assume that the converse is true." He reached forward and, without hesitation, broke the seal and pushed open the hatch.

When the three of them stood in the dim, cold light, the

Martian wilderness spread out before them, cracked and bouldered, serrated with rugged mountain ranges. The thin and frigid air made Jane shiver, and Wells held her close. He wished he had a coat to give her. Although Huxley stood only in his thin lounging robe, he didn't seem to mind the chill.

A grinding, clanking sound came toward them from the distance, like heavy industrial pistons pounding. Nine tall metal tripods strode across the ground, converging on the cavorite sphere. Turrets atop the moving legs spun, scanning the landscape. Jointed mechanical arms sprouted from the nine turrets, extending a complex apparatus made of lenses and generators. To Wells, the three-legged machines resembled nothing so much as nightmarish milk stools careening over the uneven ground.

"We won't have much trouble finding the Martians, Professor," Wells said. "It appears that they've found us."

"Guard dogs coming to attack the intruders." Jane swallowed hard.

From speakers in the turrets, the Martian drivers let loose a thunderous cry of *"Ulla! Ulla!"* The unearthly sound vibrated through Wells's bones, striking in him an atavistic fear.

Towering several stories high, the ominous tripods clanked into position around the cavorite sphere. They had no possibility of escape. Jointed metal arms directed the complicated mirrored apparatus at the humans, as if it were a weapon. The tripods let out another titanic hooting cry. *"Ulla! Ulla!"*

Huxley stepped forward, waving his hands and directing his gaze up at the turret of the nearest tripod. His movement startled the alien operators, and several of the camera-like devices swung into position. One emitted a blast of blinding heat from the arrangement of lenses. The almost-invisible fire roared into the sand near where they stood, melting the iron-oxide dust into a smoking trough of hardening glass, like dark blood congealing on the ground.

Huxley did not flinch. The ominous battle tripods ratcheted and fidgeted, and the heat-ray projectors remained focused on the three visitors. Wells said out of the corner of his mouth, "Now what are we going to do, Professor?"

"I believe surrender is the most intelligent course of action." Moving with extraordinary caution, Huxley raised both hands. Wells and Jane did likewise.

Cables spun down from the turrets like wiry metal tentacles, each tipped with a grasping mechanical claw. Remarkably adept, the claws snatched Wells by his shirt collar and yanked him into the air like a child grasping a kitten. Two other tentacles hoisted Huxley and Jane high above the stilt legs and plopped all three of them unceremoniously into a metal basket affixed to the bottom of the control turret.

"Now I know what it feels like to be snagged in a rat catcher's net," Jane said.

"Take heart that the Martians did not kill us outright, Miss Robbins. We must be quite a curiosity to them."

"Considering that we are trying to save the Earth from a deadly invasion, I had hoped we'd be a bit more than a mere curiosity," Wells grumbled. With lurching strides, the first battle tripod carried the captives away.

As they were jostled and bruised inside the carrier, Wells grasped the metal lattice and peered out. Behind them, the remaining three-legged contraptions stood as if scrutinizing the cavorite sphere. Using extended cable-like arms to manipulate chains, they hooked a grappling apparatus to the sphere. Like oxen pulling a plow, the battle tripods dragged the spacecraft with its open gravity-attracting panes to the ground. The machines lumbered with their prize toward the steaming ice cliffs.

The main tripod approached a large industrial center, like a mine in the polar cap. As if it were a broad chalk quarry, battle tripods stood with their stilt-like legs anchored on the frozen shelves, raising segmented arms and using their heat rays to blast free chunks of the ice walls. Heavy frozen blocks, each one the size of a house, tumbled down gracefully in the low Martian gravity to crash in a debris pile at the bottom of the pit, where other swarming machinery processed the chunks.

Below, in a great plume of escaping steam, heat rays further broke up the mounds of excavated ice. It seemed to be an enormous strip mine, scouring away the antarctic cap. The recovered water poured into the canals and spread like blood through an artificial circulatory system for a dying planet.

Even from far away, the thunderous noise of the complex sounded tinny in the thin air, clamorous explosions of collapsing cliffs, the buzz and roar of heat rays, the thudding and hissing of distillation factories. Huxley stared in wonder at the expanding spokes of the canal system that extended from the polar ice to the Martian cities. "No human endeavor could match this. I've seen the marble quarries of Italy. By comparison they are no more than a tiny anthill."

The ratcheting tripod finally came to a halt. Metal tentacles quested out from the control turret, and claws dipped down to grasp the cage. With no apparent regard for the safety of the prisoners, the battle machine dumped the three of them on a high platform overlooking the immense ice quarry.

Wells brushed himself off and helped Jane to her feet; Huxley cinched his striped robe tighter around his waist to protect against the frigid breezes. Behind them, the guardian tripods loomed, raising their heat-ray projectors in a clear threat, but the professor could not contain his curiosity. Ignoring the three-legged machines, he walked eagerly to the edge to get a view of the sweeping operations.

"Their civilization must indeed be taking its last gasps if they must butcher their arctic regions for water." He shook his gray head. "Here is the root cause for the Martians' plans to invade Earth. They have no other choice. Their minds are at the end of the tether."

Wells took Jane's hand and they joined him, looking across at the Herculean project. Below them, under the mist and smoke, they could see swarms of workers manning the pumps and performing manual labor. Wells instantly recognized the creatures. "They're Selenites!"

"I count more down there than we saw in all of the catacombs of the Moon," Jane said.

Huxley nodded grimly. "And almost certainly, this is but a fraction of their captive Selenite population. They seem to have adapted well enough to their slavery here."

Around the Selenite crews, ominous Martian battle tripods stood ready with their heat rays to destroy any unruly laborer. The white drones went about their tasks like mindless termites, showing neither resistance nor initiative. Without guidance from the Grand Lunar, the drones had no choice but to obey the evil Martians who had kidnapped them from their world.

Wells looked behind them to the open desert, where the

group of tall tripods dragged the gravity-anchored cavorite sphere toward an expansive warehouse hangar at the ice quarry. While he watched with a sinking heart, the Martians took the spacecraft into the dark hangar. A heavy metal door rolled shut, sealing the cavorite sphere from view and cutting off their hope of returning home.

CHAPTER TWENTY

IN THE LOWELL OBSERVATORY

FROM THE JOURNAL OF DR. MOREAU

The American landscape is vaster than I imagined. Heading westward from Boston, our train took days to cross the expanse, stopping at cities and small towns, stockyards and river ports. We traveled through Chicago, then Kansas City, and finally into the wilderness in the company of hardy pioneers, miners, lumberjacks, and cowboys. Henceforth, we supposed we would face wild grizzlies, bloodthirsty Comanches, stampeding bison, and lawless gunmen.

Lowell relaxed in his plush private car, unconcerned, as he jotted daily letters to be dispatched back home to his mother.

On the way to Arizona Territory, Lowell told me about

his assistant, Andrew Ellicott Douglass, a young astronomer on loan from Harvard. William Pickering, the head of Harvard's observatory program, hoped that by offering Douglass's services, he could add Lowell's privately funded observatory to his astronomical army. Pickering assumed that Percival Lowell would be no more than the financial backer, while he himself would be in charge of all the science. Pickering was a deluded fool.

After construction started on the Arizona observatory, Lowell rebuffed Pickering's suggested names for the facility, saying, "We shall call it Lowell Observatory, in honor of my father. There will be no further discussion."

Lowell is like a bee whose attention flickers from one bright flower to another. But, unlike the bee, he has the financial means to make any fleeting interest into a major production. Upon becoming interested in Mars, he immediately diverted his wealth and furious diligence to the construction of an observatory that would stand as a monument to his contributions to science. If the Harvard Astronomy Board expected to make any decisions, they would be in for quite a shock.

In the private coach, Lowell traced his fingers along a map of Arizona Territory. "I dispatched Douglass to the American Southwest in search of a suitable location. He investigated Tombstone, Tucson, Prescott, and Tempe before finally discovering the perfect conditions at a northern mountain town called Flagstaff. While you and I were in the Sahara, Douglass was establishing the framework for my observatory."

"I shall relish the solitude," I said. "Once we secure the

cooperation of our Martian friend and colleague, we will have the freedom to achieve breakthroughs in many areas of science. Once we learn how to communicate, we will have much to share that can benefit both of our races."

* * *

Our train finally clattered into Flagstaff after dusk, grinding to a halt with a loud whistle and hissing belch. I emerged from the private car with Lowell beside me, looking immensely pleased with himself. I found this primitive, isolated town lacking in many things, despite its reputedly excellent conditions for astronomical observations.

The San Francisco Peaks rose behind us, silhouetted in the last light of day. Mingled with the oil, sawdust, and hot metal smells of the train yards, I caught the scent of pine in the dry air. This place was far more pleasant than the brutally hot Sahara, the miasmic smokes of industrial London, or the noisy bustle of New York or Boston. Still, it was very far from civilization.

The town had no more than a handful of buildings: a whitewashed church with a single steeple, a general store, shacks, saloons, and boarding houses. According to reports, Flagstaff even had a hotel that was "nice enough for a lady to stay in." (Apparently, this was unusual in the West.)

Flagstaff's main business was the lumber industry; tree cutters and sawmill workers settled in squalid camps that ringed the hills. The men cut down the ponderosa pines, and wood products were shipped on the Santa Fe railroad to construction sites back east.

Once we disembarked from the train, our primary challenge was to transport the Martian, now fully recovered from its surgery. We cloaked the cage again with a tarpaulin so that no curiosity seekers could peer inside.

Men lounged around the train yard, looking for jobs of work, and Lowell decisively hired two of them. One of the burly men casually spat tobacco onto the ground and looked at the covered cage. "What's in there?"

Lowell stood stiffly. "My colleague and I are transporting an unusual animal specimen caught in the wilds of Africa."

"Circus just came through here last month. Saw a lion, a dancing bear, even an elephant."

"This is . . . something like that."

"Let's have a look, then."

The man stepped forward, but I stepped between him and the tarpaulin. "Mr. Lowell's paying you well, but your wages don't include free admission." As far as these uneducated men were concerned, the Martian might be an item of interest rather than horror and revulsion. Still, we did not want our secret exposed.

The man grumbled, more incensed by my attitude than at being rebuffed. "Suit yourself. I wasn't never a customer for the freak show tent anyway."

The second carter guided his wagon up to the cargo car, and the two men loaded our restless cargo on the wagon bed. Lowell rode on the buckboard next to the driver, while I remained in back with the cage, watching the curious worker.

The horse plodded without enthusiasm up a rutted dirt road that took us away from the train yards to a higher elevation above Flagstaff. Douglass had selected the round-topped rise as the site for the new observatory. Appropriately, Lowell had dubbed it "Mars Hill."

Most of the construction crew lived in shacks closer to town, where they could go to saloons and provision houses, but a few men who had little desire to trudge up and down the steep path each day made their campfires on the hill.

I saw the lights of the construction area as we approached. Several buildings had already been completed, with glass in the windows and kerosene lamps burning inside. Lowell had wired ahead to Douglass, informing him of our imminent arrival. Fabricating a story about having captured a new species of bear, Lowell insisted that Douglass arrange for utmost privacy so that I could study the beast. By the time we arrived, the young Harvard astronomer had prepared rooms for us and fitted an outbuilding to serve as a secure holding pen.

Hearing the wagon arrive, the young man emerged from the main house to welcome his benefactor. "Mr. Lowell, welcome back to Mars Hill." Douglass had short brown hair, glasses, and a thin, uneven beard. His eyes were intent and intelligent, his movements fidgety, and he appeared to be a meek person, a follower of orders—not an actual leader like Lowell or myself.

Douglass gave me a quick appraising glance. "And this is your companion? Mr.—?"

I shook his hand, and the strength of my grip surprised him. "It's *Doctor*, actually. Dr. Moreau. I am a surgeon and a biological specialist, an experimental physician, if you will." I gave no further details and neither did Lowell, though the assistant's curiosity was plain.

"Is there a new project of which I am not aware, Mr. Lowell?" Douglass took off his glasses and vigorously wiped them clean with a handkerchief. "Why does an astronomical observatory require an . . . experimental physician?"

Lowell frowned at him. "Mind your place, Andrew. Dr. Moreau is a world-renowned expert. There is no one comparable to him. I require his assistance and advice on a matter so important that it may even supersede our work with the telescopes."

The young astronomer was astonished, but I could see that he was familiar with Percival Lowell's changing passions; he surrendered his objections like an animal baring its throat to a dominant predator.

Just then the Martian stirred in its canvas-shrouded cage. "I trust you have arranged for a quiet and secure place to store our specimen?" Lowell said. "I want it to be inside a building where no one can see. I must be confident that no one will disturb it, not even you, Andrew."

Douglass was affronted at being kept from this new discovery, but Lowell makes a very clear distinction between colleagues and underlings. Though he trusted the young astronomer to choose the observatory site, manage the construction, and handle all the workers, Lowell did not wish to let Douglass share in our private triumph.

Similarly, I had long kept my vivisection research confidential from faint-hearted colleagues and subordinates. In London I used the services of a drunken lout named Montgomery; despite his unreliability and rude behavior, he was a talented surgical assistant, and many of my experiments succeeded because of his efforts. But Montgomery was killed in Borneo by a surgically modified puma. The pain-maddened beast got loose and tore the man to shreds as he lay in a gin-induced stupor, after which the puma fled into the jungle, where it bled to death from its torn incisions.

Having experienced the destructive meddling and ineptitude of a poorly prepared assistant, I did not question Lowell's decision to keep this young man in the dark.

Douglass led us to a secure outbuilding made of wooden planks with two small windows that had been boarded up, per Lowell's telegraphed instructions. "This was to have been our equipment shed. I believe it is sufficient for your needs, Mr. Lowell."

Lowell brushed his moustache and peered inside, holding up the lantern to reveal a large empty space with a dirt floor and a few unused shelves on the walls. "This is acceptable, Andrew."

After inspecting the wall boards and sturdy hinges on the shed door, I whistled for the wagon driver to pull up to the outbuilding. While the two burly men unloaded the shrouded cage, Douglass produced a padlock and chain with which we could secure the door. Lamplight reflected from his glasses. He was keenly interested, but too cowed to defy Lowell's strict instructions.

After the cage was moved into the shed, Lowell paid the wagon driver and the carter, then sent them away down the hill. Gruff and preoccupied, he dispatched Douglass to prepare our beds and see to it that we had a good meal waiting for us in the main house.

Alone again with the Martian, we removed the canvas

covering. The creature sat motionless inside its cage, staring into the dimness and assessing its new surroundings. Searching for a way to escape? The sutures had healed, leaving jagged scabs across its brown-skinned back. Thankfully, I observed no suppuration, no oozing pus or gangrene. Rarely had my surgical work been so perfectly successful, and I was pleased. The Martian was now strong and healthy—though still entirely unresponsive.

When Lowell opened the cage door to let the captive out into the shed, the Martian barely stirred. "Let us leave it to become accustomed to this place," I suggested. "It is best not to provoke an animal we do not understand. It will leave the cage when it wishes to." We slipped outside, then closed, chained, and padlocked the door. Lowell kept the only key.

Inside the main house, we dined on some rather bland and stringy venison. Douglass did not eat with us, but stayed to share a conversation. I listened with detached interest as the young man gave Lowell a full report of his work on the observatory.

Douglass seemed a competent administrator, guiding teams of workmen, following the blueprints and architectural sketches for the construction. The large dome was nearly ready to house the site's main refractor telescope, whose lenses were currently being ground and assembled by Alvan Clark & Sons in Cambridge, Massachusetts.

The Clark refractor would be the showpiece of the observatory, the instrument by which Lowell hoped to make many discoveries. Douglass had already set up two smaller personal telescopes on tripods on the veranda. He had been making nightly observations and sketches of Mars, which he showed to Lowell, who approved of most of them, criticized only a few.

Watching the two men interact, I saw that A.E. Douglass was the calm counterpoint to brash Lowell. I also detected friction between them. Douglass was talented, but Lowell refused to give him free reign. He questioned the young man's decisions and made him defensive about obvious points. How would Douglass respond when he learned of our creature from another planet?

We went to bed early. I slept soundly, my thoughts preoccupied with dreams of Martians and deserts and telescopes . . . .

* * *

The next morning as we drank our coffee and ate hot biscuits and fried eggs, Lowell dumbfounded Douglass by sending him away from Flagstaff.

"I can manage the work at the observatory, Andrew. I want you to return to the telescope factory of Clark & Sons. Supervise the completion of my great instrument. If it is humanly possible to install the refractor in time for the opposition of Mars later this year, I want it accomplished. Urge them to all possible haste."

Douglass accepted his new marching orders with bad grace. "But Mr. Lowell, there is so much activity here, so much I have not yet completed. The work crews, the carpenters and blacksmiths, the lumber that must be shipped from the forest, the sawmill owners, the—"

"My father trained me to run a large textile industry,

Andrew. A simple construction site should not tax my capabilities."

Douglass's shoulders sagged, and his teeth were clenched as if to hold his anger inside. "But what is the purpose of this, sir? Have I disappointed you in some way?"

"Not as of yet," Lowell said coldly, "unless you continue to question my orders. I deem my reasons for secrecy to be sufficient, and I'm sure Dr. Moreau will agree with them."

"I do agree," I answered, affirming my superiority over his rank and position. "Beyond that, it is none of your concern."

Clearly, Douglass's inquisitive mind would have threatened our secrecy and stifled our continuing efforts with the Martian. The local laborers might be frightened or curious, but our explanation of some exotic animal from Africa would satisfy them. Douglass, though, was far too bright for that. Upon glimpsing the Martian, he would know that this was not a creature born of Earth. Lowell was correct: we had to get the young man away from Mars Hill.

Later that day, his feathers ruffled but his bags packed, Douglass descended to the rail yards in Flagstaff, where he caught the next eastbound train.

* * *

Inside its shed, the Martian settled in. Now that I had time to experiment more comfortably, I practiced by giving it samples of fresh animal blood obtained from Flagstaff's butcher shop; though this seemed to nourish it sufficiently, the Martian was not pleased, as if the life fluid of inferior animals was simply not acceptable. Also, the butcher began to ask many unwelcome questions, and so I returned to regularly giving our specimen vials of my own blood, injecting sustenance into the creature's veins, just enough for it to survive. By now, Lowell had become accustomed to the ghastly feeding ritual, and when I grew weak from loss of blood, he volunteered to donate a pint or two for the Martian's continued existence.

Lowell always kept his distance from the creature, remembering the hideous sight of the redheaded crewman aboard the steamer, his neck snapped like kindling. But I approached the Martian without fear. I felt we had an unusual sort of understanding, and I knew it would not harm me.

During my attempts at communication, the creature would twitch its tentacles and meet my gaze with its large eyes. "We are making some progress, Percival, though this is going more slowly than I had hoped. We have no common ground, no point of comparison with which to begin a conversation."

Lowell took out the lovely crystal egg we had removed from the crashed cylinder. He held it in the light, turning the object in his hand. "I wish it could explain this to us."

Seeing the crystal egg, the Martian once again perked up. Its tentacles brushed briefly in the air and then one extended forward tentatively, then insistently, as if it wanted to touch the object. I was excited. This was the clearest reaction I had seen so far from this creature, much stronger than its previous reactions. "Let him have it, Percival."

He extended his hand with the crystal egg in it. With one tentacle like a lover's fingertip, the Martian caressed it, then reached out second and third tentacles to cradle the crystal egg. It held up the cloudy ellipsoid and somehow found unseen controls in its surface. When it activated a mechanism or energy source within, a faint shimmer of light glowed from the crystal egg.

"What has it done?" Lowell asked.

The Martian extended the crystal egg again, encouraging me to take it. I felt a surge of smug pride. Lowell may have been its financial benefactor, but the Martian realized that *I* had saved its life.

But then, what it showed me!

The crystal egg felt warm and tingly in my hand, as if it were connected to a voltaic pile. When I looked down, I saw astonishing images of an incredible world more exotic than all the Arabian wonders Scheherazade had ever described to Sir Richard Burton. Lowell crowded closer, and the two of us stared at an amazing stereoscopic image of an alien place.

The sky was greenish instead of blue. The landscape of red rock and towering cliffs was scored with breathtaking canals, watercourses distributing a liquid lifeblood to grand cities strung across otherwise dry continents. Never had I seen towers stretch so high, or arches so ethereal and delicate, poised in a gravity lower than our Earth's. The architecture, the building materials, the streets paved with gems and tiles of jade—I am not a man prone to hyperbole, but even I found myself transfixed.

We saw domed cities easily withstanding the blast of incredible dust storms. Large flying things like hawks cruised in the skies, circling to scavenge food. Fantastic industries manufactured treasures beyond anything our minds had imagined. And we could see only the broadest detail in the crystal egg—how much more might await us if we actually went to this land of marvels?

"What is this place?" Lowell asked in wonder. "What are we seeing?"

I shall never forget the thrill I felt next as, clear as a bell, the Martian spoke directly into our minds.

That is my home.

CHAPTER TWENTY-ONE

THE MASTER MINDS OF MARS

Held in the excavation site at the Martian pole, Wells stood close to Jane and waited for their fates to be decided. Towering guardian tripods marched about the giant ice quarry, their heat-ray projectors raised ominously; smaller two-legged Martian walking machines, each of which carried a single Martian like a man astride an iron ostrich, clanked back and forth. It was the first Wells and his companions had seen of the hideous creatures Moreau had described in his journal.

"It looks like a bloated bag of brain covered with oilskin," Jane cried. "And the eyes! Look at the eyes! I wish I could make a sketch of it. Have you ever seen anything so hideous?"

"One cannot apply human standards of beauty to an alien

world," Huxley pointed out.

"Even so," Jane said, "they are still extraordinarily ugly."

Unable to tear his gaze from the approaching bird-like contrivances, Wells countered, "Knowing what these Martians have done to the Selenite utopia and what they mean to do on Earth, I find their *minds* particularly loathsome, regardless of their physical appearance."

Four of the small walking contrivances clomped up to the captives, extruding electrical tentacles from the machine core. Inside the transparent control dome, the Martian driver activated controls: the whips lashed, and sparks cracked; Huxley hissed in pain from a sudden jolt that left a red weal on his cheek.

Fearful but desperate to do something, Wells tried to interpose himself to protect the old man, but Huxley stopped him. "Don't do anything foolishly futile, Mr. Wells. I believe they're attempting to herd us." He gestured toward a steep ramp that descended to the canal levels. "We may as well be on our way."

In the water below, anchored barges and bubble-topped floating craft rested in the numerous feeder channels that led into the primary network of canals. Martian walking machines moved along the docks, loading and arranging cargo.

The static whips cracked again, and Wells took a jolt in the shoulder. "Bloody hell, we're going!" He kept himself where he could take the blows instead of Jane, but once they started walking, the Martians did not strike again.

"Apparently, they assume we're docile, like the Selenites," Jane said.

"Personally, I *want* to go meet one of their representatives," Huxley said. "It's the only way we may accomplish our mission."

When the strange procession reached the docks on the frigid canals, two Martians, looking like overfed spiders, crawled out of the control domes of their walking contrivances and scuttled down a ramp into a bubble-topped floating craft. The remaining pair of guardian walkers clanked back and forth in front of the captives, cracking their static whips to drive the humans toward the boat.

"Professor, we can't go far from our sphere," Wells said with increasing anxiety. "The Martians will dismantle it in that hangar, and then we'll never get back home."

Huxley gave him a stoic look. "Ah, young man, we came here to save our Earth. Before we can devise a plan, we require a great deal more information about the Martian society."

"There's only one way to find out what we need to know," Jane said. She was the first to step aboard the domed boat, and the two men followed. "The human race is at stake."

The vessel's interior was made of a strange, smooth metal. It boasted no furnishings except for sturdy platforms designed to accommodate the shapeless and bulky Martians, but the three sat on them anyway. Once the prisoners were inside, the faceted domes clicked into place, sealing them in. Mechanical anchors disengaged from the docks, and the floating craft lurched forward into the swift current.

Back at the docks, guardian walkers stood observing them as the domed boat departed. Then they clanked away, static whips lashing at hapless Selenite slaves.

"I know we replenished ourselves just before landing, but I do wish we'd brought some food supplies from the sphere," Huxley said, wrapping his striped bathrobe tighter around his chest. "A bottle of beer and some dried meat would certainly restore my energy right now." Wells searched in his pockets and found some forgotten old biscuits he had taken from the supplies in the cavorite sphere; he shared the food around, but it only served to whet their appetites.

As the domed boat rushed down the main canal, the three stared out at the rubble of ancient cities worn to bare geometric silhouettes. Abandoned towers stretched into the gray-green sky, silent and barren. Scavenger birds, practically the only animal form they noticed, circled about the ruins. The current of thawed antarctic water swept them through oasis intersections where lush plant life abounded in stark contrast to the dry red deserts all around. Large-eyed creatures ducked into the shelter of vegetation.

"A living civilization was born here, matured, and is now dying," Huxley lamented. "At one glorious time, this landscape could have been covered with plants and forests, but it's now entirely played out, drained dry." He shook his head. "Did the Martians mine the nutrients out of the soil, cut down all the trees? No wonder they need to go someplace fresh and new. Like Earth."

Contemplating the factory smokestacks around London, the dirty industries, the constantly belching furnaces and the sluggish, polluted waters of the Thames, Wells wondered what the Earth itself would look like in a few thousand years.

The bubble-topped boat finally approached a huge metropolis whose buildings rose in dagger-like points and spheres. The primary construction materials were a type of glass or crystal, but considering the loads placed on them, it must have been stronger than forged steel. Wells thought the skyline looked like a cluster of minarets created by a blind glassblower.

Whirling antennae spun about on the tops of tall structures—perhaps a form of weather forecasting? Mirrors and prisms rotated, flashing the dim sunshine into sharp beams like a spotlight. He saw trapezoidal gates and long sloping ramps, walkways that spiraled around and up the highest spires. No doubt with their slumping bodies and tentacular appendages, the Martians would not have been able to negotiate stairs or ladders.

"From its very grandeur, I would guess this metropolis is the Martian capital." As the vessel slowed, Huxley combed his fingers through his sideburns and hair in an attempt to make himself look presentable. "Where else would they take emissaries from another planet?" He fretted over his rumpled lounging shirt, trousers, and slippers. "I do wish I had brought more formal clothes."

Wells tried to console him. "No matter how sophisticated the Martian telescopes may be, Professor, I doubt they care about the latest fashions in London."

From a control dome above the boat, the unseen Martian pilot guided the vessel into an apparatus that closed like lips and locked the floating craft against the metal-plated dock. When the hemispherical covers opened, Huxley stood first. "Ah then, we are . . . here." Wells took Jane's hand and, stepping into the yellowish artificial illumination of the Martian metropolis, they waited for what might happen next. Would they be received as ambassadors, or as spies and saboteurs?

A trio of small walking contrivances met the prisoners at the dock gate. Riding inside the control seats, the inhuman creatures stared at them with cold hunger. Crackling metallic bullwhips snapped out, shooting sparks, and by now the three needed no encouragement.

"I do not choose to meet the Martian leaders as a downtrodden prisoner or a captured enemy." Huxley squared his shoulders, then marched briskly and proudly along the sleek-looking and streamlined street. "I prefer to think of myself as a visiting emissary, regardless of how these creatures treat me." Wells copied the older man's demeanor, taking Jane's arm. The three strolled along as if they were invited guests, ignoring the crackling whips behind them.

They listened to the hum of machinery in the air. Liquid lines of blue electricity flowed up the sides of buildings in some form of circulatory system for the alien metropolis. Rotating faceted crystal spheres spun rainbows from the tops of towers. But the city had no babble of conversation, no drone of voices, no bustle of living people or daily business. The Martians were an eerily silent race, moving about with secret thoughts and sinister plans.

At the center of the metropolis several intersecting canals flowed in a frothing, churning rush. Towering over this nexus stood a prominent Martian building, like a scientific cathedral of mathematically precise swooping towers, embedded domes, and laboratory spires.

"Note the unique architectural style, which takes into account the lower gravity of Mars and the different ores and stone available for construction," Huxley said.

Wells drank it all in with his eyes, hoping that someday he'd be able to describe such marvels in prose: how the *Pall Mall Gazette* would pay for an eyewitness account of the civilization of Mars! If he, Jane, and the professor ever got safely home, he would sell his memoirs, perhaps even demand an increase in his pay rate.

Inside what he thought of as the scientific cathedral, tunnels and tubes rose upward like wild beanstalks made of transparent substances softer and more flexible than glass. Bubbling fluids spewed into large cylinders, before being pumped downward by heavy pistons. Standing inside the nave of the wondrous structure, Wells could imagine they were inside a giant machine, like a life-support system for the Martian culture.

The small walking contrivances herded them through a reception chamber and up a long textured ramp like an alluvial fan to a flat platform, like a sacrificial altar in one of the newly discovered Mayan ziggurats of Central America. There, in a shallow circular pool with a golden rim, three hideous Martians floated in a honey-colored bath of nutrients, soaking in the syrupy substance. The trio of Martian brains—Wells ironically thought to call them the "heads of state"—regarded the humans in silence. Their thin tentacles stirred the nutrient bath.

After invisibly conferring amongst themselves, the trio of master minds wallowed to the edge of their communal pool and climbed with rolling, flopping motions out onto the wet floor of the dais. The ungainly Martians crawled to three empty walking contrivances at the opposite edge of the dais, and used tentacles to heave their swollen brain-bodies into the open control domes. After the master minds had seated themselves at the controls and closed the dome covers tightly, the walkers activated. Heavy legs clomped toward where the three humans stood waiting.

"Not much for conversation, are they?" Wells muttered.

The alien council members marched the three captives up a winding ramp to a laboratory spire that looked out over the Martian metropolis. After Wells and his friends were unceremoniously dropped onto the smooth floor, the three walkers strode over to a set of high silver pillars, that reminded Wells of perches for pet vultures. The Martian master minds slid out of the walking contrivances and rested heavily atop the pedestals, like a tribunal.

Huxley was most interested in the laboratory around them. Aquarium tanks contained ghoulish specimens of odd life forms floating in preservation solutions. One entire wall was devoted to representatives of Selenite castes, all studied, dissected, and then placed in specimen bottles like the invertebrates and fish Huxley himself had collected on the *Rattlesnake*.

Jane, though, turned her attention to the trays of gleaming tools and probes. Three tables rested in the middle of the room, etched with channels and sloping funnels to drain away unwanted fluids. "What will they do to us, H.G.? Or is it as obvious as I think?"

The old professor's gaze was dark and sharp. "It seems clear enough that they mean to dissect us, young lady." His shoulders sagged. "After all, it is what I would have done with new and interesting specimens."

A door slid open at the rear of the laboratory dome to admit a new Martian walker—this one far more frightening than the others they had seen. Wells immediately thought of it as the Grand Inquisitor. The new machine bristled with robotic arms, claws, syringes, and probes. The Martian riding like an imp on its back had numerous controls at its disposal. Electrical fluids pulsed along its outer skeleton, trailed by flashing lights and hissing hydrodynamic pulleys.

The Grand Inquisitor faced the three Martian master minds on their pedestals, then strode over to the three humans, who clung together. Scanners roamed up and down, measuring, assessing, and recording images of their bodies. "Painless so far," Jane said.

After studying them for some moments, the Grand Inquisitor lurched forward and reached out a set of four limbs for Jane. Wells pushed her aside. "Leave her alone. Take me first."

"H.G., don't!"

The Grand Inquisitor was perfectly satisfied to take Wells as the first specimen. The ominous walker hauled him to one of the three dissection tables. With a flurry of arms, claws, and sharp scalpels, the analytical machine poked and stroked and studied him, gaining tactile records as well as visual ones.

Though he tried not to show it, Wells was terrified. He squirmed and was seized by a fit of coughing, which the Grand Inquisitor seemed to regard as an attack, a show of futile resistance, or an abortive attempt at communication.

Huxley pleaded with the three alien leaders, attempting to appeal to their reason. He formed triangles and circles with his fingers to demonstrate simple mathematical relationships that the Martians might understand. He tried to express the concept of pi, then the Pythagorean Theorem.

The master minds remained entirely preoccupied with Wells, leaning forward to peer at him helpless on their analytical table. They observed every moment in complete silence.

Two large-bore syringes plunged into the soft skin of his neck, and Wells writhed in agony. Jane threw herself forward, but Huxley restrained her. Through his fog of pain, Wells called in a strained voice, "Don't interfere, Jane—you'll put yourself in danger too."

Samples of his blood flowed into the syringes and through

tubes back into analytical compartments. With a horrible sliding and clicking sound, two more sets of metallic hands rose from the interrogation machine. Wells strained to see, but the long needles in his neck prevented him from struggling. Twelve sharp robotic fingers extended into his field of view, each one terminating in a needle that glistened with a droplet of white fluid.

Again Wells tried to squirm away. Like sharp stingers, the Inquisitor's new needle-hands brushed his scalp, the contours of his skull, as if looking for something. Then with a sudden sharp movement—and a torrent of excruciating pain—the needles plunged into his skull, drilling deep.

Wells peeled his lips back in a grimace. At first he struggled and thrashed, but then he forced himself to remain still, heroically surrendering to the Martian's analysis for the sake of Jane and Professor Huxley. Although his own brain was much smaller than the Martians' superior organs, he hoped that if they could obtain the data they required from *him*, then the evil master minds wouldn't need to torture his friends. Cold tears trickled out of the corners of his eyes, and he shuddered, his whole body spasming.

The needles dug deeper, through the skull and into gray matter, stimulating thoughts, dreams. Visions surged through his optic nerves, though his eyes were shut. Without any volition of his own, information surged out of his brain as if he were a book being casually skimmed by the Grand Inquisitor.

In a flash before his eyes, Wells saw glimpses of his youth, his brothers and parents . . . breaking his leg when he was a boy, reading books and discovering the joy of stories. The drudgery of working in a draper's shop with other abused apprentices.

His disappointing love and marriage to Isabel, and then meeting Jane . . . his love for her, the wonders and happiness they had together.

But the Martian was not interested in such thoughts. This was not an attempt to establish communication. This was the interrogation of a prisoner of war.

The silver fingers dug deeper yet, uncovering information about politics and warfare, the technology available to the British Empire and to the Germans: siege machines and ironclads, explosives, rifles, cannons. More and more thoughts were drained from his deepest brain, inspected, and recorded for later analysis by Martian invasion planners.

Realizing the crucial information he was revealing, Wells struggled. "No!" He tried to clamp his memories away, fighting the sharp probings of the deep needles. No matter how he resisted, the Grand Inquisitor's apparatus was able to steal all it needed to know about Earth's defensive abilities.

Finally the silver spikes withdrew from his brain and skull, and Wells collapsed like an invertebrate to the cold dissection table. His frustration and disgust at what he had unwittingly divulged made him feel even weaker. The Grand Inquisitor retracted its surgical and analytical limbs into storage cylinders mounted like gun barrels on the sides of its dome-turret, then clanked away.

"H.G., are you all right?" Jane rushed to his side and helped him to his feet. "What have they done to you?"

Tears still streamed out of his blue eyes, and he hung his head. "They know everything, Jane. *Everything*. We have no way to fight them."

Huxley inspected his wounds, the small needle punctures,

and nodded with faint satisfaction. "I believe you will heal, Wells."

Jane held him close to her. "I thought they were going to kill you, H.G."

"It's worse, Jane. They let me remain alive, knowing that *I myself* doomed the human race to slavery and defeat."

CHAPTER TWENTY-TWO

MARS AS THE ABODE OF LIFE

FROM THE JOURNAL OF DR. MOREAU

Once the captive Martian specimen finally began to communicate with us, our world—indeed, our view of the universe—changed entirely. After all my tedious and patient labors, the creature at last understood I was its benefactor, and must have resolved to confide in me. With the Martian's incredible revelations, my previous conceptions of evolution and biological adaptations were both reaffirmed and thrown into confusion. It was a heady time.

Lowell took notes as furiously as he could. Closed within the shadowy shed, he and I listened intently while the Martian described his withering civilization. Using the crystal egg to display remarkable images, the Martian spoke into our minds, telling of his race.

Since it was half again as far from the Sun as Earth, Mars had cooled much more swiftly and had become an abode of life long before the first primordial creatures stirred in the ooze of our oceans. Martian civilization had grown swiftly from primitive encampments to small agricultural settlements that eventually expanded into cities filled with technological wonders. Through tremendous advances in science and mathematics, their race had accomplished great things.

Any scientist knows that crisis and deprivation are the driving factors of evolutionary improvement. As their red deserts became more arid and their survival was threatened, Martian minds were forced to evolve and enlarge to meet the challenge—or perish.

Employing their most advanced industrial techniques on a massive scale, they excavated and installed an immense network of canals to distribute the remnants of moisture from the north and south poles. The peaceable Martians worked together, building upon what they had developed so that each system worked with increasing efficiency.

In the crystal egg, Lowell and I saw vibrant images of canals and pumping stations, ice quarrying and melting operations at the polar caps. As their brains enlarged and their bodies atrophied, the Martians constructed walker machines in order to move about more easily.

I realized that in this small hand-held observation device I had access to an amazing laboratory of evolution. Watching how the Martian race had changed, I could see adaptations that had arisen after perhaps a thousand generations, or more. As their civilization grew and became more and more sophisticated, their bodies had dwindled away, becoming dependent on more efficient technological innovations. And why not? Did not our arboreal simian ancestors once have prehensile tails, which had gradually vanished as our intellect created better solutions to obtaining food?

The Martians could no longer sustain themselves through entirely natural means, but they had not allowed this to hinder their development. Through incredible intellect and a powerful drive for survival, they had designed and constructed everything they needed . . . and their race had survived the catastrophic drought that would have destroyed Mars.

Lowell's breathing was shallow, as if the very concepts drove him into a feverish state. "Oh, if only there were some way to record these pictures! But no camera apparatus would ever be sufficient to the task."

Everything I saw in the crystal egg made me feel an increasingly acute disappointment at the lack of progress and foresight my fellow humans had shown in their constant squabbles. Mortal man had always been more fundamentally composed of apathy than of determination. Only a few great men, such as myself, were willing to devote their lives to the advancement of our world.

Though I did not want the Martian to stop regaling us with the details of Martian history, the constant flow of ideas numbed my mind. The revelations were like a banquet on which I had gorged and gorged, and I needed time to digest it all. Day after day, when we finished our discussions and retired to the main house, I was exhausted and brain weary.

Lowell obviously felt the same. He had some history of nervous distress, and I feared that this wonderful adventure might push him into another breakdown, but his skin was flushed and his gaze as intent as that of a jungle predator. I could not in good conscience suggest that we stop.

We ate dinner together alone with our thoughts and paying scant attention to the taste of the meal. Lowell had been correct in sending away A.E. Douglass, for we could never have been so candid with each other. With his beefsteak and beans only half eaten, Lowell pushed his plate away and looked over my shoulder, out the window to where the sky was darkening.

The tall ponderosa pines bowed and danced with the rising wind, whispering secrets to each other. The windows were open and the veranda stood empty, waiting for us to begin our nightly observations of Mars. I could hear night birds beginning their dusk hunts as insect songs taunted them.

"I find myself utterly fascinated and pleasantly surprised by this first contact," Lowell said. "Although this Martian is an enigma to me, just as the Japanese were—alien and incomprehensible to the Western mind—already, I am finding common ground with this creature."

He dabbed his lips with a linen napkin. "We are both, after all, of the higher social classes. Our Martian is a respected explorer and ambassador, as am I." He stared out the open window, sniffing the night breeze. "And, the old Boston Brahmin way of life—not unlike the Martian civilization—is in decline. Perhaps I can use this Martian's insight to form an alliance and strengthen the greater families of Boston and New York." He smiled. "Yes, that would be a marvelous result of all this work, wouldn't it? My father would certainly approve."

I nodded noncommittally, for I felt that such frivolous goals in the face of tremendous potential benefits to the human race were laughable. Once again, Lowell had shown he was not a true scientist at his core. He was a rich young man merely dabbling in the sciences. Other upper-class playboys purchased yachts and took extended trips. Being more eccentric, Lowell poured his funds into the toys of research, determined to purchase a spot for himself in the history of science.

Our Martian explorer was a far different sort of creature, with a much nobler purpose: it was trying to save its world.

When full darkness finally arrived, Lowell and I went onto the veranda to enjoy cigars. The wind had died down, which would still the atmosphere and improve the quality of seeing for our two tripod-mounted refractor telescopes. Douglass had left them for our amusement, and Lowell made nightly observations with a tenacity that I found admirable.

With the stars sparkling above us and the thin crescent Moon setting on the western horizon, I could barely see the outlines of the buildings across the observatory site. The largest dome, which would house the impressive Clark refractor, was already constructed, its outer paneling nearly finished.

As instructed by Lowell, Douglass had by now arrived on the east coast and telegraphed a progress report. The telescope's lenses were poured and cooled and currently being ground to the proper curvature. The huge yoke and cradle for the telescope barrel would be shipped by rail soon. Lowell grumbled his impatience, wishing that Douglass showed enough backbone to make the manufacturers work harder.

Lowell himself, however, had been so engrossed in his work debriefing the captive Martian, that construction activities at the observatory site began to fall behind after Douglass's departure. When Lowell finally noticed the failings, though, he turned his ire upon the irresponsible work crews with an outraged sternness that shocked the lazy laborers into redoubling their efforts. Like a stampeding bull, Lowell strode from one building site to the next, shouting at workers and threatening to withhold pay unless they got the project back on schedule.

A.E. Douglass was a quieter, meeker supervisor, not a man to strike fear into the thick-muscled carpenters and haulers. Lowell had a much stronger personality; I did not doubt that all of the buildings would indeed be ready for operation by the time of the Martian opposition . . . .

In the meantime, he and I glued our eyes to the smaller telescopes. I observed the rusty orange orb, seeing only murky shadows and none of the fine detail that Lowell discerned. Even knowing what the Martian had showed us in the crystal egg, I could not make out the webwork of canals, the fertile shadings of each oasis. But Lowell saw them—and how could I question his eyesight? For I knew that such things were truly there.

Lowell no longer had any doubts about why he had gone to so much work and expense. He felt completely vindicated. "Imagine the response of the public when I publish these discoveries. They will be excited to learn about the idyllic Martian society and all the achievements that they have brought about through diligence and cooperation. Perhaps humanity will find some way to help this dying society, make a union between Earth and Mars for the benefit of both planets. I will see to it that my book is published and widely disseminated so that everyone can know Mars as well as they know Japan from my previous popular descriptions."

I did not want to discourage him, but his exuberance was a bit naive. Having been censured so many times in my career, I understood that the public was not always receptive to radical new ideas. "I am more skeptical about how this news will be received, Lowell. What if the readers and your fellow scientists don't believe you?"

Lowell straightened from the refractor telescope and looked at me with surprised indignation. "But these are *facts*, Moreau. If I tell them the truth about Mars and its canals, how could any sane person doubt my word? One might just as easily argue against a statement that the sky is blue or the desert is dry."

I gave him a thin smile. "I could show you men who would do exactly that, Percival."

CHAPTER TWENTY-THREE

ENSLAVED WITH THE SELENITES

After ransacking the brain of H.G. Wells, the Martians knew that Huxley was the mastermind of their expedition from Earth. They also understood, from Wells's own assessment, that the old professor would never survive long under the rigors of heavy slave labor. The Martians considered Wells and Jane, however, to be fit workers for the underground industries of the red planet.

Lashing with static whips from their small walkers, taskmaster Martians drove the two young lovers away from the laboratory spire, leaving Huxley to shout after them, "Use your intellect and your imagination, Wells, and we will find a way out of this."

Wells struggled as padded claws clamped around his arms, pulling him and Jane down the sloping ramp that led out of the scientific cathedral. "We'll break free and rescue you, Professor!" His thin voice cracked with desperation.

"And I shall do my best to reciprocate. One of us is bound to succeed."

As the mechanical walkers marched the two of them along, Wells discovered that it was useless to struggle. The machines were not much larger than a human, but their lashing whips made them far superior. The Martian taskmaster in the control seat of the walking contrivance showed no evil glee at its position; it merely forced the new human slaves to obey.

Wells and Jane matched the rapid pace set by the Martian walkers, circling down level after level. He looked at her, taking her hand and half-fearing that their captors would prevent this brief contact. "At least I'm with you, Jane. Together, you and I have a better chance than the average person to succeed at impossible things."

She forced a laugh. "And if there was ever an impossible situation, H.G., this one qualifies."

They finally reached their destination deep beneath the Martian surface, a network of artificially bored passages fused into glassy reddish-black smoothness and lit with artificial illumination crystals. Wells remembered the soothing blue-white phosphorescence in the tunnels of the Grand Lunar; here, though, the light was reddish and dim, as if the window of a lamp had been smeared with fresh blood.

From within the labyrinth, they heard the hissing of exhaust plumes and steam jets, the creak of heavy copper and iron gears ponderously turning, the clank of pistons, the rattle of chains and pulleys. In the catacombs, the air was close and humid, smelling of dust, chemicals, and grease. Though the heat from the machinery made them truly warm for the first time since they had arrived on Mars, Wells still shivered.

All around them scuttled the thin Selenite drones, working underground and out of sight from the extravagant surface city. The miserable conditions reminded Wells of the conditions faced by spinners and weavers and textile workers, as well as workers in the infamous phosphorus matchstick factories in London. His voice held a dull anger. "This is slave labor, pure and simple. Mindless, wearying. It will crush our spirits and wear us down to nothing."

"The Selenites have survived all this time. Perhaps they just need a Moses to free them from their bondage."

Wells let out a bitter chuckle. "Of all the grand goals I had imagined in my life, being Moses was never one of them."

Mechanical slave masters in grimy iron-ostrich walkers observed all the tunnel activity. They transmitted implacable instructions that crackled through the air, reinforced with blows from their static whips.

The dull Selenite drones worked, making strange squeaking sounds that were not responses or complaints, but utterances of weary, hopeless pain. The lunar slaves took no more notice of their new human comrades than they did of their tasks.

Food and water stations provided meager nourishment, and Wells and Jane replenished themselves for the first time in nearly a day. The water tasted flat, and the pasty food wafers were bitter, but sustenance was sustenance. "We must survive, Jane," he said quietly. "We will need our strength."

Martian slave masters loomed over the two humans in their

walking contrivances. Wells forced himself to stand straight and tall, showing bravery for Jane's sake. The nearest Martian extended robotic arms and clamped a thin metal ring around his neck in a swift, confident movement. Wells had not seen it coming and reacted with surprise, grabbing at the collar. A sharp shock of pain discouraged him from further resistance. He noticed that the Selenite slaves also wore the silvery band. A second slave master fitted Jane's slender neck with an identical circlet. In its streamlined simplicity, the torc might have been an ornamental piece of jewelry.

From a small device mounted in the walker machine, the silent Martian taskmaster issued a harsh communication. Jolting words came from the collar, burrowing into Wells's mind. *These collars facilitate your reception of our commands.*

"The Selenites are bred to follow the will of the Grand Lunar. For generations, they have been listless but cooperative slaves," Jane observed. "The Martians seem to expect the same from us."

"I shall be happy to disappoint them, but I don't want you to be injured or punished. For now, let us do what we're told—and observe. Remember what Professor Huxley said. We must use our intellect and imagination to discover our way out of this predicament."

But as he looked around himself in the shadowy catacombs, at the mechanical slave masters and the hordes of cowed Selenites, he doubted the two of them could find any simple solution.

All that day Wells and Jane performed mindless but difficult labor alongside the Selenites, maintaining the great machinery that ran the Martian civilization. The slave masters did not care that the two humans remained together, nor that they talked or took comfort in each other's presence, but their large yellow eyes watched them like a starving hawk, and their static whips crackled menacingly.

Slave masters marched through the smooth tunnels, using devices in their walkers to transmit bursts of complex instructions through the communication collars. Wells and Jane instantly comprehended and followed the commands, though they had no wish to assist the invaders. They fed fuel into generators, cleaned pumps and immense dynamos, built power conduits, and adjusted the water flow and distribution from the canals. The Selenites toiled without rest.

These captive Moon drones were a pale, weak underclass that bore the burden of labor for the superior thinking class. The Martians had atrophied so badly they required artificial machines simply to move about. These Selenites, if they ever realized their power, were truly in control of civilization here. But not so long as they obeyed every command of the overlords. If this kept on for centuries more, Wells suspected that the pampered Martians would be utterly dependent upon the Selenite workers, and the roles of master and slave would be permanently reversed.

Weak and weary after long hours of labor, Wells began to wonder if the Martian slave masters would ever feed them. From Jane's paleness, the shadows under her eyes, he could see that she was forcing herself to keep going; he tried to pick up the slack in her tasks, but she would have none of it.

Suddenly heavy, hollow gongs began to ring. The insistent signal reverberated through the tunnels. The Selenites instantly paused in their labor as if hypnotized. They straightened, standing in ranks like toy soldiers.

"What is it, H.G.? What does it mean?"

"Let us hope it means no harm to either of us."

Slave masters marched through the tunnel in their small walkers and led a shuffling column of Selenites upward. Wells had received no instruction through his communication collar, but he did not want to be left behind, always keeping his eyes open for a chance at escape. He and Jane hurried after the drones as the work crew approached an open red rock arena surrounded by white ceramic seats and ramps.

Hundreds of bloated, spidery Martians had gathered there, all of them dismounted from their walkers, eerily silent. Martian drivers thrashed the Selenites with unnecessary static whips, herding them into the arena. The outside air was dry, dusty, and cold. It carried a foul taint, a stink not of sweat or fear . . . but of anticipation exuded by the sinister Martians.

"This makes me uneasy," Wells said to Jane.

Martian walkers culled out a group of fifty Selenites, who marched into the center of the open area like cattle. Feeling a shiver down his spine, Wells clutched Jane's hand. "It's like a spectacle in an ancient Roman gladiator arena," she said.

Loud gongs rang again as the chosen Selenites stood waiting, staring motionlessly ahead. Then the tone changed.

A startling roar came from the previously silent Martians, a hungry howl of "*Ulla! Ulla!*" The Martians stampeded out of the stands and rushed onto the field. They moved like a pack, lumbering along with their soft bodies. They squirmed down the ramps from their seats and out into the open area, where they surrounded the defenseless drones.

All the Martians were armed, not with swords or guns, but with crystal-barreled instruments similar to hypodermic needles. Ravenous predators, the Martians fell upon the lunar creatures, stabbing their hypodermics into the pale flesh. Their bulk held down the squealing Selenite victims as their apparatus drained the flowing vital liquor from the hapless creatures. Unable to escape, the drones squeaked and squirmed as the Martians swarmed over them, waving their tentacles.

Unable to tear away his gaze, Wells tried to understand how the Martians could ever have evolved such a method of acquiring sustenance. It could not be natural, but the Martian race had adapted themselves drastically to changing conditions— building walkers to maintain their mobility, erecting canals to distribute water long after their planet should have died, and now feeding upon the blood of their slaves.

Perhaps they had found the hypodermic ingestion of blood to be more efficient, or more enjoyable, than feeding in a more natural fashion. It was even possible, Wells supposed, that they had altered or bred their physical forms into these new shapes that depended upon the blood of their captives.

No matter what the answer, he found it monstrous.

The other Selenites, those not called into the arena, stood motionless, incapable of resistance.

Though it made him want to vomit, Wells could not tear his eyes from the frenzy of tentacles and thrusting needles that drew out thick, greenish blood and injected it into themselves. He clenched his teeth together in outrage.

"This is horrible, horrible!" Jane cried. "We have to find some way to stop them."

Wells took deep breaths to keep the dizzying black spots from his vision. He clenched his fists and bunched his muscles, thinking furiously. If the Martians launched their invasion of

Earth, they would conquer mankind with little difficulty. The Selenite drones no longer resisted, but humans would fight. It would be a bloody war between Mars and Earth . . . but given their amazingly sophisticated technology, how could the Martians lose?

Scenes like this feeding frenzy would be played out all across England and America, Europe, Africa, Asia—human beings rounded up and herded into similar slaughter arenas. They would struggle, they would run, but they would all die in the end.

Unless Wells and his companions could stop the invasion.

Rabid with glee, the Martians kept hooting their raucous "*Ulla! Ulla!*" as they stabbed their hypodermics again and again. Although the Selenites had all fallen to the red dust by now, the Martians continued feeding, sucking every last drop of life fluid from their victims. Soon the dead Selenites were little more than trampled husks, leathery lumps that had been living beings . . . creatures who once served a benevolent and enlightened Grand Lunar. Now they were no more than garbage, the remnants of a feast for hideous Martian master minds.

Finally the gongs rang again to release the Selenites from the horrific feeding ritual. The drones marched back into the dark and oppressive tunnels, where they were forced to continue their infinite labors.

Sickened and fearful, Wells led Jane toward the dubious safety of the catacombs. He expected to see panic in her lovely brown eyes, but instead they flashed at him, and he saw the strength and determination that had endeared her to him throughout their long adventure. "We have to do more than just protect Earth, H.G. If it is in our power, if it is humanly possible, we've got to save the Selenites too. We have to rescue them from this horror."

Wells took her arm and nodded, just as determined as she. "And I want to see the Martians not just defeated, but utterly destroyed."

CHAPTER TWENTY-FOUR

THE MARKS OF PLANETARY DESTRUCTION

FROM THE JOURNAL OF DR. MOREAU

Though the Martian had told us of its race and its world, still I did not feel we understood it. This alien being was more exotic than anything either Marco Polo or Jonathan Swift ever described. Its words and images were comprehensible to us, but the deep thoughts within that immense brain remained a cipher.

I sensed the Martian was keeping secrets from us, but Lowell was so overjoyed by the marvels revealed in the crystal egg that he failed to consider all the information he did *not* know.

Attempting to become friendly with our interplanetary guest, he proposed an expedition out into the desert.

Though I didn't understand what Lowell had in mind, I had no objections, so long as the logistical details could be solved. He looked at me with his bright eyes. "We will take my new motorcar."

* * *

Most travel in Arizona Territory is done on horseback or in carriages. The dirt roads are rutted wagon tracks; even Flagstaff's Main Street, crossed by the railroad tracks, has no paving stones or gutters.

While we'd been in Boston visiting his family, Lowell had grown enamored with Karl Benz's new vehicles. Rattle-wheeled models with capricious engines had recently been shipped over from Europe. Lowell became determined that he must be the first to own one of the four-wheeled motorcars, as a mark of his superiority.

On the day the motorcar reached Flagstaff via the Santa Fe rail, a crowd of curious spectators gathered to see the contraption. They watched as Lowell assembled the components according to instructions, added the oil and gasoline, and, after several abortive tries, succeeded in starting the popping, fluttering engine. Wearing an immensely pleased smile, sitting straight and tall, Lowell drove the rattletrap vehicle out of town and up the steep road to Mars Hill.

Thus far, Lowell had had little opportunity to use the motorcar on expeditions. Being intent on our conversations with the Martian, he had not yet taken the mayor of Flagstaff for a ride, or the saucer-eyed Methodist minister, or the railway executive who had stopped on his way through town. Today, though, he proposed to take the *Martian* for a ride out into the dry Arizona desert.

In the coolness of dawn, with light just beginning to edge the San Francisco Peaks, Lowell started his motorcar while I unlocked the outbuilding. By now, the Martian understood that we were its friends and allies, that it would get no better treatment if it broke out of its confinement and ran loose across the wild countryside. But the lock kept curiosity seekers out.

Construction work continued at the observatory site and, knowing how tight the schedule was, the workers did not dare risk Lowell's impatience. So close to dawn, however, the men had not yet come up from their camps, and we guided the cumbersome Martian to the humming motorcar without incident.

The creature perched in the vehicle's back seat, its tentacles exploring the upholstery and framework. Lowell pulled up the fabric rain covering in order to hide the Martian, then engaged the clutch and put the car into gear, whereupon we rolled off downhill, clattering and popping.

No doubt the sounds woke many lumberjacks and train workers trying to sleep off hangovers in saloons and boarding houses. But Lowell never had a care for how his activities inconvenienced other people; the man wasn't arrogant, so much as oblivious.

I looked through the thin windscreen, watching the dark pines rush by as we continued at a speed of well over twenty miles per hour. I feared my teeth would be jarred loose, but Lowell seemed confident in his vehicle. The Martian's large

242

eyes stared at the terrain with fascination. Perhaps the dry rocks and parched landscape reminded it of Mars . . . .

Flagstaff fell behind, as did the ponderosa forests. The rising sun cast long shadows across the flat scrubland, and Lowell followed wagon roads and horse tracks. He had put several rolled-up maps beside him on the seat, though he rarely consulted them.

As we drove along, Lowell was in high spirits. He had packed a picnic lunch, including some bottles of water and one of wine. I hoped the Martian would not require any nourishment during our journey, for I had not brought along the blood-drawing apparatus.

Lowell chattered at great length about human society, our various countries and governments, our industries and inventors and artists. With a detached sadness and scorn, he discussed human conflicts and the political disagreements that led to wars. The Martian listened intently, but did not communicate with us, as if such things were greatly beneath its intellect. To be fair, I doubted either Lowell or I would have been interested in, for example, the tribal dances of primitive people.

Lowell gestured out the left side of the Benz car. "North of Flagstaff, half a day's journey away, is a canyon so grand and vast it is considered one of the wonders of the world."

Our telescopes have studied your geography, and I have no interest in canyons, the Martian communicated. *Mars has canyons far superior to any minor scratch on Earth.*

Lowell frowned as if his hospitality had been rebuffed. "Nevertheless, we humans consider it quite magnificent." He sounded deflated.

The Martian's behavior had grown more confrontational of late. I wondered what made the creature so irritable. Of course, it was all alone on this planet, its cylinder crashed, its companion killed. It had been beaten, taken prisoner, hauled across the globe under less-than-pleasant circumstances. Though we had tried to be accommodating, surely this was not what the Martian explorers had expected.

The day grew warmer until I felt we would be broiled out in the open. At least the dry heat seemed less miserable than the humid, insect-infested miasmas of sweltering tropical islands where I had been forced to work after fleeing London. I searched the flat sands dotted with sage and mesquite, but could see no object that might be of interest to an extraterrestrial visitor. "So where are we going, Lowell?"

"You can just see it in the distance." We hit a rut and bounced, but he pointed without slowing the vehicle. I discerned a distinct raised landmark, the lip of a symmetrical mesa. "It is known to the locals, a most perplexing and scientifically interesting landmark: a perfectly symmetrical depression, a strange crater. I thought our visitor might find it interesting."

The dirt roads soon dwindled into mere paths used by Navajo shepherds or rugged white settlers. I reserved my own opinion about the crater. This seemed a long journey just to look at a hole in the ground, and I was about to say as much when the motor car broke down. The engine shuddered, coughed, and then hemorrhaged steam.

Lowell shifted his gears and attempted to start the engine again without bothering to ascertain the problem. When this proved unsuccessful, he hurled insults at the machine, as if he could command it just as he issued orders to his underlings. But the engine lay still.

We were far from commonly traveled roads, far from the rail line. In the past hour, we had seen no towns, encampments, or isolated homesteads. We couldn't simply wait and hope for rescue. It would be a long time before someone found us.

"I didn't plan for this part," Lowell said petulantly.

I raised and rejected possible solutions in my mind. Perhaps I could find a shepherd or a prospector; another alternative would be to head straight north until I encountered the railroad tracks, where I could flag down the next train. But I would have to walk for untold miles across this rough terrain, which was filled with rattlesnakes and scorpions, during the most intense heat of the afternoon.

In the meantime, what if the Martian grew ill? What a pathetic end for such a priceless specimen.

For the moment, I withheld my recriminations, but if we escaped this predicament I intended to have words with Lowell in private.

The Martian stirred, as if understanding the problem. It raised tentacles to detach the weather covering and, with a mighty heave, crawled over the motorcar's door. It dropped to the ground and began questing around with ungainly movements. Its every move seemed sinister and frightening. The Martian was an intimidating thing, as large as a bear, and its tentacles could easily snap our necks. We were all alone and defenseless if the beast should turn on us. However, the creature ignored us and used its tentacles to fold back the hood and probe inside the motorcar's engine.

"What is it doing?" Lowell asked.

"It's curious," I said.

"What if it damages the engine?"

I pointed out that neither of us had any hope of fixing it. Though he took pride in his motorcar, Lowell himself knew very little about how the vehicle functioned. My own expertise lay in biology and surgery; I knew nothing about engines.

I had a sudden inspiration. "Lowell, don't you have a small kit of tools in the rear of the motorcar? Give them to the Martian."

Lowell resisted the idea, then realized that we had little to lose. Though it did not comment, the Martian accepted the tools with apparent scorn, as if we had just handed it stone knives and bear skins. But it quickly determined the purpose of each tool, then attacked the engine, dismantling pieces, rerouting hoses, connecting filters.

The Martian applied itself with amazing intensity, rebuilding and redesigning the Benz engine according to some incomprehensible plan. I was reminded of my own efforts in vivisection, grafting organs, stretching the plasticity of living creatures.

The Martian did the same with the engine. Lowell and I sat in the minimal shade of the car. The desert air was hot and oppressive. The whole idea of an alien acting as our road mechanic seemed ridiculous, but the creature displayed an extraordinary technical aptitude, and was able to use our tools to construct a functional, if unorthodox, propulsion system.

When the Martian finished its ministrations, the

motorcar's engine started easily. And although the pistons purred and vibrated at a higher pitch than before, it seemed smoother, faster.

"Bravo!" Lowell brushed dust from his jacket as he stood. He hesitated, as if considering whether he should pat the Martian's back or somehow extend his appreciation. In our minds, the Martian said, *We go again*.

"Of course." Lowell climbed behind the driver's controls, and after the Martian had settled itself in the rear seat again, we were off toward the unusual landmark ahead.

* * *

My skepticism about the crater vanished as we approached the base of the rim's sudden and steep uplift. Our faint, rocky road petered out into a scattered maze of trails and footpaths.

When we had driven as far as we could go, Lowell locked the brakes. Snatching our picnic basket, he set his hat firmly on his head. "We will have to walk the rest of the way to the top. I look forward to your opinions and your reactions."

The Martian must have made a strange sight as it crawled out of the motorcar and followed us with an odd, lurching gait. We switchbacked right and left, ascending steeply. I could see the desert all around us, but I do not enjoy frivolous sightseeing. I hoped Lowell had not gotten it into his mind to convert our Martian ambassador into a simple tourist.

But when we finally reached the top of the crater, the sight robbed me of my breath. The change was abrupt and startling. The ground dropped away into a huge open bowl. I could see layers of strata like the rings of a cut-down tree, tan and reddish rock exposed as if a giant scoop had removed a perfectly round divot from the Earth's skin. The interior was speckled with juniper and sage all the way to the bottom.

Lowell set down our picnic basket. "Speculators have called this the remnant of a long-extinct volcano, but I have seen Sunset Crater and others here in Arizona. Personally, I believe it is the scar left by a tremendous heavenly impact, similar to the craters visible on the Moon."

The Martian remained on the rim, tentacles waving, its large round eyes studying the site. When the creature finally responded, its comment did nothing to dispel my uneasiness about its worsening mood and attitude. *Greater dangers than this can come from space.*

Lowell asked what it meant, but the Martian would say no more.

CHAPTER TWENTY-FIVE

SCIENTIFIC INVESTIGATIONS

T.H. Huxley was left alone in the laboratory spire with the three Martian master minds. Even though the Martians intended to invade Earth, destroy human civilization, and enslave mankind, the professor could not help but find them fascinating. They were as far from human beings on the evolutionary ladder as he himself was from the jellyfish he'd studied aboard the *Rattlesnake*.

He was deeply concerned about young Wells and Miss Robbins, not to mention his own fate. He supposed that these large-brained creatures intended to dissect him and perform a symphony of exotic and excruciating tests. In a detached way, he could understand the Martian curiosity, but he found it immensely bothersome to be a specimen instead of a colleague.

Since his younger days, Huxley had advanced his scientific knowledge by studying the works of other researchers. When those answers did not satisfy him, he embarked on his own journeys of discovery. By the age of fifteen, he had been apprenticed to his brother-in-law—a doctor—and later won a free scholarship to the Charing Cross Hospital's medical school. By twenty, Huxley had joined the Royal Navy's medical service. It was just the beginning of a life of scientific investigations.

Though he professed to be an agnostic—in fact, he had invented the term for popular use—Huxley felt that these Martians were *evil*.

From the Grand Lunar he already knew how the Martians had swept from the red planet, conquered the Moon, and raided all the healthy Selenites, stealing them to be slaves on another world. The Martians had exploited the drones, forcing them to reproduce, then to run all the burdens of their high-technology civilization. Huxley was sure, from what he had seen, that the Martians could no longer survive without their slaves.

But what had driven them to such a dire situation? What had the Martians done before stealing the Selenites? He did not know what sort of catastrophe had created the environmental disaster on Mars, but he had a deep-seated suspicion that the rapacious Martians with their short-sighted consumption and their urge to conquer and destroy had brought the tragedy upon themselves.

Perhaps other breeds of Martian had once lived on the red planet, creatures secondary to the bloated master minds. The superior Martians could have enslaved them first, exploited them, then driven them to extinction. Their industry could have caused the ecosystem to collapse, forcing the Martians to take extravagant gestures for their own survival. And for that, they required a vast pool of laborers. Hence, the lunar invasion.

And now, perhaps, the Selenite drones were no longer adequate for the Martians' new plans. They had to look elsewhere, deeper into the Solar System.

Huxley doubted these desperate creatures would reconsider their impending invasion of Earth, but nevertheless he held out hope, for combat never seemed a viable solution. He would hear what the master minds had to say, if they deigned to communicate with him at all.

From Wells's brain, the master minds had apparently extracted a general understanding of the human race, its temperament and biology; therefore, the creatures were aware of the work Huxley had done. No doubt, they found the old scientist much more valuable as a knowledgeable resource than as a manual laborer.

He thrust his chin forward and addressed the three alien leaders perched before him on their pedestals. "Go on, then—what do you have to show me?"

The nearest Martian reached its tentacles into a concealed alcove in its podium and removed a transparent ovoid object, a crystal egg like the one Moreau had described in his journal. "Ah, that is your observation and communication device!"

The Martian twisted the curved object so that images formed and flowed within, then held it out. Huxley saw that the crystal egg contained thousands of tiny facets, like the segments of a fly's eye, each one tuned to a specific "channel" that could connect to sister crystal eggs.

Squinting into the strange lens, he witnessed scenes of

Martian cities, canals, and industries, and hordes of Selenite workers completing gargantuan construction projects, like Israelite slaves forced to build Egyptian pyramids. The Martian master mind rotated the egg so that Huxley could see many views of the world. For an instant, he caught a glimpse of Wells and Miss Robbins standing together, dirty and sweating on a work line, but still alive and apparently unharmed.

The Martian's eyes brightened with a flare that seemed almost like anger. The image jolted and changed, sweeping to another planet entirely—and Huxley looked with amazement upon the bearded face of Dr. Moreau!

Standing amid the wreckage of what was clearly Cavor's laboratory at the Imperial Institute, the bear-like man peered into a counterpart crystal egg. Others paced through the ruins, poking about in the burned timbers, fallen bricks, and shattered glass. Several downcast scientists and engineers stood in the room. In the image, Cavor's assistants appeared particularly disheartened. Huxley saw their mouths moving but could hear no words from their lips.

The fire from the nitroglycerin explosion was extinguished by now, of course, but he saw singed papers and laboratory notebooks strewn on the floor, waterlogged in oily puddles. Holding the crystal egg, a scowling Moreau tromped about, kicking aside pieces of wreckage.

Judging from the visible damage, both Griffin and Cavor must have been killed in the frightful detonation. Huxley swallowed his anger, unable to conceive how even the mad invisible man could have worried about stealing weapons for Kaiser Wilhelm when the fate of the Earth hung in the balance!

Moreau gestured to where the missing cavorite sphere had

been cradled, pointed up into the sky. The other scientists looked at him skeptically, but the rogue biologist was insistent.

"Ah, I believe he's guessed it," Huxley shouted at the egg, but before he could see if Moreau reacted, the Martian snatched the object away. When it turned the egg again, the images vanished, showing only the greenish Martian sky.

The three master minds climbed into the control seats of their small personal walkers and, motioning for him to come, lurched off. Huxley accompanied them willingly, curious as to what they meant to show him next.

In a different room of the laboratory spire, the Martians showed him an enormous telescope the size of a giant cannon poking out of the tower, directing its lenses and mirrors toward Earth. In his travels, Huxley had seen the impressive Avu Observatory near Borneo; these observational devices were vastly superior to the best equipment Earthbound astronomers had.

Next, the creatures presented long maps to him. Huxley recognized the contours of England and Ireland, France and Spain. He saw mountain ranges and river valleys, the mosaic of cities, uneven roadways. Even the best maps drawn by the most meticulous explorers could not boast such precision and accuracy.

Huxley could identify some notable buildings—the cathedrals of Rome, the bridges and towers of London, immaculate Versailles in France—but the Martians were not interested in architecture. They paid greater attention to the British Navy, fleets of warships at sea, the fortifications of cities.

Huxley looked at the master minds in their thrumming walkers. Were they waiting for his assessment? Did they hope to intimidate him into surrendering on behalf of the human race, without even a fight? He hid any expression of dismay on his face, though he doubted they could interpret human emotions. "Clearly, you are drawing your plans against us."

Leaving the map surveillance room, the master minds guided Huxley out of the scientific cathedral. Looking upward, he saw one of the towering battle tripods as high as a tall Martian building. The high tripod stood with an open turret at the top of its three long legs, waiting to receive passengers. The three Martian leaders crawled out of their walking contrivances and onto a detachable platform; when Huxley joined them, the whole platform was levered upward on a jointed arm. He heard the rumble of engines, the groan of gears. The ground dropped dizzyingly away from him as they were lifted to the height of the tripod's control turret.

The Martians pressed him forward into the open door in the side of the turret. "I will say it's better to be inside than in a cage slung below." Working together, the three master minds grasped motivating levers and operated mechanisms until the side door of the turret sealed shut. Huxley braced himself against a curved metal wall as the towering tripod set off.

With its strangely awkward three-legged gait, the battle tripod lurched away from the Martian metropolis and out onto the rusty flatlands, covering distance swiftly with each extended leg. Holding on to maintain his balance, Huxley stared through the low windows until finally the tall machine reached an immense industrial site, where clouds of dust and smoke boiled upward.

"Now what are you trying to show me? Another mine or quarry?" No doubt such superior creatures as the Martians could communicate with him, if they chose, but they remained silent, as if to increase his fear.

In a veritable beehive of activity, amidst the smokes of factories and smelters, Selenite slave crews bustled about—building, installing, constructing in a never-faltering line of mass-production. They worked with metal presses and hot riveters, turning out and assembling huge sheets of red-hot armor that swiftly cooled to a silvery luster in the frigid air.

The battle tripod strode along, cresting a rise. As the turret tilted downward, Huxley could see the extent of the flat crater, a holding area, a landing field. There, a brand new war fleet was being constructed: row upon row of silvery cylinders gleamed, ready for launch—an entire invading navy, just like the one that had conquered the Moon centuries ago. A terrible rain of cylinders would descend upon Earth, pinpointing target after strategic target from the incredibly detailed surveillance maps the Martians had compiled by observing through their giant telescopes.

Huxley felt an inconsolable dread and helplessness. What could he possibly do against such an enemy? Selenites were completing the construction of hundreds of spacecraft, while sinister battle tripods watched their every move, forcing them to cooperate.

Occasionally, the towering guardian machines let out small blasts of their heat rays, but Huxley could see that the lunar creatures were already working as swiftly as they could. They had no choice in the matter.

With thousands of clever hands and strong bodies, the Selenites had assembled this war fleet, and it would certainly launch as the opposition of Mars approached. The three Martian master minds were looking at him, assessing his reaction. They must have sensed his primal fear, for they appeared to be smug and satisfied.

CHAPTER TWENTY-SIX

THE EYE OF THE GRAND LUNAR

"The longer we remain captives, the less chance we have to escape," Wells said. "Our time is short."

Jane labored beside him at the pumping station as heavy pistons chugged up and down, and foul-smelling steam hissed into the close catacombs. It had been only a day, but they were both very hungry. "I'm ready to escape when you are, H.G.—as soon as either of us thinks of a way."

If thousands of Selenite drones had been unable to break free after centuries of bondage, he couldn't imagine how two humans might manage it. Still, he said, "We should concoct a scheme together—our collaborative ideas are much better than anything I come up with alone."

Her arms and face were splattered with dark grease, and her chestnut hair had come undone, hanging loose around her face, yet even under these difficult circumstances, he found her more beautiful than ever. Jane was a strong woman and would endure whatever was required of her.

Isabel, on the other hand, would have wilted like a flower in such an ordeal. She would not have lasted an hour in the work catacombs beneath the cities of Mars. Grave and lovely Isabel was a product of her times, with no aspirations or interests other than planting a flower garden, doing embroidery, or sipping tea with her lady friends. Wells blamed himself for their fruitless marriage, too blind to recognize that his cousin would never fit comfortably with his intense curiosities. His own dissatisfaction, not Isabel's personal failings, had driven him from her.

Jane, though, had always been willing to share her ideas, and if she disagreed with his grand pronouncements, she would debate with him as an equal, though she had been only his student. When she needed more explanation, she boldly asked him questions, insisting that he go over a lesson again and again until she understood the topic. And in parrying her probing questions, Wells often found that he himself didn't comprehend the subject as well as he had thought.

"Remember when we resolved together to cure each other of ignorance?" he said to her now. "Let us similarly resolve to get ourselves free of this predicament and destroy the Martian threat."

"I accept the challenge," she said, making him smile. Her eyes were bright with determination instead of hopelessness.

A tone resonated through their silver collars, and a wordless but nevertheless clear command summoned him, Jane, and the Selenite drone crew to the surface levels. Wells's stomach tightened as he feared that the ravenous Martians were staging another butchery. How long would it be before the Martians grew curious as to what human blood tasted like?

He tugged unsuccessfully on the hated slave collar. "Once they take over the Earth, they'll have all the fresh red blood they can stomach."

But when they reached the street level and stood surrounded by the strange twisted spires of Martian architecture, he spotted that one of the glowing energy conduits had slipped from its track. A thick containment pipe was knocked out of alignment, sparking a bluish-white power flow into the air.

Jane also seemed relieved. "Just repairs. They want us to fix the conduit."

Wells grumbled. "Is it possible they have grown so dependent on the Selenite workers they can no longer maintain their own technology?"

"It may soon come to that," Jane said.

Hundreds of Selenites scurried around the power conduit supports, climbing the sides of buildings and tinkering with the components. Two drones touched the naked pulsing energy and died, spasming. Other Selenites carried off the twitching soot-stained bodies of their fallen fellows, while more of them climbed up to take their places.

The alien buildings were huge, and shadowy forms of Martian brains stirred behind the glittering segmented windows, but still the city seemed like a gigantic empty house, with far fewer Martians than Selenites. Only three of the slave-master walkers watched over the entire work crew, static whips ready.

Jane saw it, too. "Maybe this is our chance."

Wells did not know if the slave masters were eavesdropping. "We greatly outnumber the Martians, even with their heat rays and powerful machines. If only we could rally the Selenites."

Jane lifted her eyebrows and proudly reached into the folds of her tattered dress and withdrew the faceted gem, the petrified jewel-eye the Grand Lunar had removed from its face. "I've been wondering how we can use this. The Selenites won't do anything without a command from the Grand Lunar—maybe this is close enough."

Wells brightened, excited by the possibilities. "If only we could communicate with them, tell them what to do."

Following the instructions through their collars, the drone workers moved down the winding Martian street, adding supports and making repairs to other dilapidated power conduits that ran from building to building. The three slave masters in their small walking contrivances spread out, lashing static whips whenever necessary.

Moving close to a drone, Jane guardedly cupped the purplish gem in the palm of her hand and held it out so the Selenite slave could see. "This is from your Grand Lunar. Do you recognize it?"

The Selenite turned its ant-like head toward her, directing large burnished eyes at Jane's face, then down at her hand. The thin white creature froze. A dozen other drones stopped working as well. Now a rattling chitter began, at first quietly, then growing to a strange excited hum. The Selenites backed away from her, bowing their smooth heads as if in awe.

Wells was amazed at the reaction. These Selenite drones had been in captivity on Mars for many centuries, many generations. None of the creatures here on the red planet had ever seen the gardens on the Moon, or the Grand Lunar. Yet it immediately recognized the talisman from the powerful leader of all Selenites. He wondered if the drones possessed a form of racial memory transmitted from one generation to the next . . . or perhaps they were just one interconnected hive mind, a sentience distributed across the numerous Selenite components. Individual drones might die, but the hive brain continued.

He would have to remember to discuss the matter with Professor Huxley, once they had all escaped.

"Can you help us?" Wells said, sure the drones would never understand his words. "We must find a way to break free. We have to stop what the Martians intend to do to Earth." He made broad gestures with his hands and arms.

The Selenites looked at Wells, but found him lacking in some way. When Jane spoke again, though, the drones responded with genuine interest. "We need your help. Please." It seemed as if her possession of the talisman, the eye of the Grand Lunar, made her a worthy commander.

A humming discussion swept up and down the alien street to the entire Selenite work crew. As the twittering mutters continued, Wells noticed a difference in the character of the city itself. Before, the metropolis had been eerily devoid of voices, with only the hiss and grind of machinery. Now, though, like a jolt from a battery, the Martian city seemed to have come to life again . . . angry, restless life.

A clanking echoed down the curving, crowded streets. One of the ominous fighting tripods stalked among the tall buildings and structures. It let out a loud "*Ulla!*" to announce its arrival and careened down the boulevards toward the Martians' central cathedral of science. As it stopped next to a high platform outside of the immense building, they could just make out tiny figures emerging, a tall human herded by three bulky Martians into the main cathedral building. "Look, it's Professor Huxley!"

Relieved to see his mentor safe, Wells said, "This is not a time for rational planning and analysis. If the Selenites can help us, now is our chance. With any luck, we can rescue Professor Huxley and get away from this city."

"With any luck," Jane repeated with a sardonic laugh. "That's only one of many pieces of luck we'll need to get out of this."

"Jane, my dear, we are attempting to overthrow a planet and save our race. One must hope for a bit of good fortune. Now, if only you could convince the Selenites to create some sort of massive distraction."

Jane gestured to the nearest slave master clomping toward them in its squat walking machine. "We need to get away from the Martians. Do you know how we might break free?"

The silent drone turned its blank insect face at her, as if incapable of making a response. She asked another Selenite, and a third, but received the same silence.

"These are *drones*, Jane—docile, cooperative, and hardworking. They don't know how to respond when you ask for suggestions. They need a master mind to command them, whether it's the Grand Lunar or these Martian slave masters." His blue eyes narrowed, and he clutched her arm. "Or *you*, Jane. They listen to you. So, give them instructions."

Jane's hard anger and disgust with what the Martians were doing found its focus; Wells saw it on her face. She raised her voice to rally the Selenites around her. "The Martian city functions only because of your labor! I command you to ignore all instructions the Martians give you, for I bear the talisman of the Grand Lunar. Listen only to me."

Though they still made no answer, the Selenites ceased their work and looked up at her. Disturbed by the odd restless behavior of the Selenites, the three slave masters strode about, slashing with static whips. From their walker domes, the Martians sent stern commands vibrating through the collars again. But the Selenites did not budge. They had received other orders from Jane.

"Now shut down the machinery. Cut power to the city." Jane looked over at Wells, who nodded vigorously.

The Selenites threw themselves into their new task, falling to their uprising as if it were simply another job. The drone crew spread out and methodically began ripping free the conduit supports they had just installed and knocking down the heavy power channels. Sparks rained out in all directions. Shimmers of energy in the tall Martian turrets went dark.

The slave masters strode about in their ostrich-like walkers, vigorously trying to impose order with static whips. One of the gushing power conduits fell down upon the nearest slave master, and the machine jittered and sparked. Inside its now-darkening dome, the bloated Martian brain lay in a smoking heap. When the power surge died, the Selenites banded together and pushed until they toppled the walking contrivance to the ground.

The other two slave masters sounded a loud alarm of "*Ulla! Ulla!*" Wells ran toward the fallen walker. "Jane, if you use the communication device, you can send specific commands through the collars." The Martian had opened the dome of the small walker halfway in an attempt to escape before being electrocuted. Wells shoved the dome the rest of the way open and found the small apparatus with which he had seen the slave masters issue their hateful orders. He held it up. "It still appears to be functional. Here, try it."

Jane held the device, saw how it was designed to resonate with all the slave collars, and then continued with the fervor of a syndicalist labor organizer. The Selenites around them finally understood precisely what she wanted them to do. "Destroy the generators and the atmosphere-pumping stations! Break down the water-distribution network, block the canals! You can all do it. Bring these evil masters to a standstill."

Now the Selenites excelled in their methodical mayhem. Drones smashed through crystal sheets that formed large windows. They cracked open the streamlined canal, spilling water like cold, clear blood all down the Martian streets. Selenites splashed through the vital water as they moved to other targets.

While Wells and Jane cheered in delight, the lunar slaves raced about in diligent silence just like the ominously quiet Martians.

From the work tunnels beneath the metropolis, explosions rang out. Pistons and underground generators were sabotaged, their gears jammed, their couplings frozen. Geysers of steam poured out of hydrothermal vents, blasting the paving mosaics of the Martian streets.

Within minutes the alien city was caught up in a hurricane of rebellion. Wells had expected Jane's command to affect only the drone workers around them, but he could see that the revolt was spreading with amazing rapidity throughout the metropolis. Apparently, the signal had traveled among all the nearby slave collars, and the Selenites had spread the call.

"You certainly know how to create a diversion, Jane."

She fixed her eyes on the huge tripod that had just returned to the cathedral of science. "Come on, H.G. Let's get Professor Huxley."

CHAPTER TWENTY-SEVEN

AN UNFORTUNATE DISCOVERY

FROM THE JOURNAL OF DR. MOREAU

With problematic expediency, A.E. Douglass returned from Massachusetts. We had hoped he would tarry for many weeks inspecting the great lenses for the observatory's largest refractor. Now we had to deal with the assistant's irritating curiosity again.

"Old Mr. Clark and his sons are doing an admirable job. However, they work best—and faster—without meddlesome observers like myself." Douglass pushed his glasses up on his nose, as if to gather courage. "Since you insisted that the telescope be completed with all possible speed, Mr. Lowell, I decided you would want me to return here."

Lowell's moustache bristled as he took umbrage at the

young astronomer's attitude. "Please refresh yourself and unpack your things. I wish to speak with Dr. Moreau alone."

I watched out the window of the main house as the thin young man hurried to unload his traveling trunk. Douglass scanned the observatory construction site to determine how well the work had progressed while he was gone. When he thought no one was looking, he furtively glanced at the shuttered outbuilding where we kept our Martian.

Lowell spoke in a cold and brittle voice. "I'm afraid that young man will cause trouble, Moreau."

"Yes, he will. And it behooves us to deal with it in a manner of our *own* choosing, rather than let Douglass make a mess of things because of his persistent curiosity." I poured myself a glass of brandy from a decanter. "It would have been best if he'd remained back east, but he is here now, and he knows we are hiding something from him—something of extreme importance."

Lowell had turned his back to me and was staring out the window. "Then I will have to dispatch him on another errand."

I shook my head. "If you send him away again, either he will not go, or he will quit. After which, he will certainly report your mystery to others."

"All men talk." Lowell declined the brandy I offered him. "All men pass rumors. There is enough gossip around here with the townspeople."

"*Think*, Lowell! When a drunken man in a Flagstaff saloon speaks of ghosts and monsters, no one of importance listens to him. But what if Douglass talks to Pickering at Harvard, or to the officials at Yerkes Observatory? The news that you have a captive Martian hidden away would invite outright scorn for you." I could see by his troubled expression that my words had an effect. "You are already viewed as eccentric in Boston society, but no one can fault you for your keen observations about Japan. You've earned a certain amount of respect, but that can vanish as swiftly as ice on a hot sidewalk if you are not careful. We cannot risk it, especially now that we are on the cusp of a great announcement."

His voice was low, but no longer so antagonistic. "You obviously have some plan, Moreau."

I came to stand beside him at the window. Douglass had retired to his rooms in the newly completed guest house. "You and I have had the Martian to ourselves here for a month. Three times that long, if you count from the date of the crash in the Sahara and the trip on the steamer. By dissecting the other specimens, I have learned much about alien physiology. We have made thorough inquiries about the Martian civilization. The time has come for us to announce our results—and, by God, receive the accolades we deserve from the scientific community!"

Thunderstruck, Lowell looked like a spoiled boy who did not wish to share his toys. "But . . . but we have so much more to learn from it."

"There will be more to learn for the rest of our lives. Look at the size of its brain! However, even if we deliver our specimen to the London Zoo or the Smithsonian Institution, you and I will forever remain a dozen steps ahead of our competitors. No matter what else happens, *we* are the ones who rescued the Martian from the cylinder. *I* am the one who performed the grafting surgery and cured it from its near-fatal illness."

I took a sip of brandy and sighed, trying to sound conciliatory. "This is not the time, the place, or the method by which I would have chosen to reveal our prize specimen, but that cannot be helped. Let us enlist Douglass and turn him into an ally instead of an enemy."

Lowell's shoulders sagged, and he looked defeated. "Very well."

* * *

The young astronomer's owlish eyes were wide as he stared at the crystal egg. "Truly astonishing!"

"This is only a fraction of the amazing things we have," Lowell said.

I was a bit gruffer. "Now perhaps you will understand our initial reluctance to let anyone else in on our secret. Observe." I turned the crystal egg so that the fly-eye facets across its exterior showed the fantastic images of Martian landscape. Douglass saw canals and rust-laden sands, massive construction projects, and the dying cities of a once-glorious civilization.

The young man's face was so full of excitement I was afraid he might have some sort of breakdown. "This crystal egg is the most astounding new observing device I have ever seen! A simple viewing ellipsoid that one can hold in the palm of a hand, is superior to . . . to everything!"

Lowell had been so engrossed in the Martian specimen that he had not considered the straightforward implications of this subsidiary technology, how this crystal egg would revolutionize all of astronomy. Observing through the eyepiece of a telescope would become a quaint old custom.

But even as Douglass saw the possibilities of the observation device, I was more concerned about the suddenly inferior images in the crystal egg: the details were blurred and distances smeared. Perhaps a dust storm was sweeping across the Martian terrain. Or were the Martians—either our captive specimen or others on the red planet—directly distorting or blocking the signal? Were they trying to hide something from us?

Lowell sounded paternal instead of stern and testy. "Believe me when I say to you, Andrew, that this crystal egg is only one of the new things we will show you. But you must be patient. One cannot consume an enormous banquet all in one gulp."

Douglass agreed—too quickly. To my everlasting shame, neither Lowell nor I saw fit to issue sterner warnings or keep a better eye on the young man. We should have known better. The worst thing one can possibly say to a man of obvious curiosity is to tell him to leave certain things alone.

* * *

Screams rang out in the dead of night, blood-curdling shrieks that woke me from a sound sleep. At first I thought I was having a nightmare about my unsuccessful vivisections, but as I sat up in the darkness listening to a breeze hiss through the pines on Mars Hill, the shrieks came again like the cry of a tortured soul . . . or a man being flayed alive.

I was up in a flash, throwing on trousers and a shirt and bursting out of the main house. Lowell appeared beside me, and we both ran into the night.

A final fading gurgle came from the shuttered outbuilding. Then we heard splintering wood and a scuffling, thudding sound as of something large and ungainly rushing about.

Afterward, piecing together the evidence, I determined that Douglass must have waited until we were fast asleep, then crept out of his room to approach the shed. Foiled by the padlock on the door, he had gone around the sides to peer through the high boarded-up windows. He had worked a small, flat pry-bar into the crack of the shutters, finally pulling the boards apart. He must have held the edge of the window, standing on tiptoe to squint into the gloom.

The Martian had grabbed Douglass's arms and yanked him inside with superhuman force. The creature's strength was surprisingly great—sufficient to splinter the wooden slats inward. The Martian had dragged Douglass into the darkened outbuilding. That was when the young astronomer had begun his terrified screams, but the alien was not finished with him.

When Lowell and I finally arrived at the scene, the shed door had been smashed outward, the padlock snapped. I was astounded to realize that the Martian must have been able to escape at any time, but had chosen not to. Until now.

Standing inside the empty chamber, we heard only a faint, quiet dripping. Nothing stirred. Lowell struck a match. The Martian was gone, as I had feared. So intent was I on the disappointing loss of our specimen that I did not immediately see the battered body of Andrew Douglass lying on the packed dirt floor. But Lowell did.

In the fading light of the match, I recognized that Douglass had been strangled. When its victim stopped struggling, the Martian must have ripped open the young astronomer's jugular vein and torn a gouge in the young man's chest, attempting to drain as much fresh blood as it could, even without hypodermic syringes.

But the sinister creature must have known we were coming: it had fled. Therefore, it understood that it had committed some sort of crime. I was shocked. "Why would it do this? It makes no sense. We fed it as much blood as it needed."

Lowell stared in horror at the corpse of his assistant. "This wasn't done for food. This was just to demonstrate . . . power, malice. The Martian has been toying with us, stringing us along. It saw its chance, and it struck—"

"Don't be so quick to judge what an alien thinks, Percival."

"Perhaps not. We thought we were establishing trust with it—and now poor Douglass is dead."

I looked to the door. "Worse yet, the Martian is out there loose right now."

As he let fall the limp hand of his assistant, Lowell looked as he had when we'd come upon the dead crewman aboard the transatlantic steamer. That was a crime we had managed to hide, however. We had protected the Martian . . . only to let it kill again.

Unlike a rude and penniless crewman, however, the murder of a young Harvard astronomer would not go unnoticed. Douglass's connection to Percival Lowell and the Flagstaff Observatory was well known. My mind was already racing, wondering if we would be forced to announce prematurely our visitor from another world. If so, perhaps we could portray Douglass as a tragic victim of scientific curiosity . . . .

We heard the boom of a gunshot and angry shouts from the construction camp out among the pines. Some of the workmen must also have been roused by the screams. Unfortunately, they had found our escaped specimen first.

We ran from the outbuilding toward the shouts as a second loud shotgun blast erupted. "Hurry! We must get to the Martian before they kill it."

Lowell set his jaw and hurried after me, though he now seemed willing just to let the workmen do what they would to the murderous creature.

We caught up with the scattered mob. Some workers carried kerosene lamps; others waved flaming brands they had grabbed from their campfires. Most held makeshift weapons: wooden boards, a pitchfork, a tree branch. A broad-shouldered man with a shotgun pushed his way to the front of the group, looking full of superstitious fear.

The workmen had cornered the Martian in a dense stand of ponderosa pines. The bloated alien backed against the rough sap-studded bark, raising its tentacles as if in surrender. Pale starbursts of splintered wood showed where a shotgun blast had struck the trunk. Scattered pellets had already injured its hide, and the burly man aimed his gun again.

I charged in like a bear on a rampage. "Stop! Not another shot, you fool! You'll hurt it."

"It's a monster, sir!"

"Kill it before it kills us," said someone else. "We heard the screams. It's already done murdered three or four for sure."

"If you harm my specimen, you will answer to *me*—and I promise you a more fearsome fate than anything this creature can do to you."

The workers muttered, looking cowed. Showing no fear, I grabbed the shotgun out of the startled man's hands. Seeing the wounded Martian helpless and trapped, Lowell reluctantly supported me. "Do as he says."

I passed the shotgun to Lowell, and he clung to it in a daze while I stepped closer to the injured Martian. Having seen Douglass's broken body, I knew full well that I was risking my own safety, but I needed to maintain my dominance over the creature.

I turned to the frightened workers, speaking for the Martian's benefit as much as mine. "Yes, this creature was provoked into killing a man. Is it surprising when a circus lion rears up and turns upon a trainer who has been abusing it? Of course not! You know how dangerous a mother grizzly can be when she protects her cubs." I lowered my voice, hoping to placate them. "Our friend Andrew Douglass was brash and unwise, and he paid for it with his life. This . . . animal is far too valuable to be killed for your petty vengeance."

The men began muttering and grumbling. By morning, word of this story would spread, but Lowell and I could prepare our own documents, submit our discoveries to newspaper reporters and the scientific community. We had crossed the Rubicon, and there could be no turning back.

"Go! All of you," Lowell said angrily, still gripping the

shotgun. "Dr. Moreau and I will handle this matter."

After the men hesitantly drifted back to their camp, Lowell and I glowered at the cornered Martian. "Regardless of what I said, Moreau, it may be in our best interests to shoot that monster for what it has done." I was disturbed by his expression of utter defeat.

Too many times I was reminded of the narrow-minded fools who tried to destroy me because of my unorthodox but necessary work. I turned and commanded the Martian. "Back into your building, where you will remain! We will face many difficulties because of what you have done tonight."

As if recognizing that Lowell truly meant to kill it, the Martian scuttled back toward the outbuilding. I saw that its injuries were minor from the shotgun pellets, and decided not to waste the time or effort dressing them. Perhaps a bit of suffering would make the creature contemplate the outrages it had committed.

When we got back to the splintered door of the shed and somberly removed Douglass's wretched body, I barricaded the opening as best I could, nailing board after board across the openings. I replaced the hasp and added several more chains to keep our captive securely inside.

I hoped the Martian—and all of us—would now be safe.

CHAPTER TWENTY-EIGHT

REVOLT ON MARS

Wild alarms continued to ring through the thin air, echoing off the curved buildings. A monotonous *"Ulla! Ulla!"* resounded from the turrets as the Martian city began to fall in the astonishing Selenite insurrection.

Wells and Jane couldn't have been more pleased with the result.

Insistent messages from other slave masters continued to buzz through their communication collars, but the Selenites paid no attention to any of the commands; they heeded only the orders given by Jane, who carried the eye of the Grand Lunar.

The drones raced about in oddly coordinated and regimented confusion, like wind-up toys. Though they had no ultimate commander, the Selenites acted in concert, all following a vague but consistent plan. Chittering now, they raced through central buildings and up sloping ramps. The white drones far outnumbered their bloated masters, despite the Martian walkers and weapons. They swarmed in a mad parade of sabotage.

They barged into the main complexes where Martian generals had developed plans for invading other worlds. Selenites uprooted projection apparatus, tore apart map displays. Fifteen of them wrestled with the huge, high-resolution telescopes through which the Martians had spied upon Earth. First they disconnected the support struts, broke the aiming gears, and then by brute force they shoved the telescope barrel through the crystal window of the high tower. Like an astronomer's cannon, the telescope fell out of its yoke and toppled to the street far below, smashing with a tremendous clang. Then the drones destroyed everything else in the war room.

Heedless of their own safety, Selenites crawled over and then toppled the iron-ostrich walking contrivances of Martian master minds that attempted to flee the scientific cathedral. Rousted out of their squat machines, several lumbering creatures scuttled along the streets. A bloodthirsty mob on Earth would have chased after the large-brained slave masters and torn them limb from tentacled limb, but the lunar denizens thought differently. They went about their revolt with an efficient and intense swiftness, without unnecessary frenzy.

Knowing what the Martians had done to the utopia on the Moon and having seen their horrific method of feeding on the Selenites, Wells felt inclined to do a bit of smashing himself. Years ago, when that brutish student had kicked him in the kidneys, Wells had not understood what could provoke such mindless fury. But now he himself felt a need for vengeful violence. Perhaps he was not after all the socially enlightened human being T.H. Huxley had always taught him to be. Perhaps he was a savage animal inside. Perhaps all men were.

Explosions continued to rumble through underground tunnels; tiled street intersections collapsed into deep sinkholes. A clamor of groaning machinery rose from below as heavy industries hammered to a stop. Tendrils of smoke and steam curled upward, like the last gasps of fetid breath rising from the dying in a plague ward.

Jane grabbed his arm, and they ran down the street, dodging swiftly methodical Selenites in the process of wrecking sophisticated machinery. The drones gave Jane a wide berth, as if she were visiting royalty.

Ahead loomed the immense cathedral of science, where Huxley was still being held. Beside the main laboratory spire stood the lone battle tripod that had recently returned with the professor from the desert. Through the cathedral's transparent walls and faceted windows, Wells spotted groups of Martians splashing out of their nutrient pools and scrambling into walking contrivances or mechanical cars, evacuating. Others climbed down into enclosed bubble-dome boats and launched into the canal systems to escape, some raising their weapons to quell the revolt.

Even with their sophisticated technology, the Martians could not react swiftly enough. The Selenites were too widespread, too entrenched in all the nooks and crannies of the metropolis. Through their strange linked minds, the drones had risen up with unrestrained violence, and their attacks became coordinated.

Wells yanked Jane aside as crumbling shards from a broken

wall pattered onto the streets. They huddled under an overhang until it was safe again to run forward and pick their way toward the ornate complex.

A dozen more Martian battle tripods marched in from the red desert to impose swift order. Taller than the highest steeple, the majestic but frightening machines let out a resounding *"Ulla! Ulla!"* Segmented arms bent upward, tilting the rotating lenses of their heat rays. Jane cried out a warning into the communication collars, and just before terrible yellow waves of incineration smote the squealing drones.

The Selenites scattered, then regrouped, despite the flaming death carved by the heat rays. The drones had no interest in individual salvation; other lunar rebels congregated and struck the Martian facilities again and again, wrecking the ancient infrastructure. Striding like goliaths through the streets, the battle tripods continued their blazing retaliation, but even twelve of the huge machines could not root out every group of lunar saboteurs.

Amidst the terrible struggle, Wells looked up with alarm to see a bloated Martian scramble onto the balcony of the cathedral's laboratory spire and work its way toward the standing tripod that had recently returned with the professor. Wells growled, "I intended to commandeer that tripod. Imagine how fast we could escape across the desert—if I can figure out how to make it work."

He tugged Jane's arm, and they ran with redoubled speed. When he reached the base of the stilt-like leg, Wells gazed upward, intimidated. This was much taller and more imposing than he had expected. The thick metal leg was studded with small grooves and depressions that served as steps for nimble feet—probably so Selenite workers could polish and maintain the tripod.

Wells had no fondness for great heights, but after everything he and Jane had been through, this was a relatively minor fear. Taking her hand to help her up, he began to ascend the tripod's leg.

"I hope the Martian doesn't get this contraption moving while we're still climbing," Jane called. "It would shake us off like a beetle on a trouser leg."

Wells tried to sound optimistic, for her sake. "We're in the middle of a grand adventure, Jane! Such a fate would be much too embarrassing an end for intrepid heroes."

"Life isn't always like a story."

"True enough. Life rarely offers neat resolutions to problems."

The tripod began to vibrate as the Martian took its place inside the control turret. It activated the powerful engines to drive the war machine into the fray.

Wells scrambled higher. "Hang on, Jane! It's going to take a step."

"Just don't fall and knock me down with you."

Gritting his teeth, he held on as the tripod leg lifted up and clanged down; then the rear leg swept forward past them in a clockwork motion that pulled the giant walker along. The Martian was apparently unaware of its passengers.

Sweat dripped into his eyes, but he saw the bottom of the control turret immediately above him—with an access hatch offset from where the three stilt-like legs converged in the engines. With renewed determination and an increased sense of urgency, he pulled himself to the juncture where the three legs fit into lubricated sockets. The trapdoor was now within reach.

Swaying sickeningly, Wells waited for the Martian to pause between its rhythmic steps, grasped the hatch and pushed hard. The cover flung open with surprising ease and smashed down onto the turret's metal floor. Wells hauled himself up into the control chamber, afraid the tentacled Martian would rush over to defend itself. He turned to help Jane, but she shouted for him to go.

Seated amidst its levers, the alien master mind yanked the heavy control rods with a flurry of tentacles to keep the tripod moving. Noticing Wells as he climbed through the bottom of the turret, the creature spun about. It thrashed in agitation, huge yellow eyes glaring.

Wells stepped forward, squaring his shoulders, bunching his fists—and didn't know what to do next. The master mind released its grip on the controls and raised itself, lashing its appendages like whips. Without the direct control of its driver, the tripod shuddered to a halt, and behind him, Jane climbed to safety inside the turret. The naked Martian scuttled away from the controls in full retreat but with nowhere to go. Without access to its armored protective machinery, its body was soft and vulnerable. Wells chased the creature, while Jane seized the opportunity to detach one of the heavy control rods from its socket.

As the Martian lurched backward in the confined space of the turret, Jane came up behind it and lifted the metal lever like a club. She set her face in a firm scowl and, without remorse or hesitation, swung the lever sideways like a cricket bat. She landed a blow across the front of the Martian's head above its yellow eyes. "Superior race, indeed!" She sniffed.

A dark stain oozed across its brown, leathery cranium. As the stunned Martian fumbled about, disoriented, Wells and Jane kicked the alien master mind to the open hatch; then, with a united shove, they pushed it through. Its tentacles flailed to catch itself, but the bloated brain slid out of the dome. The Martian tumbled from a great height and struck the ground, where it broke open like a heavy, rotten fruit.

Jane wiped tangled hair away from her grimy face. "That was unpleasant."

"But necessary. Now we must learn to control this machine ourselves."

Jane replaced the control lever she had used as a club, snapping it back into place. Wells scrutinized the mechanisms, pulling rods and levers. He succeeded in lifting one of the tripod legs, and by pulling another lever he set it down a large step forward. Without coordinated balance, though, the tall walker wobbled and swayed like a drunken man balancing on top of a barrel.

Wells tried other controls, hoping to stabilize the battle tripod. With successive attempts, he moved one leg, then the other two without toppling the big machine. It was like performing an unfamiliar court dance, but as he guided the tripod through several more steps, he began to grin like a boy. "I could become accustomed to the complexities of walking with three legs instead of two. It's like riding a bicycle for the first time!" He painstakingly retraced their path down the chaotic street, dodging rubble.

Jane stooped to look through the low turret windows set at a Martian's eye level, trying to find their way back to the laboratory spire and Huxley. While they climbed up the legs of the contraption they had traveled a surprising distance. "Over there." She pointed back to the crowded skyline. "Head in that direction."

As Wells clumsily guided them toward the scientific cathedral and its uniform towers, Jane inspected the rest of the tripod's controls. One set raised and lowered the jointed arm that terminated in the heat-ray projector. As she experimented with the small levers, a blurry and distorted display moved across a highlighted projection screen. Her brow furrowed, and Wells remembered that look of intent concentration from when she had struggled to understand a new concept of chemistry or mathematics. Then her face lit up. "Oh! It's the targeting circle!"

Ahead, two squat Martian walkers were harassing a group of Selenites. They lashed out with static whips to drive the drones away from a generating station. With anger tightening her expression, Jane adjusted the bright targeting point on her screen, aiming at the much smaller walker devices on the street. Then she depressed several buttons until she discovered how to activate the heat ray.

A gush of thermal energy poured out to engulf the cruel Martian slave masters. Within seconds, they and their contrivances had melted into unrecognizable blobs like solder. Jane seemed quite pleased with herself.

Wells finally managed to maneuver their swaying tripod up against the spire where they had last seen T.H. Huxley. Toying with controls, Jane discovered the booming voice projection system. "Professor! Professor Huxley, we're here to rescue you." Her feminine voice sounded strange and unexpected from the stilt-legged war machine. "We're in the tripod."

From behind the curved turret window, Wells saw a distinctly human silhouette moving swiftly but erratically as slouching hunchbacked shapes chased him. "He's broken free, but we've got to get him out of there. Jane, can you control the heat ray well enough to open up the wall for him?"

"The professor would insist that I try." Jane swiveled the jointed arm to point the heat ray at a nearby Martian building, away from the laboratory spire. She operated the controls, centered her aim, and let loose a burst of incinerating fury. The structure exploded in a shower of fire, sparks, and shrapnel.

"Just a bit of target practice." She brushed hair out of her eyes. As she aimed the targeting point, she shouted a warning through the loudspeaker system. "Stand away from the window, Professor!" Through the murky glass, they saw Huxley's figure duck away, and Jane fired a brief burst, just enough to blast an opening in the wall.

The older man immediately appeared at the smoldering hole, flapping his hands to disperse the fumes and smoke. Under one arm he cradled rolled charts and maps he had grabbed from his captors.

Jane opened the turret's side door, only to see that they were dizzyingly high above the ground. Wells nudged the controls, and the battle tripod wavered and shuddered. "I don't dare maneuver it closer!"

Holding onto the metal wall of the turret, Jane leaned out over the gulf, extending her hand beseechingly. Huxley looked at the wide, dangerous gap. "Alas, we aren't on the Moon . . . but gravity here is still lower than Earth's."

"Jump, Professor!"

Inside the laboratory spire, the Martian master minds that

had been driven back by the heat ray blast now converged upon their prisoner again. Huxley seemed uncertain until the malicious Martians squirmed up behind him. One of them seated itself inside the hideous contraption the Grand Inquisitor had used to probe Wells's brain.

Huxley raised his chin, clutched his maps more tightly, gathered his resolve—and jumped. The distance seemed impossible, and Wells's heart lurched, but Huxley easily cleared the gap. He landed inside the turret still holding his maps, exhilarated by the spectacular leap. "I feel like an Olympian!"

Jane drew the old man to safety, closing the side hatch behind him. "Go, H.G."

Catching his breath, Huxley observed the mayhem in the streets, noted the stolen battle tripod, and nodded with gruff satisfaction. "Ah, I see that you two have everything perfectly under control."

"Remember, our intent was to bring down an enemy civilization, Professor." Wells pivoted the tripod, and it lurched drunkenly away. "One cannot overthrow an entire world without stirring things up a bit." He quickly fell into a rhythm, and they strode on a trio of stilt legs along the streets, seeking a way out of the city.

One of the dozen other battle tripods moved on a perpendicular course to intercept them. Apparently, the Martian driver suspected that the war machine had been stolen. "We have trouble," Wells said. "But they can't know who we are."

"Let us hope the Martian hesitates," Huxley said.

"I don't intend to give it a chance to hesitate." Grimly, before the other Martian fighting machine could take aggressive action, Jane blasted with her heat ray. The intense beam decapitated the enemy tripod, turning its turret into a splash of cherry-red metal. Out of control, whirling and spinning, it crashed into a tall building before collapsing in a gargantuan heap on the streets.

They left the metropolis behind, heading into an open wilderness laced with carefully laid canals. Behind them, more Martian alarms sounded as the aliens climbed into mechanical bodies, operating heavy cars, installing weapons to be turned against the Selenite rebels.

Worse, against a backdrop of smoke and turmoil at the skyline of the Martian metropolis, the humans could see four powerful battle tripods raise their heat rays and set off in pursuit of the escapees.

Still trying to master the coordination of the alien controls, Wells did his best to flee out into the open desert.

CHAPTER TWENTY-NINE

THE MONSTER OF MARS HILL

FROM THE JOURNAL OF DR. MOREAU

We made many mistakes with our Martian, Lowell and I. As I write these last entries, I recall numerous things we should have handled differently, obvious risks that led to dire consequences. Our worst error, though, was that neither of us was suspicious enough. Not until it was too late—much too late.

After locking up the Martian, Lowell and I discussed what we must do. The shaken construction crew had returned to their camp settlement, but we would lose many of them. They'd refuse to work, afraid the "monster of Mars Hill" would go on another rampage. By the following night, the stores, streets, and saloons of Flagstaff would be abuzz with the terrifying story of the hideous alien beast.

As I feared, the construction site sat idle the next day. Mars Hill was eerily silent. The support buildings and sheds were built and painted; the largest dome was finished, waiting to receive the Clark refractor from Massachusetts. But all the workers had stayed away. The observatory would never be finished in time for the alignment of Earth and Mars later this year.

Lowell stewed with indecision, pacing about the main house. The Martian stirred and thumped within its padlocked shed, but Lowell and I avoided the creature, letting it brood over what it had done to poor Douglass. Foolishly, we imagined it might have feelings of guilt or remorse. We were so stupid.

I am a scientist, a biologist; some even call me a genius. I am not, however, an undertaker. But since I knew Lowell would be loath to do it, I prepared the young man's body. I understood the need to prevent questions and superstitious terror from hindering our work here.

I cleaned up Douglass's fatal injuries, wiped away the blood, and tried to disguise his worst bruises and contusions. With his face still somewhat pliable, though rigor had begun to set in, I did my best to erase the expression of terror, making him look much more at peace.

After Lowell had already fortified himself with at least one snifter of brandy, we wrapped the corpse and placed it in the back of the Benz motorcar. No doubt after hearing the rumors, the sheriff of Flagstaff expected us. I was surprised he hadn't already come up to Mars Hill to make inquiries.

We stopped the puttering motorcar in front of the jailhouse

and told the sheriff of our companion's murder. The man had a drooping moustache and grizzled whiskers so thick that he was either attempting to grow a beard or avoiding the prospect of a regular shave. I did most of the talking, for I had a cooler head. When I described how Douglass had provoked and been attacked by a large exotic animal ("from Borneo") we kept caged at the observatory site, Lowell simply agreed with the story. The "monster" had escaped, and the men from the work site had assisted us in rounding it up.

"I assure you, Sheriff," I said, "the specimen is now properly caged. We have added additional locks and chains to ensure that it has no further opportunity to escape. Much as we grieve for our lost colleague, the blame for his death lies in his own misadventure."

The sheriff sucked on his lips, considering. He didn't seem to want to make extra work for himself. "And both of you gentlemen guarantee that this creature of yours will cause no further danger? If it's like a rabid dog, we need to put it down."

"It is not a rabid animal. This entire mishap was a fluke, nothing more."

Lowell had said little, and the sheriff turned to him with narrowed eyes. "Do you agree with this gentleman's account, Mr. Lowell? Is that exactly the way things happened last night?"

With only the briefest hesitation, Lowell nodded. "You can take the word of Dr. Moreau."

The man sat up in his chair. "All right then. You'd best take the body over to the undertaker's and get him prepared for burial."

The sheriff's lack of questions did not surprise me. While he might have met Douglass once or twice, everyone in Flagstaff knows that Percival Lowell is a wealthy man with a great deal of influence. His observatory project was welcomed by the town, and the local economy had prospered greatly from it. If the sheriff had any sense, he would take Lowell at his word.

"We won't be burying young Andrew in Arizona Territory," Lowell said. "I'll have the undertaker build a sturdy box and pack him in salt for shipment to Massachusetts." He turned to me, his face set and determined. "He doesn't belong here. We will send him back to his own people. Let Harvard take care of him."

We spent the afternoon in town, taking care of the arrangements. I sensed that no one in Flagstaff was willing to be hurried even at the best of times, and when it came to a dead man about to be sent across the country, no one understood why we needed to be impatient.

In a noisy local café, we ate beefsteaks, eggs, and beans spiced with hot chiles. Lowell looked exhausted and diluted of stamina. Finally, late in the day as clouds were gathering for an afternoon thunderstorm, we climbed into the motorcar and headed home.

With the construction workers gone, Mars Hill seemed like a ghost town. By the time we drove up to the main house, rain had begun pelting down. Lowell disengaged the Benz's gears and shut down the engine. As I climbed out of the car and into the downpour, the wind picked up, making the pines scratch and rustle together.

I shouted, "Shouldn't we check on the Martian? We've left it alone all day."

"I have no further interest in that creature."

Not wanting to push him, especially now, I joined Lowell inside the main house, where we sat together in the withdrawing room. Our small telescopes stood under the shelter of the porch, but with the dense clouds and rain, we would have no opportunity for any observing this night.

Finally I raised the question. "We must make our announcement to the world, Lowell. If rumors of Douglass's death strike anger or horror in the astronomical community, we will not be heard objectively. But if we reveal our Martian now, the sheer excitement will make the young man's murder a mere footnote to the story."

"Yes," Lowell said, his voice empty, "it will be a sensation. We have the Martian itself and the preserved cadavers of the other specimens. We can even send an expedition out to salvage the silver cylinder that crashed in the Sahara."

I frowned. "Let us hope Tuareg scavengers haven't stripped all the metal from it and destroyed any scientific benefit we might gain."

Lowell refilled his brandy snifter and swallowed another large gulp. "Most importantly, we have the crystal egg."

He went to the cabinet and took out the lovely, shining object. We sat together as he turned and tilted the ellipsoid. By now we had lit all the lamps in the room against the early darkness from the continuing rainstorm.

Thunder rattled the windowpanes like blows from a hammer, and water poured down, streaking the glass. I thought about the Martian confined in its outbuilding. On its arid, dying world, had it ever seen a summer rainstorm?

Was it terrified or delighted to see droplets of water falling from the sky?

Lowell hunched over the crystal egg, turning it under the lamplight. "Look, the images are sharp again today, clear as a bell. Not like the blurred pictures Andrew saw." He heaved a despondent sigh. "And I gazed with him, helping him gently turn it to study different views."

Everything seemed sharper and brighter now, and I wondered if the denizens of Mars had previously been blocking or distorting the signals. The red planet was a place of grandeur, open and vast . . . but it seemed far too empty, too dead. How could a superior technological civilization thousands of years old have accomplished so little? Even the Egyptians left huge pyramids, the Greeks and Romans their temples and coliseums.

The Martians had cities and canals, but given the fact that they had been capable of constructing such things for millennia, shouldn't the red planet have been a utopia, with cities and parks spanning all the open continents? Instead, Mars was just a . . . skeleton, the landscape entirely dead.

When Lowell turned the crystal egg, a new image astounded us into speechlessness. There on a vast open field, we saw row upon row of silver cylinders ready for launch. Newly constructed ships, all of them outfitted and ready to launch en masse toward Earth.

To me it was readily apparent that these ships were not designed to deliver Martian delegates and scientists to mankind. No, this was a massive invasion fleet, hundreds of ships, all of them filled with Martian conquerors. I felt my face grow hot with disbelief and then anger.

The Martian cylinders would fall like rain from the skies, descending upon an unsuspecting blue planet. The crashed ships would crack open, and the Martian invaders would build towering war machines. What we saw in the image was an incredible armada that would easily engulf the British, German, and Russian navies combined.

Lowell's eyes went wide, then hardened into ice chips. "It is a full-scale invasion fleet. There can be no doubt of it, Moreau! With such a force, they could conquer the whole Earth."

"But . . . but the one cylinder that crashed in the Sahara—" I stammered, then realized. "Of course! Our captive Martian is a scout sent to study our defenses and our weaknesses."

I imagined it being launched on what was sure to be a suicide mission, with no possibility of return to Mars—at least not until the rest of the invasion fleet arrived. Our Martian had been packed aboard with a comrade and numerous white drones—for food? Yes, the bodies had all been drained and desiccated, just as the Martian had drained the hapless redheaded crewman on the Atlantic steamer, and like poor Douglass.

But the voyage had been longer than anticipated, and so the drones had all been consumed. Our Martian had killed his comrade to drain it of its lifeblood, sustenance for its own survival, until it could complete its reconnaissance mission of Earth. Had the two superior Martians drawn lots, deciding the survivor in a civilized fashion? Or had our Martian attacked its companion unawares, murdering it and then drinking its blood?

My fists knotted. "It has come to study us, and we have told it everything. It has sent its report through the crystal egg to its superiors back on Mars. Even now they must be planning their attack! What naive fools we have been, Lowell!"

Lowell set the transparent ovoid on the desktop, his face flushed. "The villain has deceived us with all it has said. While we listened entranced to the propaganda about its venerable civilization, the Martians were completing their invasion ships."

I wanted to disbelieve him, but could find no evidence to the contrary, no better explanation. Our Martian specimen was evil, an enemy of mankind.

Lowell's brow furrowed, as if he were doing mental calculations. "We still have time. It is months until the opposition. The Martians will surely launch their ships then." He marched to the door and flung it open with murderous intent. Lowell was always bullish once he made up his mind. Heedless of the cold rain, or the possible danger our alien spy might pose, he stepped out into the dusk. "We'll see what the Martian has to say about this." I ran after him.

Heavy rain came down like wet gunshots. With a splash of lightning, white light flickered across the construction site, illuminating the empty buildings. Behind us, the only light on Mars Hill came from the lamps in the main house. Thunder boomed like a cannonade, and we splashed through the mud together. Lowell ignored the weather entirely and strode ahead, ready to accuse our specimen.

But when we reached the locked shed, the Martian was gone. The door had been smashed open again, cast aside like kindling, discarded and useless. The chains and lock were removed, all metal gone.

"Damn him!" Lowell peered into the musty building, but we knew it would be empty. I did not doubt that it could have escaped us at any time . . . possibly even from the moment we took it prisoner out in the Sahara. The creature had played us for fools.

Another lightning flash illuminated our surroundings, and I could see that many things seemed to be missing. Construction tools had vanished, as well as equipment left lying around the observatory buildings, scrap metal and pipes, all stolen. "The Martian is doing something, Lowell."

"It's been planning this all along. We would be well advised to prevent whatever mischief that creature intends." When he frowned, his moustache formed a bridge over his lips. "No one will make a fool out of me, Moreau—not even a creature from another planet."

The rain pounded harder, and I shielded my head, wishing I had brought a hat or an umbrella. Water streamed down my face. I turned around, searching for any movement. "Martian! Where are you?" I shouted into the night. We could hear no sounds other than the fury of the storm.

When lightning flashed again, accompanied by an almost immediate crack of thunder, I turned to where Lowell had parked his Benz motorcar only an hour earlier. To my astonishment, the vehicle lay *disassembled*—not torn apart in fury, but carefully dismantled, components removed, resources stripped.

Lowell looked angrier than I had ever seen him. "Come with me, Moreau." He stalked off.

The roaring storm fell into a lull, as if the rain and wind were taking a momentary rest before returning with redoubled strength. I heard the clanking sounds of labor: metal upon metal, heavy objects clattering against each other. Then the sounds were drowned out again by the thunder and downpour.

"Over here!" Lowell switched direction, striding off with determination.

We arrived at the observatory dome to see the Martian busy at work out in the open in the pouring rain. I instantly saw why the alien had ransacked the construction site for materials and torn apart the motorcar's engine. It had used the scavenged components to construct an ominous device of its own, taller even than the observatory dome.

"What is that ghastly thing?" Lowell said. "A . . . tripod?"

Crawling up on the structure like a bloated spider, the Martian worked its tentacles, pulling together girders and struts, pipes and wires. I realized with horror that I had seen this awful thing before, back in the Sahara.

Ingeniously resourceful with construction equipment around the observatory site, the Martian had built another ray weapon.

CHAPTER THIRTY

THE TRIPOD CHASE

While Wells wrestled with the battle tripod's controls, whispering to himself to keep calm, Professor Huxley bent over to peer through the low rear windows of the control turret. "Those other war machines are still coming, Mr. Wells. Four tripods. As near as I can tell by marking off the seconds as we pass landmarks, our pursuers are gaining on us."

Wells grabbed the wrong lever and lost the rhythm of his lurching walk. "These blasted controls were designed for a dozen Martian tentacles, not two simple hands!" The tripod reeled like a spinning stool, then caught its balance again. "And as you're so fond of reminding us, Professor, the Martians have superior brains to my small primate organ."

"Don't get discouraged, H.G.," Jane said. "Besides, if those others come any closer, I'll be able to use the heat ray."

"Unfortunately, Miss Robbins, when those tripods are in range of our weapon, then the converse is also true."

The tripod legs pumped up and down like pistons and slammed into the rusty sands with pile-driver blows. "At the moment, I'm just trying to get away. But I would appreciate any guidance in getting us to the south pole, where the Martians are holding our cavorite sphere."

"Ah, I have just the thing!" Huxley spread out the rolled documents he had stolen from the laboratory spire. "These detailed topographical maps may be of some use, if we can decipher them and determine our current location."

"Show them to Jane," he said, then lurched the stilt legs to dodge a field of loose boulders. "She's always good with maps."

Jane fiddled with the weapon controls. "A minute, H.G." With a grim set to her jaw like a lioness protecting her cubs, she pinpointed the nearest pursuer and sprayed the heat ray like water from a fireman's pump. The throbbing blast melted and bent one of the war machine's legs; before the tripod could tumble, she refocused her aim and exploded the turret. "I got it!"

"If you can manage any greater speed, Mr. Wells, now would be the time to use it. I expect the Martians to retaliate at any moment."

The remaining three battle tripods raised their jointed arms in unison and directed the rotating lenses. Fortunately, by virtue of Wells's uncoordinated gait, he reeled and lurched, accidentally dodging a direct hit from the converging heat rays. The red sands turned molten around them, and Wells staggered away from the target zone. Without caution or care, he raced ahead at a frantic pace, fearful of missing a single step. The pursuing Martians increased their own speed.

As he ran headlong, the southern sky grew dark and murky, a brewing cauldron of dire weather. Wells would have been more concerned about the storm if he hadn't been so intent on simply fleeing for their lives. From behind, the heat rays lanced out again, but struck wide, catching them with only a fringe of thermal energy.

The three tripods chased after them in a three-legged gallop. The terrain became more rugged, cracked with canyons carved long ago by rivers that had fallen into arid extinction. Along the rim of a wide gorge, one of the artificial canals that carried clear water from the polar excavation sites turned west over the flat terrain.

"Ah, a good landmark." Huxley studied his unrolled maps. "In theory, we can follow the canal network southward until we reach its antarctic terminus."

"We have to outrun the tripods first." Jane scanned the charts and diagrams, trying to match what she saw outside. Finally, she pointed to a canal line running in the right direction, along the rim of a labyrinth of gorges and canyonlands. "I think that's it, Professor. See if you can match the details any more clearly." She ran back to the heat-ray controls, hoping for a chance to take another shot.

Wells hunched over to peer through the turret windows as he worked the controls. "Maybe we can hide in that maze." He struck out toward the sloping paths into the deep ravines, while Huxley continued to study his maps.

"I will do my best to navigate you through them, Mr. Wells."

As she looked toward the edge of the gorge, Jane grinned with an idea. "H.G., take us close to the canal. I'll create a . . . a smokescreen to hide us before we drop into the canyons. It might buy us some time."

Wells didn't debate with her. Jane often had unorthodox and quite admirable ideas. Huxley's eyes were bright with amusement. "I believe you mean *steam* instead of smoke, Miss Robbins—but the concept is an excellent one."

Rushing along with first one leg in front and then two stretching to take its place like a freakish pole-vaulter, the battle tripod made for the canyons. The three pursuing war machines gained ground with every step.

Wells mentally marked the best place to descend unseen into the tangled maze of deep ravines. Behind him, the Martians came into firing range and raised their terrible heat rays. Jane was ready with her own targeting systems. Instead of shooting at the pursuing tripods, though, she unleashed an intense blast of heat into the channel of water, playing the beam across its chill surface.

The result was like a boiler explosion. Gouts of steam blasted into roiling clouds that billowed all around, engulfing them in an impenetrable white fog. Wells lost all sight of his surroundings—as did the Martians. Jane drew the incinerating knife back and forth along the canal. Water continued to evaporate in a boiling storm that would expand and spread across the bleak landscape.

"Thank you, Jane." Wells grinned at her.

"Don't lose our advantage, Mr. Wells," Huxley said. "Move forward with the proper balance of caution and panicked haste."

Wells set off, searching intently for the shadows of land forms, relying on his mental map of the best path to take.

Finally, as steam curdled around them, he found a sloping descent into the canyons and soon ducked out of sight, before the pursuers could find them again.

Manipulating the three legs, he could negotiate rubble and boulders. He was wary of tilting too far on the slope, for fear that the ungainly battle tripod would tumble over.

As their tripod moved deeper into the tangled canyons, they passed beneath the thick steam bank, and Wells could see their way ahead again. When he could dodge the worst of the obstacles, he moved off with all the speed and practice he had acquired, leaving the pursuing tripods to muddle their way out of the blinding hot fog.

* * *

Hours later, after playing a cat-and-mouse game through the canyons, they faced the onset of the cold Martian night. Wells was forced to find shelter in a narrow cul-de-sac and wait out the darkness, hoping the hunting tripods would not find them.

He had guided their stilt-legged walker on a meandering path through the twisting canyon labyrinth, taking random turns but careful not to blunder into dead ends or slots too narrow to pass. The now-barren watercourses tended generally south toward the ice caps, but with many blind and confusing turns. Huxley diligently marked each direction on his charts to keep them from getting entirely lost. Jane studied the terrain maps to find a viable course to their destination.

They had seen no sign of the pursuing Martian tripods since foiling them with the canal smokescreen. Releasing the controls at last, Wells felt his extraordinary weariness. He and Jane snuggled together for warmth, resting for the first time in what seemed like weeks; they began to feel momentarily safe, though they wished they had something to eat.

Overhead, the stars came out, then dimmed and faded as if a blanket of dirty mist had been drawn over the sky. A pattering sound like birdshot struck the metal turret. Before Wells could even ask a question, a blast of wind charged through the canyon like a steam locomotive.

"Dust storm!" Huxley cried.

The wind shoved against them like a flood surging from a broken dam. A hail of rocks and sand scoured the outside of the hull, scratching the low turret windows. When shutting down for the night, Wells had stopped the great walker in the sheltered corner of a canyon. Now, the blunt rocks deflected the dust storm's fury, and the three splayed legs of the battle tripod kept them anchored, though the machine rocked and swayed as if it was about to be knocked over.

Wells held onto Jane. There was nothing to do but wait and endure. Even in the howling gale, Huxley was intrigued and took meteorological notes on the back of one of the rolled maps. Mercifully, after less than an hour of the loud howling and scraping, the dry hurricane passed, racing away like a stampede in the night.

Wells finally said aloud, "I believe we can be confident now that our tracks have been erased."

* * *

The next morning, as wan sunlight crept through the sheer-walled canyons, they set off again, picking their way southward.

Huxley and Jane had spent hours scrutinizing the maps. Now, the professor directed Wells into convoluted channels that led toward the pole. With mechanical strides, the young man guided the tripod across a landscape that had been scrubbed clean by the high winds and rough dust.

As Wells lumbered down the bottom of the gorge, hoping their peace and safety would last, he suddenly saw the three pursuing tripods reappear out of a side canyon. Seeing the hijacked war machine, the Martians charged forward, bellowing a triumphant "*Ulla!*"

"They are certainly persistent," Huxley said. "I would have hoped the rebellious Selenites were giving the Martians too many other things to do."

Jane looked in frustration at the command apparatus they had taken with them in the battle tripod, sure they were out of range of the silver collars. She groaned, touching the device as she saw their chances slipping away. "We're all isolated here. If only the Selenites could defend us now, distract the Martians."

The heat rays blasted at them again, blackening the canyon walls. Wells dodged from side to side, staggering and wobbling, as Jane tried to fire their weapon back at the attackers. He ducked their tripod into tangential canyons to elude the pursuit. But the Martians were much more adept at running in their three-legged war machines, and Wells was trapped inside the confining canyons, racing down unknown channels. If he made a single mistake and ran into a closed gorge, the three hunters could disintegrate them.

Wells was astonished when the Selenites appeared, just as Jane had commanded.

Drone work crews had been dispatched all up and down

the canal network, monitoring substations and maintaining the machinery that distributed fresh water across the Martian landscape. Now, sudden swarms of the white-skinned Selenites surged out of side canyons and over the rim, working together as if with a unified mind. They would die to defend the humans who carried the talisman of the Grand Lunar. Groups of drones lifted boulders in the low gravity and tossed huge stones into the paths of the enemy tripods, battering them from the cliffs above.

"I will personally thank the Grand Lunar next time we get to the Moon," Wells said.

Under the sudden attack, the three Martian hunters reeled and turned their heat rays upon the unexpected rebels. The incinerating beams vaporized many valiant Selenite allies, but the delay and confusion gave Wells a chance to surge ahead.

Jane touched her collar, perplexed. "The Selenites are sending me a message! It's so faint it's nearly incomprehensible, but I think they have figured out how to communicate with me, just barely. H.G., they want you to get us out of the canyons as soon as you possibly can. Up over the rim and out into the open. They'll help us."

He hesitated, aware that on the plains above he would have less chance of hiding or finding shelter.

"H.G., hurry!"

He scrambled up a sloping boulder-strewn path on which he found purchase for the machine's three legs. As he gained elevation, the pursuing Martians blasted aimlessly with their heat rays along the walls of the canyon.

When the Selenites saw that the three humans had climbed high enough for safety, they transmitted chittering messages to other lunar slaves upstream at the head of the canyons. Those drones began their sabotage work.

Responding, Jane delivered her commands for them to defend the humans. Continuing their precise mayhem, the Selenites destroyed a primary pumping station in the canal distribution network. The ruined grand canal diverted a surging wave, and all the water poured into the narrow canyons, funneled forward and picking up force.

Wells and Jane stood together, gazing out the turret's low windows. From their higher vantage, they watched a furious wall of water gush through the canyons and sweep aside the three pursuing tripods, as if they were mere feathers in a cyclone. The giant metal contraptions crashed into each other and into the rocky walls, slammed about like toys, until they were dashed to bits.

Sadly, as the Martian war machines were knocked helter-skelter, hundreds of the Selenites were also sacrificed—just to give the three humans time to escape. Wells felt weak watching the destruction. He clasped Jane's hand.

"An excellent solution to our predicament," Huxley said. "Now we have a bit of breathing room. It should be safe enough for us on top of the plateau now."

The tripod climbed out of the canyons, and the Martian morning spread out before them with a greenish sky and rusty-red landscape that extended to the horizon.

"Somehow," Jane said, deeply disturbed, "we must find a way to show our appreciation to these Selenites. They have saved our lives. They fought to the death for us, for *me*."

* * *

They traveled due south all day, homing in on the ice cap. Remembering how many Martian fighting machines and slave-master walkers kept the Selenite work crews in line, Wells knew they would be in for a fight as soon as they arrived. But the cavorite sphere—their only means of returning to Earth—had been hauled inside a hangar at the vast ice quarry. No matter how dangerous it might seem, they had to go there.

When they arrived at the ice quarry and water excavation industries, they found total destruction.

Only days ago, they had seen the enormous Martian labor pits here at the polar cap, the diligent work that created fresh water. Since then, a complete holocaust had taken place. All of the sophisticated Martian works had been utterly ruined.

Wells cried, "The uprising took place here, too!"

Jane stared, nodding slowly. "I told them to protect us, to help us get away. The Selenites knew we were coming here, and so they rebelled against their slave masters. They destroyed all the Martian walkers and tripods and took over the whole antarctic facility, just to make the way clear for us."

"Have they risen up everywhere? Sacrificing themselves to destroy all Martians in all cities?" Wells wondered.

Jane looked at him aghast, thinking of the appalling bloodshed. "No! At least . . . I hope not."

Huxley pursed his lips. "It seems that thanks to you, Miss Robbins, Mars itself is at war."

CHAPTER THIRTY-ONE

A WAR OF WORLDS

FROM THE JOURNAL OF DR. MOREAU

Looking at the tripod structure of the Martian weapon, Lowell was appalled. "Not only has that creature ruined my motorcar, it's stolen my telescope's clock drive! And part of the cradle for the Clark refractor!"

Thunder cracked again, and I had to shield my eyes against the rain. Seeing us approach, the Martian scrambled to its controls with amazing nimbleness in its ungainly body. Lowell glared indignantly up at the towering machine. "Come down from there!"

The Martian turned the camera-like lens device on its segmented arm, and I looked up into the dangerous eye of the ray weapon. Before Lowell could bellow again, I knocked him out of the way, and we both went sprawling in the mud just as a burst of sparks and heat sprayed out, vaporizing the rain and baking the mud into brick.

The Martian fired its heat ray again, but the stress and vibration had knocked the uncompleted armature loose, spoiling its aim. Instead, the heat ray set alight two of the tall pines, which crackled and snapped like torches in the storm. Despite all the care we had lavished upon it, the creature meant to incinerate us, like a child burning ants with a magnifying lens.

I grabbed Lowell's arm, and we began to run. As the thunder continued to boom and the cloudburst reached its climax around us, the Martian raised its heat ray high, hoping for a better aim. I was certain we were doomed.

But the metal tripod itself was already taller than the observatory structure, which made the three-legged machine the highest thing atop Mars Hill. When the Martian raised the heat ray, its articulated arm acted as an irresistible lightning rod. Like the spear of Zeus, a blinding blue-white bolt lanced down to strike the Martian's contraption, sending sparks and cinders flying.

The resulting thunderclap knocked me flat, and I blinked dazzling colors from my light-blinded eyes. I could not find Lowell and assumed he had scrambled off into the night.

On the blackened tripod structure, the Martian stirred like a stunned insect, amazingly still alive. It dangled by two tentacles, then dropped partway before catching itself. Its body was smoking, burned—defenseless. I knew we had to act. Unable to see Lowell in the darkness and the rain, I decided to take care of matters myself.

By the time I reached the ruined tripod, the Martian had already dropped to the wet ground and scuttled away through puddles, seeking shelter. Then I saw it move, battering down the door of the empty observatory dome before it scrambled inside. I didn't know where it expected to run here. Perhaps it was dying, or just going to ground so that it could heal.

I followed the thing cautiously, not wishing to be killed in the same manner as Douglass. I stepped through the door quietly. The interior walls were made of carefully lapped pine boards, and I could smell the sap and resin. The rain had already made everything dank and damp. The floor of poured cement bore only the ruins of the cradle for the giant Clark refractor; in constructing its tripod, our Martian had taken many of the telescope's support components. I could discern little in the dimness, but my dazzled eyes were adjusting after the lightning flash that had ruined the battle tripod.

I heard something heavy moving within the shadows, dragging itself along with wet scraping sounds. Then with a skitter and a clatter, the Martian found a metal ladder that led up to the tracks on which iron wheels and heavy cranks could turn the great dome. During a night of observing, astronomers would be able to swivel the dome's opening to view any desired section of sky.

Apparently the work crew had abandoned their jobs without bothering to close the dome, for the dome itself was open. A slit of cloudy sky shone down. Though the storm had come up unexpectedly, Lowell would be furious if his observatory was damaged.

I saw the bloated creature finish clambering up the ladder before it scuttled along the tracks of the dome. It moved with a drunken sluggishness, having been injured by the lightning strike. The crawling thing made its way to the opening through which only lightning and rain could be seen. Perhaps it wanted to see the stars or Mars one last time . . . .

I put my hands on my hips. Now that the creature had no place else to run, I demanded, "Why? Why are you doing this? Have we not helped you? Did I not save your life?"

Holding on with its tentacles, the Martian glared down at me with wide, round eyes like signal lamps on a train. It simply heaved, as if trying to withstand the pain.

I shouted again, "I know you can talk. Explain yourself."

You have helped our Martian cause.

In a horrific succession of images transmitted by its superior brain, it confirmed my worst fear: the impending invasion. The Martians' intent was total domination of Earth. Now I understood more fully what Lowell and I had seen in the crystal egg.

Our cylinders will launch soon. Mars will conquer the human race, as we did the Moon. Weak and juicy humans will be our workers, our food.

I could not argue, for I knew that what the creature described was true. No army on Earth could stand against the Martian invasion force. No military, no battleship, no weapon would be great enough to withstand this onslaught.

Your civilization, your science, *is too primitive to stop us.*

Suddenly, Lowell appeared in the doorway. "No—but I can stop you."

A glint of flickering lightning through the dome

showed me that he carried a shotgun—the same one he had confiscated from the unruly worker the night before. He raised the weapon and, in the instant the next flash of lightning showed him his target, he fired. Inside the enclosed dome, the gun's boom was louder than any thunder.

The shotgun blast smashed into the Martian, driving it against the wall and splattering dark fluids along the lapped wooden boards. Calmly, without hesitation, Lowell loaded a second shell into the barrel and fired again, pulverizing the enormous brain that had concocted such terrible plans, snuffing out the intellect that meant only to crush humanity.

The dying Martian held on for just an instant more before finally releasing its grip with rubbery tentacles. It slowly slid, then dropped to the cement floor of the observatory, where it twitched and shuddered. The creature bled from numerous ruptures and gashes torn by the shotgun blasts. Already injured and weakened by the terrible lightning strike, it squirmed briefly and then died, curled up like a giant spider.

"I did that not in the name of science, Moreau." Lowell turned to me. "But in the name of humanity."

* * *

The proof is abundant, and I will not waste time and effort convincing a skeptical public of the truth of my story. However, with the coming opposition of planets the Martian invasion is imminent, and the greatest question now in my mind is how to proceed.

In what possible manner can human beings prepare for

this attack from the red planet? When the cylinders come raining down, how will we defend ourselves? It is not a matter for one man to decide, but for all the leaders and greatest scientific minds of Earth.

I believe that human resolve and ingenuity is sufficient to meet even this challenge, but all countries and governments must be united immediately, no longer concerned about a war between lands and ideologies, but a war of the worlds. Even if the human race is not ultimately victorious against this interplanetary threat, I am confident that we can at least put up a valiant fight.

I have decided to return to London, where I am still a wanted man. Perhaps, given the terrible news that I bring, they will forget such foolishness and realize that I, too, can contribute to this fight. Lowell will offer all the funding at his disposal.

I will share all of this information with my rival and former colleague, T.H. Huxley. He is a brilliant man. Perhaps he will know what to do.

CHAPTER THIRTY-TWO

THE STOLEN BACILLUS

Using the Martians' own command collar and their enslavement devices, Jane had issued her rebellious call to all the drone workers in the canal industries, the ancient cities, the polar ice quarries. Unleashed with the same relentless efficiency they devoted to every task, hordes of Selenites had overrun the ice cap operations, swarming over the tentacled slave masters and toppling their short, sturdy walking contrivances.

Jane's skin paled, turning the color of milk. "Good heavens, look at the damage they've done. Did I . . . incite all this?"

Wells looked through the scratched windows of their stolen turret as he marched to the work site. "It would appear so." He squeezed her arm. "These Selenites were kidnapped generations ago and put to work. They had no instructions from the Grand Lunar, no guidance. You gave them new orders—and their freedom."

Smoke curled into the greenish sky from fires lit by heat-ray blasts. The drones had thrown themselves against the defending Martians until they brought down the guardian tripods.

Jane's voice was thin with disbelief. "But thousands have been slaughtered, all because I carry the eye of their Grand Lunar."

Armored cars and pumping machinery lay scattered about. Only a few of the swollen brains lumbered off in wild flight across the desert, their squat walkers or tall battle tripods destroyed.

Huxley smiled. "We can only hope, Miss Robbins, that this insurrection will thwart the Martians' plans to invade our Earth. You may well have saved the human race."

"I pray they didn't accidentally damage our cavorite sphere in their mayhem," Wells said.

Down below, he saw that the drones had blocked off the central water-distribution network, so that the icy current melted from polar cliffs flooded the stippled plains. Even as he watched now, crowds of pale Selenites surrounded two sealed Martian bubble boats and tore them from their docks; the tentacled Martian slave masters inside were pulled from their sheltered domes and cast into the rushing, icy water, where they were borne away helpless in the current.

Jane stood stoically. "Let's help the Selenites, while we still can, H.G."

"I wouldn't mind striking a blow or two of our own." Calm now, he brought the tripod forward into the scorched battlefield, where hundreds of white drones still ran amok. Jane spoke through the stolen communication device. "We are coming. We mean you no harm in this tripod. Please don't attack us."

Only three of the Martian battle tripods remained, and the Selenite swarms had backed them up onto the cliffs, where the slave masters were fighting for their lives. The war machines had climbed up the stair-step ledges of the polar quarry and now made their last stand on a sheer ledge where slabs of frozen water had been cut away. The three desperate tripods stood side by side, burning a swath of death all around them. But they were trapped, and the Selenites seemed inexhaustible.

As Wells brought his battered three-legged walker forward, the defeated tripods bellowed out a haunting "*Ulla! Ulla!*" as if they expected him to be their rescuer. Inside the tripod's control deck, he saw a buzzing sequence of lights. Perhaps a transmission? Questions from the cornered Martians, inquiries evolving into angry commands? And then stuttering panic as they heard no answer.

Wells scowled with determination. "Jane, with a single blast from your heat ray, you can undercut that frozen ice ledge beneath them and—"

She saw it immediately. "It'll be my pleasure, H.G." Her face hard, glancing once more at the thousands of dead Selenites lying all about, she raised the camera apparatus and unleashed a line of fire that cut through the ice as if it were butter, fracturing the solid cliffs.

The three remaining battle tripods fired back, but the ground beneath them became unstable. In a rush and a roar, the side of the frozen quarry collapsed in an avalanche of blocky ice. The metal war machines were crushed, buried under the steaming white rubble that piled at the bottom of the huge pit.

"This polar facility is ours now," Jane said.

"I should think that puts an end to it," Huxley agreed. "Now, on to business."

Wells brought their commandeered tripod to a halt in the middle of the pumping yards. He opened the hatch at the base of the turret and carefully climbed down the stilt-like leg with Jane and Huxley following. The descent was easier than expected in the low gravity, especially since there was no desperate hurry this time, no Martians battling in the streets. On solid ground again, surrounded by chill steam and fading smoke, they raised their hands like conquering heroes.

Chittering with unusual excitement, the Selenites clustered around them, touching them in strange greeting. The drones were exuberant with their new liberation.

"Like downtrodden laborers everywhere, they could have obtained their freedom all along," Wells said, "if they had simply pooled their resources and acted in unison."

Though she had safely replaced the eye of the Grand Lunar in the folds of her skirt, the Selenites still treated Jane like a queen. She smiled, returning their greeting by touching the creatures. "Aren't they so . . . charming? They are lost and far from home. For many generations they haven't known who they are. They had no hope. But now we've freed them."

Huxley seemed to be drowning in Selenites, and wishing he could be taking notes as to their taxonomy. "They are a most curious species. I wonder why they show such particular attention to you, Miss Robbins. Is it only because you carry the eye of the Grand Lunar? They are practically worshipful, as if you were their goddess."

Smiling, Wells took her arm. "Perhaps the Selenites simply have good taste in women, as I do. I worship Jane myself."

She put her hands on her hips and looked at Wells and Huxley, then rolled her eyes in exasperation. "You gentlemen spend so much time studying biology from a distance that you don't understand it in your hearts. You have the information but you don't view the picture. Where are your powers of observation that you would miss something so obvious?"

She looked back and forth between them, but both men remained perplexed. Jane let out a long sigh. Wells remembered teaching Jane a botany lesson one languid summer afternoon, and he had teasingly used nearly those same words to get her to notice the obvious. Now he waited for her to reveal her secret.

"The Grand Lunar gave the eye gem to *me*, specifically, gentlemen. She was their *queen*. A *female*." Then she gave Wells an impish smile. "To these Selenites, you men are simply my drones."

* * *

Jane relayed instructions to the devoted Selenites, and the lunar workers tore open locked doors and pried apart the walls of hangars and warehouses, searching for the cavorite sphere. They found the milky-white vessel connected to numerous analytical instruments. Thankfully, the Martian scientists had done no damage to it during their investigations.

Wells's heart nearly jumped into his throat, and he gave Jane a quick, enthusiastic hug. "At last, our ticket home, our steamer to the stars." Beside them, Huxley was grinning like a fool.

They carefully inspected the sphere, searching for any damage, deep scrapes or breaches that would allow air to leak out in space. Jane opened the hatch and climbed inside to verify that their stores and equipment remained intact. Famished, she, Wells, and Huxley sat under the dim greenish skies to have a peculiar picnic as the Selenites bustled about, putting out the remaining fires and scouring the industrial fields for any surviving or hiding Martians. It seemed the battle was over here at the pole.

Instead of being relieved, though, Wells was deeply troubled. "I fear the Martians will rally before long. If the Selenites did not rise up everywhere on the planet, then the Martians will contain them, perhaps kill all the drones."

Jane looked squeamish, but did not dispute his conclusion.

Wells continued, "They will soon know what has befallen their operations here at the ice cap. They are not a passive civilization, and they cannot survive unless water flows through the canals. They'll have no choice but to gather reinforcements and reconquer the south pole, no matter what it takes. This rebellion has caught them by surprise, but they will return with hundreds of their battle tripods, and these drones can never withstand it."

"But they need the Selenites! As slaves and as . . . food." Jane looked around at all the drones.

"They will concern themselves first with their immediate survival." Huxley nodded heavily. "I believe you have the truth of it, Mr. Wells. We know the terrible plans these creatures have made against the Earth. This violent insurrection has set their invasion plans back by decades—perhaps as much as a century—but I do not believe the Martians will give up. With so many of their Selenite drones killed in the uprising, the Martians will have a greater need than ever for new slaves, new lifeblood."

Wells took a long draught from one of the bottles of beer. "We need to escape so that we can inform the Institute of all we have learned. Let them put their minds to the problem."

Jane was alarmed. "H.G., we can't just leave these Selenites to their fates! After everything they've sacrificed in order to help us?" She looked at Huxley for a suggestion.

His face was troubled as he stared at the icy cliffs, then off to the dry, dusty horizon. "Escape is not enough right now, my friends. We might save ourselves, but we would doom all of humanity." Preoccupied, he went back to the open hatch of the sphere. "Ah, excuse me a moment. I must check something."

While the professor rummaged around, Wells noted how easily the old man moved. Ever since they had left Earth and arrived in the low gravity of the Moon and here on Mars, he seemed spry and healthy, as if his arthritic pains and the weariness of age had been stripped away.

After a few moments Huxley emerged, satisfied but grim. His conscience seemed to be weighing on him more heavily than the planet's gravity. "What is it, Professor?" Jane asked.

Wells narrowed his eyes. "He has an idea—but he doesn't like it."

Jane asked in a small voice, "What . . . what did you take from inside the sphere, Professor?"

"We have the means to end this now." Huxley reached into the pocket of his striped dressing robe and removed the six test tubes that had been carefully sealed and padded against accidental damage. "Vials of the deadly cholera germ that Dr. Griffin intended to deliver to the Kaiser."

"The stolen bacillus," Wells murmured.

Though he seemed beaten, Huxley straightened his back,

dredging up determination and justifications from deep within. "At the Imperial Institute I had many discussions with Philby about the morality of conducting a germ warfare against our enemies. If such a thing is to be contemplated, if such action is ever to be considered—what circumstances could possibly be more valid than *here and now*? We are speaking of the fate of an entire world."

"And dooming another one, Professor," Wells pointed out.

Jane looked around at the drones. "What about all the Selenites still here? If you unleash that plague, won't they die in as many numbers as the Martians?"

Huxley shook his head. "Recall what the Grand Lunar said. It—*she* made it abundantly clear that the drones and other lunar castes are immune to microbiological hazards. Their physiology is much different from ours."

Wells spoke up quickly. "And from Dr. Moreau's journal we already know that the Martians are vulnerable to Earthly sicknesses and other morbidities."

Huxley nodded, his brow furrowed. "Without the extreme ministrations and vigorous grafting surgery Moreau performed, the Martian scout would have perished shortly after exposure to our air. But if it managed to transmit information via the crystal egg, subsequent invaders will know to take precautions." He strode away from the cavorite sphere. "I don't intend to give them the chance. I will buy more than a simple reprieve for the human race."

The Selenites swarmed around them, watching their every move. With Wells and Jane following him, the professor reached the primary barricade the drones had erected to block the melted water from the ice caps. "Miss Robbins, please instruct them to open the floodgates. Have them start the water flowing through all the canal lines."

Holding the Grand Lunar's eye gem, Jane spoke into the Martian command device and passed along the request. The white drones did not hesitate or question the commands of their new female master mind.

Though some of the gears and automated machinery had been damaged in the chaotic uprising, the Selenites used main strength to force open the barrier. Surging like wild horses suddenly released from their pen, the waters of the antarctic cap gushed into the channel again, flowing back toward the Martian cities. Chunks of white ice burst along, bobbing against each other.

Without the work crews and industry to process the glaciers, the water supply would dwindle. Any surviving Martians in the cities would be forced to conserve every drop. By then Wells hoped it would be too late for them.

After the flow had stabilized into a glistening ribbon that spread along the intersecting canals, Huxley stood on the lip of the primary supply and uncorked the vials of the deadly plague. "I have to do this myself." He looked weak and beaten, crushed by the realization of what he intended to do. His hands trembled as he held the six test tubes. "I am a biologist. Since I was a boy, I have studied life in all its forms and all its wonder. This is a terrible, terrible thing for a man like myself to contemplate."

Wells said firmly, "No more terrible than the war these Martians intended to unleash upon our world. They would burn our cities, enslave our people, drink their blood."

"Alas, Mr. Wells, you are entirely correct."

Wells took two of the test tubes from the old man. "*We* must do it." Seeing what he intended, Jane took a pair for herself. Together, the three looked at each other and then simultaneously poured the deadly solution into the flowing water. The current of the Martian canals would distribute the fatal germs throughout the ancient, stagnant Martian civilization.

But when it was done, not one of them felt a sense of triumph.

CHAPTER THIRTY-THREE

PROFESSOR HUXLEY'S DECISION

Though the results wouldn't become obvious for days, nature took its inexorable course as the cholera germ spread through the Martian canal system. Faint mists rose from the wrecked ice quarries as water and carbon dioxide sublimated into the skies. Across the polar battleground, the Selenite drones began to repair the worst destruction, like ants busily tidying their mound after a rainstorm. Rebuilding the world, even if it wasn't their own.

Wells stood in the chill air beside his two companions, feeling hollow. He slipped his arm around Jane's waist and held her close. Neither of them said anything. What was there to say, knowing they had just delivered a death sentence to an ancient—if terrible—civilization?

Huxley drew a deep breath and stared toward the red-tinged horizon. The gentlest of breezes ruffled his gray hair and bushy sideburns. "It is the biological imperative to do what is necessary to ensure one's own survival. The Martians no doubt felt justified in their evil actions to ensure the continuation of their species."

"We ourselves are doing nothing less, Professor," Wells said. "So why don't I feel victorious?"

Jane frowned. "If only the Martians had asked for our help, rather than deciding to take everything they needed . . . ."

Superior Martian technology was capable of remarkable advancements, but the slave masters of the red planet had long since stopped devising new solutions. Instead, they behaved as parasites, draining the lifeblood—literally and figuratively—from Selenite society. They had intended to do the same to humankind. Given innovation and imagination, Wells was certain the Martian race could have developed alternative solutions. He mused grimly, "When a race's imagination dies, extinction itself cannot be far behind."

The Selenites helped them attach chains and cables to the sphere and drag it outside, assisted by the judicious opening and closing of the blinds covering the anti-gravity material. Wells and Jane worked together inside the cavorite ship, airing it out, taking stock of their supplies for the return journey.

Huxley remained outside, assessing the polar cap industries, studying the technology the Martians had built by the labor of the captive drones. He crossed his arms over his striped robe; by now his clothes were quite tattered and dirty, his slippers falling apart.

"Mr. Wells, Miss Robbins, I have reached a decision. You two, climb aboard now and go. There is no guarantee you'll return safely to Earth, but I am confident in your abilities. I, meanwhile, intend to stay here, on Mars."

Wells's jaw dropped. "Professor, I beg you to reconsider."

"I am a man of convictions, Mr. Wells, as I have proved in countless debates with uneducated asses. Nothing now will force me to change my mind or re-evaluate my conclusions."

Though Wells knew it was folly to argue with one of the greatest and most persuasive speakers of the nineteenth century, he said, "Professor, you are a self-proclaimed agnostic. How can you feel such devastating guilt that you would sentence yourself to permanent exile? What good does it do to remain here, to live with your conscience? Are you so eager to observe the terrible destruction we all have wrought?"

Huxley gave him a wan smile and looked contemplative. "Guilt? On the contrary, Mr. Wells, I am genuinely curious to observe what happens next here. It is the purest example of survival of the fittest . . . an experiment in a biological laboratory the size of a world. Will the Selenites manage to create their own society here, even without a Grand Lunar? Such questions are quite vexing."

Jane said, "But what about the cholera, Professor? You are just as vulnerable to it."

"Ah, I shall be careful to drink only purified water from the source here at the pole. Though this germ affects human populations in squalid living conditions, it is easy enough to avoid through proper sanitation procedures. The Martians, however, will have no way to guard themselves."

Huxley put his arm around the shoulders of his distraught young companions and spoke in a paternal voice. "Now, now, you two. Think of me. I am old, and my health is failing. Wells, you are a keen observer—you must have noticed in London how painful my joints and aches were. The stiffness in my bones, the arthritis, the rheumatism. I suffered from plentiful maladies ranging from gout to headache to hangnails. Here on Mars, though, the lower gravity and the drier air will make my life much more comfortable. I feel young, and alive, with a whole new world to explore! I believe I can survive longer. Besides, it will give me a chance to help the Selenites maintain this planet."

Jane sniffed. She withdrew the eye of the Grand Lunar and placed it in the old man's seamed palm. "Keep this, Professor—you will have much greater need of it than I do. It's the only way you can communicate with the Selenites." She smiled at him. "Besides, with a mind such as yours, I can think of no person more capable of serving as a surrogate Grand Lunar."

Huxley blushed and kissed the young woman on the cheek. "I haven't had an opportunity such as this since the *Rattlesnake*, and I do look forward to the challenge. Someone should stay behind to observe and document every moment of it for science, for history . . . in case humans ever return to the red planet."

After they said their farewells and the Selenite drones surrounded Jane one final time, she and Wells climbed into the cavorite sphere. Huxley gave them a long, meaningful look before he swung the hatch shut and sealed them inside.

They closed the blinds to block off the cavorite and thus severed the sphere's connection to Mars's gravity. The craft soared into the sky with a smooth, weightless sensation.

Though he knew it might alter their course, Wells opened one of the porthole blinds. He and Jane pressed their faces together, gazing down to see T.H. Huxley, a small figure surrounded by swarms of white-skinned drones. The professor was staring across the landscape at the canals and the water quarry, no doubt imagining the distant cities of the dying Martians. He looked up to them and waved, then turned back to his enormous task.

Staring down at the receding deserts of Mars, Wells and Jane swiftly and surely left the red planet behind. As he held her close in the confines of the cavorite sphere, he knew it would be days before their path would take them back to Earth. "Apart from thwarting the invasion, Jane, I can see one tremendous advantage for the two of us."

She looked at him quizzically, then grinned. "Of course. At last we can be alone."

EPILOGUE

THE SHAPE OF THINGS TO COME

CHAPTER THIRTY-FOUR

HOME AGAIN, WITH A STORY

By the time the sphere returned to Earth, days later, Wells and Jane had become adept enough at maneuvering that they brought themselves down safely to England, and London . . . and directly onto the grounds of the Imperial Institute itself. Judiciously, they opened and closed the blinds to block sections of cavorite and reduce their velocity. The descending vessel glimmered in the cloudy English sky and came to rest heavily in the Institute's gardens, crushing well-groomed shrubberies and ruining a bed of geraniums, petunias, and marigolds. Upper-class students with fine clothes and haughty airs viewed the unexpected arrival with a flurry of consternation and confusion.

Wells opened the sphere's hatch and took a deep breath of

the thick and familiar London air. Standing tall, he reached inside to take Jane by the hand, and helped her out onto the soft lawn. "Welcome back to Earth, my dear."

"It's good to be back home again, H.G. I hope our landlady hasn't sold our possessions by now."

With a pang of sadness, they both looked at the gutted ruin of the secret research wing. Part of the roof remained caved in, and blackened beams stood like skeletal ribs. Carpenters had boarded up the shattered windows. Wells remarked, "I wonder if the students now know about the classified work that occurred behind those closed doors."

Jane sighed. "More likely, the Institute's administration made up some absurd story about a 'tragic chemical accident' in one of the research facilities."

Jabbering students pushed closer. Two young men, clad in shorts and high white socks, brandished cricket bats as weapons. Wells raised his hands. "We are good English citizens, and we present no threat. Everything will be explained to you in good time."

"Or perhaps not." Jane gave the crowd a teasing smile. "You'd think they've never seen a spacecraft land on their school grounds before."

Before long, the commotion attracted several of the technological geniuses from the damaged research wing. Wells recognized the biological researcher Philby. "Look there! It's the sphere Cavor was building!"

A bear-like Dr. Moreau pushed forward, looking as if he belonged at the Institute after the turmoil of the explosion and the unexplained disappearance of Professor Huxley. Professor Redwood and Mr. Bensington, the scientists who had created a growth-enhancing food, followed Moreau as he nudged students aside and took charge.

Now the burly vivisectionist frowned at Wells and Jane; the only time he had met Wells, Moreau had been intent on a bristling conversation with Huxley. "What are you doing with Cavor's sphere?" He gave neither of them a chance to answer. "I thought Thomas would be with you. Where is Huxley? Or is he dead like Cavor and Griffin?"

Jane said, "Oh no, the professor is alive and well—and on Mars."

Wells added, "He won't be returning home, I fear. He has elected to stay behind, but he has accomplished his task. He has made certain—"

"As have we," Jane interjected.

"—that mankind no longer needs to fear an invasion from Mars."

"Good news indeed!" Moreau boomed. "So you believe me after all?"

Feeling strangely familiar with this abrasive stranger, Wells nodded. "Not only have we read your journal, Dr. Moreau, we have been to Mars and fought the Martians ourselves."

Moreau heaved a long sigh, as if hoping to minimize the excitement of the event. Too many of the students were already listening. He indicated his fellow researchers, then lowered his voice. "We shall be glad to hear your account—in private, of course, without so many curious ears and gossiping lips."

Philby rubbed two fingers along his pointed chin. "So something good has come of this, then. I'm relieved our efforts haven't been a complete loss. That bastard Griffin stole all our records, and then they burned up along with him."

Jane ducked back inside the sphere and retrieved the papers and plans the invisible spy had smuggled aboard. "No, here are the original reports and formulas our scientists developed for the Empire. Perhaps they can be put to good use after all."

"Well, after what we've learned of the Martians, our traditional enemies seem to be a much smaller threat," said Professor Redwood. For once, Mr. Bensington did not disagree with him.

From the courtyard behind the research wing came a shout and a scream as people ran about in terror. Wells heard a loud squeaking and a scritching of clawed feet across flagstones and then a crashing in the bushes. Bensington and Redwood looked at each other, alarmed. "Oh no, that'll be our rats again. They've gotten loose!" The two men dashed off.

"Don't just stand staring," Moreau said to the spectators clustered around the sphere. "Get some of these strong young men to rig up chains and rope. We have to bring Cavor's vessel back inside where we can polish it, inspect it . . . and keep it away from the curious." Scientists and students hurried to obey, spurred on by the doctor's forceful personality.

Hand in hand, Wells and Jane walked through the Institute's doors into the burned research wing, which was now a clamor of construction crews—glaziers, bricklayers, carpenters. Moreau followed them inside. "After the explosion, the subsequent fire wrecked many laboratories. We salvaged some of the research, but it took days for us to get the damage under control. Our scientists are already diligently back at work."

"You seem to be quite at home here, Dr. Moreau," Jane said. "Aren't you concerned about—"

He raised a meaty hand, dismissing her worry. "After

I sounded the alarm about the Martians and gave a full account of all that I've discovered, Queen Victoria offered me a provisional pardon, so long as I agree to stay here at the Institute and devote my intellect to the crisis at hand. Given the shortage of decent workers, the Institute has asked me to provide assistance . . . though the queen insists that I submit to unreasonable constraints and limitations." He drew a deep breath and let it out, calming himself. "Still, it is the only way I can be sure these men keep their research on track and don't let themselves be distracted by phantom enemies."

He frowned. "However, since you claim to have conveniently solved the Martian problem, I wonder if Buckingham Palace will change its mind." Moreau scratched his beard, then urged them down the hall. "You two have had the benefit of reading my experiences as set forth in my journal. Now you must tell me precisely what you yourselves have done."

While several Institute researchers listened in, Wells and Jane quickly explained everything. After they described how Professor Huxley insisted on remaining behind, Moreau shook his head without surprise. "That sounds exactly like him."

*　*　*

After bathing, changing into clean clothes, then enjoying a generous meal—their first decent sustenance in days—Wells and Jane spent a long, exhausted night in the Institute's visitor's quarters. They were both eager to get back home where the two of them could spend calm afternoons bicycling down the tree-lined lanes or boating along the canals—and Wells could get back to his writing.

He felt thoroughly inspired now, full of ideas that would make fictions much more extravagant than simple articles for *The Strand*, *Pall Mall Gazette*, and *Pearson's Magazine*. For a long time now, W.E. Henley at the *National Observer* had been encouraging him to revisit his fanciful story, "The Chronic Argonauts," which he had published in his school newspaper years before. He had thought about developing it into a serial novel, *The Time Machine*. Now he had new twists to add to the story, more depth to the societies he had imagined.

Yes, he was very anxious to get back to work again.

Preparing to leave the next morning, Wells and Jane were carrying their bags down the corridor when they encountered a grinning Dr. Moreau. He held in his large hands the crystal egg he had described in his journal. "Before you two return to your mundane existence, I have something to show you. The crystal egg has begun to transmit again."

They followed him into a well-lit alcove where sunlight reflected off the smooth surface of the ellipsoid. From its infinite, shimmering depths, an amazing scene emerged like bubbles from a deep pond.

"It's Professor Huxley!" Wells said.

Happily amazed, he and Jane watched the old man working contentedly on Mars, surrounded by Selenites. Huxley appeared healthy and full of life. Though they could not hear the professor's words, a youthful exuberance shone on his face.

Selenite labor crews bustled about the ruins of the majestic Martian cities. Working non-stop, the lunar drones had already reconstructed much of what they had damaged in the insurrection. Wells thought that the buildings already had a brighter, more *lunar* style of architecture.

Moreau's gruff voice startled them. "Obviously, Huxley has found a crystal egg of his own, a counterpart to this one. Thus he can remain in contact with us."

On Mars, Huxley took great strides through the streets, turning the glassy artificial eye to show the dying, tentacled Martian brains. They crawled plague-stricken through their streets, probably gasping a final "*Ulla! Ulla!*" before they succumbed to the cholera germ. The creatures faltered in their clumsy flight, their brown skin blotchy and necrotic. Some gasping Martians had crawled to their windows and dangled lifelessly out of them. In the sky a flurry of black angular shapes, the Martian equivalent of carrion birds, swooped down to peck and tear at their carcasses.

* * *

Wells and Jane stayed at the Institute until that afternoon, engrossed in the images from Mars. An impatient Dr. Moreau went back to his laboratory, loaning them the crystal egg so that they could continue their observations.

Professor Huxley went to the now-completed invasion fleet of silver cylinders resting on the Martian landing field. Instead of letting the ships be used as a military force to conquer Earth, however, the old man loaded the cylinders with masses of kidnapped Selenite drones. Rank after rank of ant-like lunar workers crowded into the projectiles, which were ready to launch. This exodus would deplete the Selenite population on Mars, but it would be a rebirth for the crumbling civilization on the Moon.

Jane smiled, her pale cheeks flushed. "The infusion of fresh workers from all castes will likely save the lunar race. The Grand Lunar will be so pleased—and so am I. After all, I was their temporary queen."

They sat together enthralled as the first wave of silver cylinders raced away from Mars on a green flash of rocket flame and hurtled toward the Moon . . . back home.

* * *

In the end, settled once more in their rented rooms in Euston, Wells and Jane sat outside, gently rocking in a bench-swing as they looked into a clear, dark night. The full Moon rode high in the sky like a radiant, pale beacon.

Thinking of all they had done and everywhere they had gone, they clasped hands and just stared out at a universe filled with infinite possibilities. They could tell no one of their fantastic adventures. It was their secret for now. Even the queen and the Royal Institute would hold all the details under the tightest classification.

Wells seemed content, though. "We did not do it for accolades, Jane. We did it because it was necessary."

Jane kissed his fingers, then leaned against him. "And I am very proud to have been part of it with you. No one would believe us if we told the story, though. Unless you can think of an innovative way . . . ."

Wells smiled at her, the wheels already turning in his mind—as they always did. "It's not such an impossible thing, Jane. Any good writer can find a way to tell the story."

AUTHOR'S NOTE

During extensive historical research undertaken by the author in writing this book, it became sadly but abundantly apparent that the events as set forth in this novel *did not, in fact, occur*.

However, with the benefit of more than a century of hindsight, one can see that this is indeed how history *should* have happened.

ACKNOWLEDGMENTS

This book—and indeed a large portion of the science fiction genre—would not exist without the groundwork laid by H.G. Wells and Percival Lowell. Wells single-handedly introduced the world to many of science fiction's best-loved concepts. Despite repeated censure and ridicule from his peers, Lowell's tireless promotion of Mars as the abode of life kindled a public fascination with Martians and their dying world.

Most especially, I must express my gratitude to the estate of H.G. Wells for allowing me to do this book. I would also like to thank the staff at the Lowell Observatory in Flagstaff, Arizona, for their help and suggestions.

I give a respectful nod to Stephen Baxter for putting me in

touch with the heirs of H.G. Wells; my editors Steve Saffel, John Ordover, and Jennifer Heddle for "getting it"; Vivian Cheung, Nick Landau, and Cath Trechman from Titan Books; John Teehan, Robyn Herrington, and Mark Bourne for helping me track down some of Wells's more obscure writings; Catherine Sidor and Diane Jones for their assistance in various stages of preparing this manuscript; and, of course, Rebecca Moesta Anderson for most everything else.

ABOUT THE AUTHOR

Kevin J. Anderson is a prolific author who has published over 115 novels, 50 of which have been national or international bestsellers. His work has been translated into 30 languages, and he has well over 23 million books in print. He often collaborates with other authors, such as Brian Herbert, Rebecca Moesta (his wife), Dean Koontz, Greg Benford, and Doug Beason. In his solo work he is best known for his seven-volume *Saga of Seven Suns* SF epic and his *Terra Incognita* sailing-ships fantasy. He is currently working on the *Hellhole* trilogy with Brian Herbert, and *The Saga of Shadows*, a new trilogy set in the *Seven Suns* universe, as well as the humorous *Dan Shamble, Zombie P.I.* series, and *Clockwork Angels*, a novelization of the recent Rush album. He has also written novels and/or comics for *Dune*, *Star Wars*, *X-Files*, *JSA*, *Titan A.E.*, *StarCraft*, *Star Trek*, *Batman/Superman*, and many others. His website is: www.wordfire.com.

WAR OF THE WORLDS
GLOBAL DISPATCHES

by Kevin J. Anderson

In the spirit of H.G. Wells's classic tale comes this anthology of accounts of the Martian invasion, as it might have been seen through the eyes of such notables as H.P. Lovecraft, Jules Verne, Teddy Roosevelt, Pablo Picasso, Henry James, Winston Churchill, Rudyard Kipling, Edgar Rice Burroughs, Albert Einstein, Mark Twain, Joseph Conrad and Emily Dickenson.

Featuring the work of twenty leading sci-fi authors including Robert Silverberg, Barbara Hambly, Allen Steele, Gregory Benford, Connie Willis, Mike Resnick, Walter Jon Williams and David Brin.

"A rollicking good compilation . . . Highly recommended."
—*Library Journal*

SEPTEMBER 2013

TITANBOOKS.COM

CAPTAIN NEMO
THE FANTASTIC ADVENTURES OF A DARK GENIUS

by Kevin J. Anderson

When André Nemo's father dies suddenly, the young adventurer takes to the sea, accompanied by his lifelong friend, Jules Verne. Verne is thwarted in his yearning for action, while Nemo continues across the continents. Years pass, and he is feared dead.

Far from lost, however, Nemo criss-crosses the globe. He discovers the lost city of Timbuktu, the hidden land at the center of the earth, and is marooned on the uncharted mysterious island. He faces bloodthirsty pirates, prehistoric monsters, Arab slavers, and serves in the British cavalry against the Russians in the charge of the Light Brigade. Against all odds he survives, and becomes the captain of the futuristic vessel known as the *Nautilus*.

"Anderson's rollicking whopper of a novel glides along smoothly in a style deliberately modeled on Verne's own . . . No one would miss the boat by signing on this fantastic journey." —*Publishers Weekly*

TITANBOOKS.COM

THE COMPANY OF THE DEAD

by David J. Kowalski

March 1912.
A mysterious man appears aboard the *Titanic* on its doomed voyage. His mission? To save the ship. The result? A world where the United States never entered World War I, thus launching the secret history of the twentieth century.

"Time travel, airships, the *Titanic*, Roswell . . . Kowalski builds a decidedly original creature that blends military science fiction, conspiracy theory, alternate history, and even a dash of romance." —*Publishers Weekly*

THE HARRY HOUDINI MYSTERIES

by Daniel Stashower

The Dime Museum Murders
The Floating Lady Murder
The Houdini Specter

In turn-of-the-century New York, the Great Houdini's confidence in his own abilities is matched only by the indifference of the paying public. Now the young performer has the opportunity to make a name for himself by attempting the most amazing feats of his fledgling career— solving what seem to be impenetrable crimes. With the reluctant help of his brother Dash, Houdini must unravel murders, debunk frauds and escape from danger that is no illusion . . . .

THE FURTHER ADVENTURES OF
SHERLOCK HOLMES

Sir Arthur Conan Doyle's timeless creation returns in
a series of handsomely designed detective stories.
The Further Adventures of Sherlock Holmes encapsulates
the most varied and thrilling cases of the world's
greatest detective.

THE ECTOPLASMIC MAN
BY DANIEL STASHOWER

THE WAR OF THE WORLDS
BY MANLY WADE WELLMAN & WADE WELLMAN

THE SCROLL OF THE DEAD
BY DAVID STUART DAVIES

THE STALWART COMPANIONS
BY H. PAUL JEFFERS

THE VEILED DETECTIVE
BY DAVID STUART DAVIES

THE MAN FROM HELL
BY BARRIE ROBERTS

SÉANCE FOR A VAMPIRE
BY FRED SABERHAGEN

THE SEVENTH BULLET
BY DANIEL D. VICTOR

THE WHITECHAPEL HORRORS
BY EDWARD B. HANNA

DR JEKYLL AND MR HOLMES
BY LOREN D. ESTLEMAN

THE ANGEL OF THE OPERA
BY SAM SICILIANO

THE GIANT RAT OF SUMATRA
BY RICHARD L. BOYER

THE PEERLESS PEER
BY PHILIP JOSÉ FARMER

THE STAR OF INDIA
BY CAROLE BUGGÉ

THE WEB WEAVER
BY SAM SICILIANO

THE TITANIC TRAGEDY
BY WILLIAM SEIL

TITANBOOKS.COM